THE
BRIBE

WILLA NASH

THE BRIBE

Editing & Proofreading:

Elizabeth Nover

www.razorsharpediting.com

Julie Deaton, Deaton Author Services

www.facebook.com/jdproofs

Karen Lawson, The Proof is in the Reading

Judy Zweifel, Judy's Proofreading

www.judysproofreading.com

Cover:

Sarah Hansen © Okay Creations

www.okaycreations.com

CHAPTER ONE

JADE

"I HATE you for making me do this," Everly hissed.

"Me?" I whisper-yelled. "This was your idea, remember? I wanted to spend a weekend glamping. But no. You thought a hike would be a more memorable experience."

She wasn't wrong. We'd definitely remember this trip.

If we survived.

Her entire body trembled by my side. "Do you think they'll come closer?"

"I don't know." I gripped her hand, clutching it as we huddled together on the trail.

Across from us, about fifty feet down the trail, stood a bison the size of a tank. He'd been farther away five minutes ago, but with every passing second, he inched closer, nuzzling the grass with his snout before taking another step in our direction. His charcoal horns tapered to piercing points, and his black, beady eyes seemed glued to our every move.

The bull snorted, causing both of us to flinch.

The minute we'd come upon the herd in this meadow,

1

we'd nonchalantly retreated on the trail, but for every backward step we took, the animals—this one in particular—took three forward.

Everly unclipped the canister holstered to her belt. "Does bear spray work on bison?"

"I don't know." But if that thing came within firing range, we'd both unleash until either he killed us or we turned him into bison jerky—pepper spray flavored. "Come on."

We eased back another foot, this time not drawing any movement from the beast. One foot became ten, then twenty. When the animal turned, whipping his tail over his ass in a silent *fuck off*, Everly and I slumped against each other in relief.

We were standing in the middle of an open plain in Yellowstone National Park. The path we were on was bordered by tall green grasses that stood above our knees and swayed in the slight summer breeze.

Everly and I had spent hours and hours doing research on trails after she'd convinced me to hike. This particular path wound through the Hayden Valley, and the online descriptions had promised an experience unique to the Yellowstone Plateau. If you wanted to see the heart of the park, this was the hike to take.

We'd been hiking since sunrise, traversing meadows and passing wide sections of pinewoods. Lunch had been by a small lake. Through it all, we'd enjoyed seeing the park's wildlife from a safe distance. Birds squawked as they flew overhead. Deer and elk stared at us cautiously before bounding away in the opposite direction. They gave us a wide berth and we returned the favor.

That was, until we'd rounded a bend, emerging from

behind one of the trail's many plateaus and found ourselves much, much too close to the bison.

"At least it wasn't a bear," I said, doing a quick sweep of the area, making sure there wasn't a grizzly in sight. "So what do we do? They're blocking the trail."

The only way forward was through the bison, and one close encounter was enough for my lifetime.

"Should we turn around? Head back to the trailhead?"

"We'll never make it back to the car before dark."

If my watch was correct, we'd hiked almost seventeen miles today and only had three to go until we reached the end. Three puny miles. Easy, if not for the blockade.

"Remember what I said about bison being majestic?" I asked. "I changed my mind."

Until thirty minutes ago, I'd loved the animals. I'd bought a bison stuffy at the gift shop at Old Faithful yesterday. But given their sheer size, if one of the ogres decided to play *chase the human*, we'd be trampled and stomped to death in seconds.

"I don't want one of those faces to be the last thing I see," I said.

"What about bears? I don't want to be bear food either. At least in the daytime, we can see them coming. I don't want to be stranded out here in the middle of the night."

"Shit," I hissed.

Though the bison had taken us by surprise, we'd been prepared for bears. Everly and I were both packing three cans of bear spray and we'd been hyper bear aware with every mile.

If my choice was grizzly or buffalo, I'd take my chances with the bison. "We have to wait for them to move off the trail."

We could try to walk around them but neither of us knew the area and the last thing we needed was to get lost. Like the park ranger had reminded us three times yesterday when we'd told him we were hiking Mary Mountain—*stay on the trail.*

So here we were. Stuck.

Beyond us, the grasslands spread for miles, eventually meeting the mountain foothills. The open wilderness had lots of space to run.

And not a damn place to hide.

Today's journey had been one of the most exhilarating and terrifying experiences of my life.

Maybe fate had intervened and brought us here. I was about to embark on a new phase in my life, and remembering this hike would help me keep things in perspective. If I could face down a one-ton bison and not pee my pants, I could move across the country and build a new life, no sweat.

We stood there, watching the animals meander through the meadow with no care for our urgency. The sun was beginning to dip lower in the sky, and though we were hours from sunset, eventually the light would fade and we'd become a tasty temptation for a passing grizzly bear.

Or a pack of wolves.

My stomach turned.

"They aren't leaving," Everly said.

"Nope."

The bison herd clustered along the stretch of trail ahead, eating and leaving their shit pies where we'd planned to walk. I'd almost stepped in a ripe one earlier, which should have been my first warning to turn back, but I'd been too busy appreciating the landscape and keeping an eye out for carnivores.

"How fast do you think we can walk slash run seventeen miles?" I asked.

"Fast." Everly nodded. "Really, really fast."

"Good. Let's get the hell out of here."

"Amen." We both spun around, ready to bolt, but froze when we saw something else on our path.

Not a bear—thank God—but a man.

"Uh . . . how long has he been behind us?"

"This is the first time I've noticed him," Everly said. "I glanced back to look for bears but that was a while ago."

"Maybe he's a park ranger."

"Or a serial killer following two idiot women from Nashville and he's going to drag us back to his lair and turn us into human stew."

"Eww." I cringed. "Thanks for the visual."

"Sorry. I've been watching a lot of *Criminal Minds*."

The man's long legs ate up the distance between us. His thighs bulged beneath his faded jeans with every stride. If he'd hiked the past seventeen miles at that speed, it was no wonder we hadn't noticed him behind us.

He wore a backpack like ours, but the straps seemed tiny on his broad shoulders, and they stretched the navy cotton of his T-shirt tight across his muscled chest and flat stomach. The baseball cap on his head shaded his eyes from view, though even from a distance, the strong line of his jaw and the straight bridge of his nose were evident.

Neither Everly nor I spoke as we watched the man get closer, his features becoming clearer with every step.

Everly clutched her can of spray in a fist as he lifted an arm to wave.

I fought to keep my mouth from falling open at this unexpected and devastatingly handsome surprise.

Everly jammed her elbow into my side, forcing me to close my gaping mouth. "You're drooling. Potential murderer, remember?"

I blinked, dropping my eyes to my feet for a long moment as I composed myself. When I lifted my chin, the guy was standing before us.

"Ladies." He kept his voice low as he looked over our heads. "Roadblock, huh?"

"Yep," I said. "And they aren't moving anytime soon. We were just going to hustle back to the trailhead."

"Seventeen miles?" He shook his head. "No offense, but you'll never make it before dark. And this is not the place you want to be after nightfall."

Everly and I shared a look. She knew what I was going to say and gave me a silent no.

I said it anyway. "Any chance we can tag along with you until the end of the trail?"

"Not a problem." He nodded, his gravelly voice sending a zing down my spine before he took a step into the tall grass.

"But the trail . . ." I pointed to the narrow dirt path.

"That's not the trail. That's a bison path. They knock down trail markers a lot." He lifted a hand and pointed toward the mountains in the distance. "The trail is over there. But you two looked lost, so . . ."

He'd come to rescue us.

Which meant the reason we were standing in the middle of a bison herd was because they'd lured us to them.

Sadistic creatures, buffalo.

"Come on." He jerked his chin and took another step. "I won't get you lost. Promise."

"Sir." Everly held up a hand, stopping him. "I really

hope you don't take this the wrong way, but how do we know you're not leading us to your serial-killer hideaway?"

A slow grin spread across his face, and he shrugged off his pack, setting it down and dropping to a knee as he unzipped the front pocket.

"Whoa, whoa, whoa." Everly aimed her bear spray at his face.

"Easy." He held up his hands. "I'm a cop. I was going to show you my badge."

"That's what all serial killers say." Everly's gaze narrowed. We really needed to find her another show to binge on Netflix.

"She's just a little on edge." I placed my hand on her wrist, pushing her arm down as I gave her a scowl. "Nature stresses us out."

He quirked an eyebrow. "Yet you're in the middle of Yellowstone National Park."

"We all make mistakes, Officer."

He chuckled, flashing me a smile of straight, white teeth before he rifled through his backpack.

I fanned my face.

"Seriously," Everly mouthed.

"What?" I mouthed back, feigning innocence.

She rolled her eyes.

In a different setting, Everly would be shoving me into this guy's arms. He was exactly my type, tall and built with an unpolished and rugged edge that had always been my weakness.

He stood and handed me a wallet, opening the front flap to reveal a gleaming silver and gold badge. "Sheriff Duke Evans."

Sweet lord, I nearly swooned.

He had a *great* name.

I'd always been a sucker for a great name.

Everly hovered over my shoulder, studying the badge. When she deemed it real, she relaxed and holstered her spray.

"What's your name?" Duke asked, taking the badge and putting it away.

"L— Jade."

"Lajade?"

"No, sorry." I blushed. One gorgeous man saving my life, and my tongue felt twelve sizes too big for my mouth. "Jade. My name is Jade Morgan. This is my best friend, Everly Sanchez."

"Nice to meet you." He rezipped his pack and shrugged it on. "Ready?"

"Definitely." I nodded and stepped off the trail.

Then I blew a kiss goodbye to the bison as Everly gave them the finger.

———

"ARE YOU GUYS CAMPING OUT?" Duke asked as we walked.

We were on the real trail now, the bison encounter forgotten as we crossed an open meadow toward a cluster of trees in the distance. The only animals in sight were the birds soaring above in the big, blue sky.

"We're staying at the Madison Campground. You?"

He shook his head. "I'm just here for the day. I had a buddy drop me off at the trailhead this morning. My rig is parked up ahead and waiting."

"He didn't hike with you?"

"I, uh . . . didn't invite him. I like to hike alone."

Which he had been until he'd rescued us. "Sorry."

"Don't be. I'm glad to help."

I smiled at his profile, then turned my attention back to the trail so I didn't trip over a rock.

Duke had navigated us through the grasses to the trail without any trouble. For the past mile, we'd had to walk single file and hadn't spoken much. I'd stayed behind him, doing my best not to stare at his ass even though it was definitely stare worthy, while Everly followed behind me. When the trail had widened, Duke had hung back a step so I could move up to his side.

Everly, my beautiful friend, had stopped to tie her already tied boot and given us a little space.

"Where are you from, Jade?"

"Tennessee."

"No accent."

I shook my head. "I grew up in upstate New York. What about you?"

"Wyoming. I grew up in a little town about an hour from here."

"Do you come here often?"

"Not as much as I'd like." He pulled in a deep breath, his chest expanding as he drew in the clean air and held it in his lungs.

"This is my first trip."

"No," he deadpanned.

"Shocking, right?" I laughed, taking in the view. "We got in a little over our heads today, but this is truly a magnificent place."

"Pure beauty."

I looked up, expecting his eyes to be on the mountains, but his gaze was aimed at me.

My focus returned to the trail as I willed the flush out of my face.

I was the furthest thing from a beauty today. My black hair was a wreck because I hadn't washed it in days, not since Everly had helped me dye it in our bathroom before we'd left Nashville. The thick locks were twisted in a sloppy braid that hung down the middle of my back and my red cap covered the greasy roots. The only makeup I'd put on my face this morning had been tinted sunscreen.

Maybe Duke was just flirting or being nice, but it was still the best compliment I'd had from a man in years because it had come honestly and without expectation.

We walked for a while without talking. Duke's strides were longer than mine, but he held back, slowing so Everly and I could keep up.

I sneaked a glance at his profile every few steps, studying the color of his eyes and how perfectly it matched the blue, cloudless sky. His toffee-colored hair curled at the nape of his neck where it escaped the confines of his hat.

"You're a sheriff," I said. "I don't know if I've ever met a sheriff before. Do you enjoy it?"

"For the most part. I'm not crazy about the politics but I'm lucky. Most people in my county think I'm doing a good job, which means I get to keep doing it."

"How long have you been a cop?"

"Since I was eighteen. I hired on as a deputy for my predecessor, then was elected sheriff two years ago."

"Impressive."

Duke shrugged. "At the time, there were some who thought I was too young for the job, but no one else would step up to take it. We'll see if they reelect me when my term is up. I'm only thirty-three and sheriffs in larger counties are generally older and have more experience. But I live in a small community."

"Something tells me you prefer it that way."

"You'd be right."

"Do you want to be reelected?"

"Yes and no," he admitted. "Some days, I love my job. Others, it's a pain in the ass. Guess you could say that about any job though, right?"

"Yep." I'd had the job most girls could only dream of, but dreams weren't always what you imagined them to be, and when there were more bad days than good, it was time to walk away. "What would you do if you weren't a cop?"

"Be a cop." He laughed. "I can't imagine doing anything else."

For his sake, I hoped that didn't change.

Because turning your back on your dream, giving it up, was heartbreaking.

We rounded a curve and the trail narrowed, forcing us closer. I slowed to get behind him, but Duke slowed too, keeping by my side. The roped muscles of his arm brushed against my bare skin. His knuckles grazed mine and I forgot to breathe.

When I looked up, those blue eyes were waiting.

Damn it, I should have picked Wyoming for my new home.

There was a spark between us, and I hadn't felt a crush on a man in ages. Duke might just be that something unexpected I'd been wishing for.

But our time together was up.

Before I was ready to part ways with this handsome and

kind stranger, a wooden sign greeted us on the trail with an arrow pointing toward the parking lot where we'd left my car —a black Range Rover I'd purchased the day Everly and I had arrived in Jackson, Wyoming.

I'd driven it through Yellowstone while she'd followed in her rental car. We'd left the rental at the trailhead where we'd started today's adventure. Our plan was to camp out tonight and cross into Montana tomorrow.

Then Everly would head to the airport in Bozeman, where she'd catch a flight home to Nashville.

And I'd continue on to Calamity and start this next chapter of my life.

There were only a few vehicles in the parking lot as we emerged from the trail. The moment Everly spotted my SUV, she sighed. "We made it. Let's never hike again. Though I am kind of sad I didn't get to use my bear spray."

Duke chuckled. "I've been pepper sprayed twice, once at the police academy and another time for a training exercise. Trust me when I say you don't want to use those cans unless absolutely necessary."

"Thanks for not being a serial killer." Everly held out her hand to shake Duke's. "And thanks for rescuing us."

"No problem." He waved as she turned and walked toward the SUV, fishing out the keys we'd put in her backpack.

I scanned the parking lot, taking note of the trees and the signs, looking anywhere but at Duke until it was time for the inevitable goodbye.

"Pleasure to meet you, Jade Morgan." He extended his hand, and I slipped mine into his grip.

Tingles raced across my skin as the rough callouses on

his palm scraped against my fingers. I met his gaze, soaking up the azure blue. "Take care, Duke."

He inched closer, not letting go as I'd expected. Instead, he held my hand, tugging me in as his focus dropped to my lips. Like maybe he was thinking of kissing me.

Maybe I wanted him to.

But then he blinked, the moment broken, and the heat of his hand disappeared.

I plastered on a smile to mask the disappointment.

It was better this way, right? Cops asked questions and I doubted Duke would be satisfied with partial answers. Over the next year or two, I needed to keep my eye on the prize. At twenty-eight years old, I was building a new life. The smartest thing for me to do would be avoiding men, especially a hot sheriff who was in the public spotlight.

But after just hours with him, I knew I'd wonder about Duke. I'd wonder what might have been. He was fantasy fodder at its finest.

"Drive safe." With a tip of his green baseball cap, he turned and walked toward a large white truck parked beneath a towering evergreen.

I stood, rooted in place, as he climbed in and drove away. "Goodbye, Duke Evans."

That really was a great name.

———

"I CAN'T BELIEVE you won't be home when I get there." Everly sniffled. "This weekend went way too fast."

"But I'm glad we did it."

She wiped away a tear. "Me too."

The two of us looked human again after long showers and sleep in an actual bed. While camping out two nights with a long hike in between had been an experience neither of us would forget, I wasn't in a hurry to see the inside of a tent again.

When we'd arrived at the Madison Campground after the hike, we'd been exhausted. Everly and I had barely mustered the energy to set up our tent and sleeping bags before we'd collapsed. The next morning, we'd woken up early, packed our things and hit the road. After collecting her rental car from the trailhead, we'd driven to West Yellowstone, where a hotel room and spa appointments had been waiting.

I'd soaked up one last day and night with my best friend before we'd come outside to say goodbye. Everly was driving to the airport.

I was heading to Calamity.

"Call me when you get home?" I asked.

She nodded. "I will. If you need anything at all, I'm just a plane ride away."

I hugged her, squeezing tight. "I'm going to miss you."

"I'm going to miss you too."

My entire life, Everly had lived less than one block away from me. First as little girls riding bikes in our cul-de-sac. Then as women living together in Nashville for the past ten years. And now she'd be across the country, living her normal life, while I was moving to a new town, a new state and a new home, hoping to find a new dream.

Hoping to find that elusive peace.

"Thanks for this," I said. "For the weekend. For coming out here with me. For keeping this a secret."

"I hope it stays that way." Her brown eyes filled with worry. "Are you sure about this?"

"No, but I have to try."

"You know your secret is safe with me, but . . . at some point, someone is going to figure it out."

"Maybe. Maybe not." I sighed. "If I'm lucky, I can hide here forever."

And if not . . .

The doubts weren't going to stop me from trying.

"Just take care of yourself, okay?" She hugged me again. "Love you."

"Love you too." I stood beside my car, watching her get into hers and drive away. It wasn't until her taillights disappeared down the highway that I finally unglued my feet.

And started my new beginning.

———

"OH, HELL." I glanced at my watch and abandoned my lazy pace.

Maybe tomorrow I'd learn how not to be perpetually late. Today was clearly not that day.

As I scurried down the sidewalk, I sent my landlord a text apologizing for being late and promising to be there soon. Then I tucked my phone away, pinned my purse beneath an elbow and ran toward my Rover.

Mom had always teased me for getting lost in my own head and misplacing time. Dad had been the same way.

Except I hadn't been lost in my head.

I'd been lost in Calamity.

Located in the heart of southwest Montana, my new hometown had charmed me instantly. Calamity was nestled in a mountain valley surrounded in all directions by towering indigo peaks. There wasn't much to the town itself, as the internet had promised—I'd driven from one end to the other in less than five minutes.

But I didn't need a sprawling metropolis. After an hour of walking up and down First Street, I'd realized the quaint rural setting suited me fine.

I'd instantly fallen in love with the easy pace. No one rushed down the sidewalks. People smiled as you passed them. In every store I'd explored today, the clerks had welcomed me to town and asked for my name.

My landlord had promised Calamity was a friendly place. She'd boasted about the stunning, short summers and sunny, albeit cold, winters. How everyone would be so happy to have a young, fresh face in their community. I'd thought she'd been blowing smoke up my ass just to get me to sign the lease agreement.

Calamity was everything she'd pledged and more.

Which was why I'd spent much too long exploring instead of meeting her on time to pick up the keys to my rental house.

Sweat beaded at my temples by the time I reached my car and hopped inside, rolling down the windows instead of using the air conditioning. Then I reversed out of my spot like my wheels were on fire and raced down the road.

The air whipped through my hair. The sun warmed my face. And the smile that stretched my mouth had staying power.

This is going to work. I felt it in my bones.

Calamity was located two hours from the nearest town of any size. It would be easy for me to hide here, living as Jade Morgan. In all my wandering, I hadn't seen a flicker of recognition on anyone's face.

According to my internet research, there were roughly

two thousand people living in Calamity and the surrounding valley. I could convince two thousand people that I was a nobody, just a single woman, new to Calamity, who'd rented a two-bedroom home on the outskirts of town. I didn't have to find a job because I was planning on telling everyone I worked from home. I'd pay cash whenever possible and simply blend in.

My foot pressed the accelerator as I glanced between the road and my GPS. In one mile, I'd take a left and in less than three minutes I'd be—

The wail of a siren filled my ears. Blue and red lights greeted me in the rearview mirror. My foot lifted off the gas pedal, but it was too late. As I slowed and veered for the shoulder, so did the imposing police truck behind me.

This was bad. This was really, really bad. "Shit. Why am I so stupid?"

My heart pounded as I came to a stop, shoving the Rover into park. With trembling hands, I reached for my purse in the passenger seat and rifled through it until I found my wallet.

Why couldn't I have just been on time for once in my life? A speeding ticket my first day in Calamity was not blending in. And if my name ended up in the local police report, my stay here would be much, much shorter than planned.

The officer's footsteps approached my door cautiously. Through the side mirror, I couldn't get a good look at his face, but I didn't miss the black gun on one hip and shining badge on the other.

"I'm sorry," I blurted the second he was close enough to my open window to hear. "I was late and—" The words disappeared as I looked up and saw blue.

"Jade?"

I blinked. "Duke? What are you doing here? I thought you were from Wyoming."

"I grew up in Wyoming, but I live in Calamity." He shook his head, clearing the disbelief from his expression. Then his gaze narrowed and intensified. "License, registration and insurance, please."

"Right." I pretended like the sharp, impassive edge to his voice didn't sting.

Maybe I'd misread that parting moment in the park. Maybe he'd just been a nice guy helping two tourists to their car, and the attraction here was one-sided.

My fingers fumbled with the plastic as I yanked my license out of my wallet, and I nearly dropped it as I handed it over.

"I'm sorry I was speeding." *Please, please don't notice.* I gave him my most innocent eyes, silently begging for him to hand me back my driver's license and forget this whole thing.

No such luck.

Duke studied my license, his eyes flicking between me and the plastic card. Then his jaw clenched and he put both of his hands on the windowsill. "Ms. Morgan. Lajade, right? Or should I call you Lucy Ross? As in the famous country singer Lucy Ross."

I cringed. "I can explain."

"Yeah. I think you'd better start talking."

"Sheriff Evans." I gave him my sweetest smile. "What would you say to a bribe?"

CHAPTER TWO

DUKE

"I'D SAY NO." A bribe? What the hell?

Her smile vanished. "I had a feeling you'd say that. Shit."

"What's going on"—I looked at her license one more time, just making sure I'd read her name correctly—"Lucy?"

"I swear I can explain everything."

"I'm waiting."

Her emerald-green eyes flicked to the clock on the dash. "I'm late. That's why I was speeding."

Goddamn, I hated traffic stops. There was always an excuse. As a general rule, I didn't bother with speeding tickets, leaving traffic for my deputies, but when I'd seen Lucy's Range Rover racing down First like a rocket, I hadn't been able to let that slide. It was early August and we had kids on summer break roaming freely.

"Late for what?" I asked.

"I'm supposed to meet my landlord."

"You're moving here?"

"Yep. I'm your newest constituent."

Well, fuck. As the sheriff, I didn't really need a famous

singer in town, drawing attention to the quiet and simple life I worked hard to maintain. But as a man, it was hard not to keep my heart from beating a bit faster.

Lucy Ross.

How could I have missed this earlier? How could I have not seen the resemblance in Yellowstone?

Probably because I'd been too busy keeping my physical reaction in check. That, and the changes she'd made to her appearance were effective.

Her hair was nearly black. The dark strands suited the color of her creamy skin and the dusting of freckles on her nose. Gone was the blonde I'd seen on a tabloid magazine cover when I'd gone to get my hair trimmed at the barber last week. Lucy's eye color was the real deal, but without the colorful eyeshadow and black liner, their shape seemed different. They were innocent and natural. Mesmerizing.

Seductive.

There was no flash in this version of Lucy. She was simply a raw beauty. Her nose was straight and slightly turned up at the end. Her lips were a soft peach color that matched the natural flush of her cheeks. Hell, even her ears were attractive with tiny points at the tips.

Especially without the enormous earrings she'd made famous as a Nashville country star.

But I couldn't unsee the semblance now.

This was Lucy Ross without the glitz and glamour.

As a hot-blooded man, I preferred this version. As a sheriff, I was tempted to run her out of town. Having a celebrity here could only mean trouble, especially if the rumors about her were true.

I listened to the radio often while I was in my office doing paperwork or when I was driving around town. I preferred country to the rock and pop music these days, and the stations had been speculating for two weeks about Lucy.

She's disappeared. Where? No one has a clue.

It must have something to do with her assistant's death.

Her publicist released a statement today asking for privacy at this time. But no one has seen her.

Where is Lucy Ross?

She'd been hiding out in Wyoming and Montana, busy facing off against a herd of bison and getting lost with her friend in the wilderness. She'd fallen off the mainstream map and landed right in the middle of mine.

"Why are you here?"

"That's a long story," she muttered. "Are you going to give me a ticket?"

I handed her back her license. "Depends on this long story."

"Please, please don't give me a ticket," she said. "I just . . . I'm here to disappear. Which, if you take a bribe, will be a lot easier."

I wasn't taking a fucking bribe. What kind of man did she think I was? What kind of cop did she think I was? I had morals, for fuck's sake.

"Please, Duke. I just want to blend in. I'll be hanging out at my house. You'll never even know I'm in town. Just don't give me a speeding ticket."

Blend in? Ha.

Her appearance, her car, screamed tourist. Lucy would stand out in Calamity like a lightning bolt streaking through a midnight sky.

A car drove past us in the opposite direction and she shielded her face with her hand.

The side of the road wasn't the place to have a drawn-out

conversation about her disappearance. It would only bring more attention to her because my truck, like her Rover, wasn't exactly subtle.

"Where are you meeting your landlord?" I asked.

"At the house."

I nodded and pushed off the side of her door. "Lead the way."

"But . . ." She looked forward, then back at me. Then forward again, down the road like it was to freedom.

If she decided to tear out of here and leave me in her rearview, I wouldn't stop her.

"What's it gonna be, Ms. Ross?"

She put both her hands on the wheel and muttered, "Okay."

I turned and strode to my truck, climbing inside and shutting off the flashing lights. I buckled up and waited. Seconds passed, enough to equal a minute. Then two. For a woman in a hurry, she was taking her sweet time. Finally, her taillight blinked yellow and she eased onto the road.

Following her down the highway was painful. She drove five miles per hour under the speed limit. I rolled my eyes, stifling a string of muttered curses, and called into the station.

"Hey, Carla," I said when my deputy and lead dispatcher answered.

"Hi, Duke. What's up?"

"I'm not going to be in for a while, so if you need anything or something comes up, give me a call."

"Will do." Had I been there, she would have given me her standard mock salute.

Carla had never been military, but she'd been saluting me since the day I'd taken over as sheriff. She was the kind who loved orders and followed them to the letter. She loved the law and she was good at enforcing it. But when it came to the gray areas, she had a hard time comprehending a bend to the rules.

It was a good thing Carla hadn't pulled Lucy over. Not only would Lucy have been issued a ticket and a fine, she would have also been arrested for attempting to bribe an officer.

Then I would have had a hell of a mess on my hands.

The people of Calamity loved their small town. I loved my small town. But we were far removed from city life and anything close to a celebrity. Our gossip centered on who was cheating on who or who'd gotten too drunk at the bar Saturday night.

News of Lucy Ross's residence would spread like a drought-year forest fire in August, and it wouldn't stop at the town limits. She'd have everyone in the county knocking on her door and poking around. The local paper would probably run a special feature, photos and all.

So before things got out of hand, Ms. Ross and I were going to have a lengthy conversation about her stay in Calamity.

Lucy's brake lights flashed and she slowed, her blinker on for a left turn.

Son of a bitch. I should have suspected this was where she was headed. There was only one place that she could have rented down this gravel county road.

Widow Ashleigh's farmhouse.

One of a few constant thorns in my side.

Ever since the widow had passed five years ago, I'd been dealing with a host of issues on the property. Widow Ashleigh had left her estate to her niece, who lived in Oklahoma. Everything had immediately been sold, and the family who'd bought the farmhouse had been from Texas.

The year they'd moved in, we'd had a miserable winter. Most rural roads, including the gravel one I was driving on now, had drifted shut. The people living in the farmhouse had called the station hourly, for three days, asking when the plow would be out to rescue them. Eventually, the county transportation department had cleared their road, but not before the owners had threatened to sue me, my deputies and basically everyone in Calamity for abandoning them.

I hadn't been surprised to see the house up for sale that spring.

But much to their dismay, it hadn't sold. Instead, the property had sat empty for years with little to no care. The neighboring farmer had reported squatters three years ago and I'd been the one to evict them. The year after that I'd gotten a call to come out because every window had been broken by vandals—I suspected the squatters I'd chased out of town had returned. Though I'd never caught them, there'd been rumors of familiar faces passing through. And lately, my trouble with Widow Ashleigh's place had been from teenagers using the property for keggers.

But about a year ago, the owners—who'd returned to Texas—had finally dropped their price to something reasonable and a local had snatched it off the market.

Kerrigan Hale had made quite the name for herself since she'd moved back to Calamity two years ago. She'd been buying properties around town to flip or lease. She'd even bought a couple of buildings on First Street. Rumor was she'd stretched herself thin, mostly because she bought the places no one else wanted and sank some money into cleaning them up.

I wasn't sure how much she'd invested in the farmhouse, but it was a hell of a lot nicer than it had been years ago, even when Widow Ashleigh had been alive.

Kerrigan was probably overjoyed to have a tenant. Word around town was that she was asking a steep price in monthly rent. As far as I knew, she'd had some vacation rental interest, but for the most part, the farmhouse had been empty. I doubted she knew her new lessee's real identity and that Lucy could probably afford twice the rent Kerrigan was charging.

The farmhouse's white paint glowed under the bright summer sun as it came into view from around a copse of leafy trees. The house was surrounded by a sea of golden wheat fields. I hadn't been out here in a month or so, and since then, Kerrigan had added a couple of rocking chairs to the wraparound porch. A planter beside the front door was bursting with pink blooms. The kelly-green grass of the sprawling lawn was freshly mowed.

The cloud of dust following Lucy's car settled as she slowed and pulled into the driveway beside Kerrigan's car.

I parked behind Lucy, blocking her vehicle in, and stepped out just as she rushed to meet Kerrigan.

"Hi." She smiled at Kerrigan. "I'm so sorry I'm late."

"It's no problem." Kerrigan pushed up from the steps where she'd been sitting, her hand extended as she walked to meet Lucy. "I'm Kerrigan Hale."

"Jade Morgan."

Lucy said the name with such effortless ease no one would question it. There was no hesitancy like there had been with me. *Lajade.* Christ, I'd fallen for that lie like a rock tossed over a cliff.

As they shook hands, Kerrigan's gaze darted over Lucy's shoulder. "Uh, hi, Duke."

I lifted a hand. "Hey, Kerrigan."

"I didn't realize you knew Jade."

I gave a single nod. "Yep."

Though Kerrigan had grown up in Calamity, we'd only known one another for a couple years. When I'd moved here to take a deputy job, she'd been in high school and had left shortly after graduation for college. I knew her parents along with the abundance of Hales in town—her aunts, uncles and cousins. As her grandfather loved to boast whenever I saw him at the café drinking coffee, their family had been here since Calamity's inception.

She was a few years younger than I was, which to most of the nosy women in town meant the two of us were eligible for matchmaking. We'd gone on one blind date, and though Kerrigan was a nice woman with long, chestnut hair and pretty brown eyes, the two of us had zero chemistry.

Lucy, on the other hand . . . there'd been an instant spark.

Too bad it was all based on bullshit.

"Let me show you the house." Kerrigan turned and started up the stairs, returning to business. "Can I help you bring anything inside?"

"Oh, no. Thanks," Lucy said. "I'll get it later. I don't have much."

I swallowed a snarky retort, following them up the porch steps. Lucy didn't have much because Jade Morgan was a whole two weeks old.

"This porch is beautiful," Lucy said, her eyes roaming over the smooth, chocolate deck boards.

"Thanks." Kerrigan beamed as she unlocked the front door. "I stained it myself."

We stepped inside the entryway and I had to remind myself where we were standing. I hadn't been inside Widow Ashleigh's place for months, and Kerrigan's updates had transformed the entrance from old and run-down to classic and stylish.

If the rest of the house was like this, no wonder she was asking for so much in rent.

"Like I told you over the phone, the lease includes the house plus twenty acres," Kerrigan told Lucy. "The house sits on the front of the property. The boundary line runs along the road so everything behind the house is yours to use. The neighbors all have good fences so it's easy to see where the property lines run. There is a barn out back if you need it, but I'll warn you I haven't spent any time in there, so it's a mess."

"No problem. I don't need a barn for anything," Lucy said, following Kerrigan deeper into the house. She cast a glance over her shoulder and if she was surprised that I was following, she didn't let it show.

"This is it." Kerrigan waved a hand toward the living room.

"It's beautiful." Lucy's smile widened, her gaze bouncing from ceiling to floor to fireplace to window.

There was a hint of paint in the air, mixed with the fresh scent of furniture polish and glass cleaner.

"Looks good, Kerrigan," I said.

"I'm happy with how it turned out." She waved for us to follow. "Let me show you the kitchen."

Kerrigan had done a lot of the work here herself, much like she had with her other properties in town. We shared a mutual friend, Kase, who owned a construction company in Calamity, and he assisted in the larger tasks that Kerrigan couldn't tackle alone. But for the most part, she was a one-woman show.

Some people in town didn't like how she was renovating some of the historical homes, this one included. But I disagreed, admiring her for taking risks.

Lucy didn't say much as she walked through the living room. Her attention seemed fixed on the large window that overlooked the front of the house, past the porch and to the driveway. When Widow Ashleigh had lived here, that window had been three. Now, the single, sparkling glass pane allowed sunlight to bathe the room. With the mountain view in the distance, it was hard to tear your eyes away.

She was so fixated on the picture outside, she nearly tripped over the corner of a rug.

"Careful." I caught her elbow in my grip, holding her steady before she could fall. A jolt of electricity shot up my hand from her smooth skin.

A red flush bloomed in her cheeks as she muttered, "Thank you," then chased after Kerrigan, this time watching where she put her feet.

Chemistry. We had it in spades.

Damn.

I gave her a head start, taking a moment to suck in a breath, then followed, finding Kerrigan and Lucy standing beside the table in the dining room off the kitchen.

Because it was an older house, none of the rooms were enormous and the spaces were all segregated by walls. Open concept hadn't been an architectural trend when this place had been built seventy or eighty years ago. Every room had at least two doorways, all adorned with ornate trim that had been painted a stark white. The crown molding had been painted to match while the walls had all been coated in a bright cream.

"Are these original?" Lucy asked, pointing to the hardwood floors.

Kerrigan nodded. "They are. I was able to restore them down here, but unfortunately, upstairs they were in bad shape, so you've got carpet in the bedrooms."

"I don't mind carpet." Lucy ran a hand over the back of a chair, then retreated into the kitchen.

The cabinets and appliances were new. They brightened the small space and made it seem more modern than the other rooms. It was large enough for a square island. Whereas the countertops around the room were granite, the island was topped with a butcher block.

Lucy opened the rear door, taking in the small patio out back.

"Should we go upstairs?" Kerrigan asked Lucy.

I stayed in the kitchen, not needing to see the bedrooms. It was going to be hard enough to mentally erase the smiling, fun, witty Jade and replace her with the scheming, famous, I'll-bribe-my-way-out-of-a-speeding-ticket Lucy. The last thing I needed was a mental image of her anywhere near a bed. Because whether I called her Jade or Lucy, that woman was sexy as hell.

As they padded up the staircase, I wandered back to the living room and stood in front of the picture window. This house wasn't flashy or expensive. It was a nice home, perfect for a couple or even a small family. Every room was furnished with quality, affordable pieces, nothing elegant or expensive.

Would someone like Lucy Ross, whose car cost more

than most homes in Calamity, actually be comfortable here? I wasn't sure how long she'd agreed to rent the farmhouse, but I was giving her until winter. Then I suspected she'd be more than willing to retreat to her glamorous life.

"The kitchen has all the standard items but if you need anything else, just let me know," Kerrigan said as the pair came down the stairs. "Same goes with the furniture."

"It's all perfect." Lucy smiled as they reached the last stair. "Thank you."

"You're from Maine?" Kerrigan asked.

"Yes, from Portland." Such effortless lies.

"That's quite the move."

"It is." Lucy laughed. "But I'm lucky that my job is so flexible. I've always wanted to see Montana and I thought, why not just move?"

My teeth gritted together, my jaw tightening with every lie. What a goddamn disappointment. I'd been so intrigued by her in Yellowstone. Instantly, she'd put me under her spell. Now she was doing the same to Kerrigan.

Fuck, I was an idiot. Gullible wasn't something I'd been much lately and it tasted awfully sour. But I was still very much intrigued, by the woman and definitely by her story. Lucy Ross—Jade Morgan—was a mystery I was going to solve.

"How are you liking Calamity?" Kerrigan asked.

"It's charming. The reason I'm late was because I got caught up exploring."

"Welcome. I grew up here and moved away after college, but there's no place like Calamity."

"I think I'll be happy here." She cast me a nervous glance, covering it quickly when she faced Kerrigan. "I appreciate all your work getting this ready for me."

"I've never had anyone rent a place via a FaceTime tour, so I'm happy you like it."

"Thanks for accommodating me and all of my, um, odd requests."

"No problem." Kerrigan smiled. "It was actually easier this way. Less paperwork."

Meaning Lucy was probably renting this place in cash.

"Okay, so you have the keys and my number," Kerrigan said. "Please let me know if you need anything at all."

"Thank you."

"I'm sure I'll see you around town. It's impossible to hide in Calamity."

The color drained from Lucy's face as she laughed, attempting to cover it up.

"See ya, Duke." Kerrigan waved and walked to the front door.

"Bye."

I waited until the sound of her car's engine drifted into the distance before I spoke. "All right, *Jade*. Time for that long story."

"One hundred thousand dollars," she blurted.

"Excuse me?"

"I, uh . . . I need something to drink." She spun away from me and walked through the house. I followed her to the kitchen, where she searched the cupboards for glasses, finding them after three failed attempts.

"Would you like some water?" she asked.

"No."

She went to the sink, giving me her back as she filled her glass, then guzzled it down. Even after the water, she didn't turn but kept her eyes on the small window overlooking the property.

She was stalling.

Fine by me. I was a patient man.

Finally, she let out a sigh and turned. Her top lip was wet and had we not been separated by the island, I might have forgotten all about her fake name, crossed the room and kissed Jade Morgan.

Something I should have done at the trailhead when I'd been happily ignorant.

I'd almost kissed her. I'd been seconds away from taking her face in my hands and tasting those peach lips. But then I'd walked away. I'd come to my senses. Jade Morgan was a stranger. And I doubted she'd want a man she'd met hours earlier to kiss her senseless, then disappear from her life.

None of those facts made her lips any less appealing now.

"I'm not going to explain why I'm here." She held up her chin. "That's my business."

"Sorry, Ms. Ross. That's not how it works in Calamity. You're in my town, which makes it my business."

"Are you going to give me a speeding ticket? Or arrest me for giving you a false name while I was hiking in the middle of nowhere?"

I crossed my arms over my chest. "I haven't decided yet."

"Then let me help you make your decision. I'll pay you one hundred thousand dollars, cash, if you forget the speeding ticket and forget you ever learned my name. I need a place to lie low, and I'd like that to be Calamity."

I narrowed my eyes.

That determined green stare, that insolent chin, didn't waver.

Christ, she was serious. She really did want to bribe me into keeping her secret.

Well, I didn't need her money. I sure as fuck wouldn't take a penny, because that wasn't the type of man I was. But I did want to know more about why Lucy Ross was in my town.

Maybe the easiest way to do that was tell her a lie of my own.

"Done," I lied. "I'll take the bribe. But I want to know your story."

"It's not up for discussion."

"Then forget the deal." I spun for the door.

"Wait." She grumbled something under her breath. "Okay. But I don't feel like talking about it today."

"Not today." I hid a triumphant grin. "But soon, Ms. Ross. Very, very soon."

CHAPTER THREE

LUCY

"LET'S SEE." I opened the refrigerator and stared at the shelves. The only things inside were a nearly empty jar of salsa and a single can of Diet Coke, something I'd known but had checked again regardless. "So much for breakfast."

My stomach growled as I made a mental note to text Everly later and thank her for always keeping our refrigerator stocked and pantry loaded. Living alone wasn't all it was cracked up to be.

I slammed the door closed, the hunger pains becoming unbearable. The salsa and a handful of sad, broken corn chip pieces were all that remained from the groceries I'd bought from a gas station in West Yellowstone before driving to Calamity. I'd been surviving on snacks for the past two days, not wanting to venture into town.

Paranoia had gotten the best of me. So had fear.

If Duke knew who I was, then it was only a matter of time until others discovered it too. I'd been a damn fool, wandering around Calamity on the day I'd arrived. What the hell had I been thinking, going into shops and giving people my name?

Fake name.

The moment Duke had recognized me, I should have hit the gas and gotten far, far away from Calamity. I'd contemplated it for a long moment. But I liked it here. That hour I'd spent exploring downtown had been precious.

No one had recognized me. No one had asked for my autograph. No one had taken my picture.

Maybe it was stupid, but I wasn't ready to give up on Calamity. Even if their sheriff knew exactly who I was. Even if that meant living like a recluse, admiring the town from afar and taking sporadic trips into public places.

Fear and paranoia aside, there was no way I could survive another day on the food in my house. As much as I loved chips and salsa, it wasn't breakfast.

The clock on the microwave read 7:23. Maybe if I limited my adventures in town to the early morning, I'd be able to avoid masses of people and go undetected.

If I could live here for a year or two without raising any suspicions, the citizens of Calamity might just believe I was Jade Morgan, and hopefully by then, the rest of the world would have forgotten all about Lucy Ross.

As long as the sheriff kept his word and accepted my bribe, things would be all right.

The bribe.

What the actual fuck had I been thinking? Was I really so jaded toward people that the first thought that had crossed my mind was to throw money at a stranger?

I could have just asked Duke to keep my secret. I could have just said, "Duke, would you please not tell anyone who I am?" But, no. Because after years and years in the music industry, I'd become a suspicious woman who trusted one and only one person on this earth—Everly.

Considering that Duke had accepted the bribe, my cynical side was struggling to see how there'd been any other option.

Everyone else just wanted a piece of me. My money. My music. My looks. My sole purpose in life had been to be *the brand.*

The Lucy Ross brand.

The irony made my insides churn. I was Lucy Ross and the brand we'd cultivated—that I'd let the record label design —was so far gone from the real Lucy Ross, I'd had to dye my hair black and move to Montana to actually recognize myself in the mirror.

The brand was the reason I'd offered that bribe. Because we protected the brand at all costs. That was the record label's motto. And for years, it had been mine.

I had protected Sunsound Music Group's Lucy Ross brand.

Even when I'd been sick to death of having my life managed by other people. Even when I'd lost the freedom to choose my own clothes except bras and underwear. Even when I'd write a song and the A&R division at Sunsound would flip it upside down and turn it inside out so that it fit the *fucking* brand.

Forget the brand. Maybe I'd offered that bribe from habit, but that money would protect this new life, the chance for me to build new habits.

As long as I could pay Duke.

As long as no one else recognized me.

Shit. What had I gotten myself into? How could I have been so naïve as to think this plan of mine would actually work? I'd been recognized on day one. Granted, he'd had my driver's license, but still . . .

There was no hiding who you really were.

Not from the outside world.

And not from yourself.

Duke had stayed away from the farmhouse these past two days, but I suspected his need for answers would soon put him on my doorstep. How was I going to keep my secrets if he insisted on knowing why I was in Montana? And that man had insisted. I'd seen the determination in his gorgeous blue eyes.

Maybe I could lie? Except I'd never been a good liar and Duke struck me as the type to see right through a bullshit answer. It was only a matter of time before I had to fess up.

My only hope was that with a huge sum of money riding on his silence, he'd honor our agreement. Was a man who accepted a bribe honorable? It didn't matter. I was out of options. The bribe had been offered and accepted. It wasn't like I could call my legal team and ask them to draft an iron-clad contract to solve this problem. My lawyer played golf with Sunsound's lead council every Thursday, and lately, I'd been questioning everyone's loyalty, with or without attorney-client privilege.

So I'd pay Duke. And since I wasn't exactly exercising my fingers on the guitar these days, I'd keep them nimble by keeping them crossed. Because if he knew anything about tabloids, he'd sell me out for well over a hundred thousand dollars.

"Ugh." I dropped my forehead to the stainless steel of the fridge and groaned. Why, Duke? Why?

The moment he'd accepted that bribe, I'd wanted to scream. He was so . . . disappointing. The noble man I'd met in Yellowstone had been an illusion. Duke Evans was just like the others—in it for the money.

Whatever. I'd spent two days pushing that crushing frustration down deep. Eventually, I'd come to terms with the bribe I'd so desperately offered and I'd pay him to keep those soft, kissable lips shut.

Now I just had to figure out how to get him one hundred thousand dollars without calling attention to my whereabouts.

I'd taken out as much cash as I could manage before leaving Nashville. Ninety thousand had gone to buying my Rover. Thirty thousand had gone into the backpack I'd taken hiking. It had probably been stupid to drive across the country with that much money, but I hadn't wanted to go to a bank.

Credit cards were too easily traced, and until things blew over, I was sticking to cash.

When I needed to replenish my funds, I'd take a road trip to Seattle or San Francisco or Salt Lake—some S-word city within a thousand miles. I could take ten or even twenty thousand out of my accounts at a time. But how was I going to get a hundred? I'd have to make a few extra trips.

Hopefully Duke would be patient and give me some time to collect. Worst case, I'd sell my car.

My stomach growled again, reminding me that priority one here was food, and I collected my purse from the kitchen counter before walking through the house. Sunshine streamed through the living room window and brightened the already well-lit room. The furniture that Kerrigan had picked was so different from the colorful and eclectic items Everly and I had shared in our apartment. We'd refused to hire a decorator and the furniture had been an odd collection we'd come up with over the years.

This farmhouse was decorated more to Everly's taste than mine, but she'd always indulged my need for bright colors. She hadn't cared when I'd bought a bold floral couch that clashed beautifully with a lemon velvet chair. I'd lost control with anything outward facing so I'd clung to it behind closed doors.

But I liked the farmhouse's look. It was simple and inviting. The modern edge gave each room a coordinating vibe and the pieces made the best of the small spaces. The couch in the living room was a rich caramel, the leather as smooth and buttery as the candy itself. The chair was a tweed fabric, the color a soft oatmeal with flecks of the same caramel as the couch. The coffee table sat on a plush, vintage-style rug with red and cream and black tones that complemented the hazelnut color of the hardwood floors and the red bricks of the fireplace.

Maybe this winter, I'd light myself a fire every morning and write songs in the living room.

Maybe by winter, I wouldn't be scared of my own guitar.

I pulled on the hat I'd worn in Yellowstone and added a pair of sunglasses before walking out the front door. Then I jogged down the five steps of the porch, checking left and right to make sure I was alone before running to the Rover and locking myself inside.

It was silly. This wasn't Nashville and the precautions I'd taken there were unnecessary in Montana. But they were yet another habit.

The Rover was parked in the same place it had been since I'd arrived, though the back was now empty. Moving into the farmhouse had barely filled an afternoon, considering all I'd brought were three suitcases and two backpacks.

I cracked the window as I drove, savoring the country air. There was a crisp chill that would probably burn off by midmorning, but at the moment, I was glad I'd tugged on a hoodie when I'd dressed earlier.

Maybe after the store, I'd venture outside for a walk or run. So far, I'd spent my time watching Netflix, avoiding my phone and all things social media. But as the fresh air blew into my face, I didn't want to spend another day cooped up inside.

Boredom's claws were coming out, preparing to scratch.

In the past, I'd kept myself occupied with music. Considering I couldn't even stand the radio now, that wasn't an option. I added a novel or two to my mental grocery list. I hadn't had time to read in recent years, not that it had ever been a priority, but my mother had loved to read. I'd like to discover why, if only to feel some sort of connection to her.

Because at the moment, alone—truly alone—for the first time in years, I was desperate for any kind of connection.

My parents had been my shelter and since they'd died, I'd felt lost. I was a woman running through a storm, searching for a haven against the onslaught of rain. For a time, I'd thought I'd found a place with Sunsound. Turns out, all I'd found was a leaking umbrella.

I reached the end of the gravel road and my anxiety spiked, shoving away thoughts of my parents and the label.

"Quick trip," I told myself as I turned toward town. I'd be in and out of the grocery store in a flash. I'd be gone an hour, tops. I didn't have to change my plan entirely. Duke had agreed to take the bribe and my secret was safe. I just had to be careful, right?

Just because Duke knew who I was didn't mean I had to move. Yet.

I slowed as the highway became First Street. Most of the diagonal parking spaces were empty as I rolled into town, the businesses not open yet. The shops in the downtown area were themed like something from an old Western movie. Square, barnwood façades. Red brick and mortar walls. On some, the original name of the business was still painted on the buildings in barely-there white letters, like the *Candy Shoppe* and *Calamity Trading Co.*

Yet restaurant sandwich boards boasted free Wi-Fi. Neon signs glowed from both of the town's bars. There was a Tesla parked in front of the bank.

Calamity was like a ghost town restored. An odd and eclectic mix of a forgotten world and modern-day society.

As I continued farther, more and more vehicles appeared. Every space in front of the coffee shop was taken and the same was true in front of the White Oak Café.

My fingers clenched the steering wheel, my heart in my throat, as I drove at exactly the speed limit to the grocery store at the opposite end of town from the farmhouse. It was the largest building on First with the exception of the hardware store across the street. It was also the most unique grocery store I'd ever seen. It was shaped like a barn and painted a loud crimson.

Thankfully, the lot was mostly empty and I parked in a space close to the front. *Get in. Get out.* I was hurrying through the sliding doors, looking for a cart, when I nearly collided with a buffalo.

I gasped, slapping a hand to my racing heart. "Stupid statue."

The animal was painted in a swirl of green and blue

from horns to hooves. I'd seen other bison like this one when I'd explored town the other day, though all had been decorated differently. Was the bison Calamity's mascot?

That would take some getting used to.

I shot the statue a scowl and continued on to the row of parked carts. With the brim of my hat pulled even lower and the hood of my sweatshirt shrugged up my neck, I took off my sunglasses, realizing it would probably be more suspicious to leave them on. Besides, my hair was draped everywhere and I hoped it would be the feature people noticed most. I'd be that woman, new to town, with the long, black hair.

Jade Morgan.

I'm Jade Morgan.

It had taken me the almost-two-thousand-mile drive from Nashville to Montana to start answering to that name when Everly used it. She'd forced me to practice, and without her here, I was on my own to rehearse.

It was nothing more than a stage name, really. Because this was all a performance.

If I could win a Country Music Award for Entertainer of the Year, I could master Jade Morgan.

I set out into the store, my hunger growing exponentially as I neared the bakery. I splurged on a dozen maple bars along with a loaf of bread. I bought the essentials from the produce section—bananas, apples and celery sticks.

Then I went up and down every aisle, filling my cart to the brim. The corners became harder and harder to maneuver by the time I made it past frozen foods to dairy for some milk.

"Morning." A man wearing a red polo smiled and

nodded as he passed me down the aisle with a clipboard tucked under his arm. His nametag read *General Manager*.

"Hello." I tensed, waiting for any sign of recognition, but he didn't slow or spare me a second glance.

I grabbed my gallon of milk, then pushed my overflowing cart to the checkout line.

"Good morning." The cashier wore the same red polo as the manager, but his was covered in a black apron. "How are you today?"

"I'm great, thanks." Once my haul was on the conveyor belt, I let my gaze wander to the magazine rack.

And my own face stared right back.

Oh, shit.

It was a picture of me from my last concert. I was smiling into the microphone. My hair was blond, curled and poofed six inches at the crown. Golden eyeshadow extended past my eyes and across my temples, dusting my hairline. My lips were colored a dark red.

I fumbled to take the first magazine down, then tried to nonchalantly put it back, this time the front cover turned inward. Before the cashier could notice what I'd done, I hurried to the end of the aisle and began bagging groceries, wanting as much distance between me and the magazine as possible.

"Anything else, ma'am?" the clerk asked as he rang up the last item.

"No, thanks." I waited for the total, then gave him a wad of cash from my wallet.

With the change in my pocket, I pushed my cart outside, the plastic sacks rustling in the breeze along with the wheels on the asphalt. I opened the back of the Rover to unload just as a deep, gravelly voice filled my ears.

"You didn't want the latest copy of *People*?"

I froze. My reprieve from Sheriff Evans was over.

Duke stood by the handlebar of my cart. The magazine from inside was in his hand. His eyes did the same thing they had with my driver's license, darting between the cover photo and my face. Then a line formed between his eyebrows, like he couldn't decide which version he liked better.

I sidestepped the cart and began transferring bags into my car.

God, I wanted to like him. I wanted to trust him. I wanted to laugh with him and smile with him like we had in Yellowstone. But then he'd taken my stupid, stupid bribe and revealed his true colors.

Would I ever learn how to read people? At least I was consistent. I'd read Duke wrong, like I had many, many others.

"Are you following me, Sheriff? Because if you're worried about your money, there's no need to stalk me around town. You'll get paid."

"Stalking? No." His jaw ticked and he lifted his other arm. There was a gallon of milk in his grip that I hadn't noticed before. "I was out of milk and I eat cereal for breakfast."

"Oh." In my defense, I was sensitive to being watched. It was too fresh and familiar.

Been there, had the letters to prove it.

Not that Duke was anything close to a stalker. No, the shivers he sent down my spine were of an entirely different brand.

The heat of his blue gaze made my pulse race. Duke was

dressed for work, but he hadn't shaved this morning and the morning sun caught the stubble dusting his jaw.

My belly clenched. I was so hungry I could eat him for breakfast.

His hair was still damp and the silky strands of that tawny brown were separated in thick chunks, probably from combing it through with his fingers. And his eyes . . . those eyes deserved a song, even if the man himself didn't.

Why? Why had he taken the bribe? Why had I offered it to him in the first place?

I hated that he wasn't the real-life hero I'd needed and wanted to know.

I hated that he was human.

Because right now, I needed a little bit of perfect. The Duke from Yellowstone had been that bit of perfect. He'd been the man I could put on an imaginary pedestal to prove to the world that not everyone was out for money or fame or revenge.

But perfect didn't exist.

Duke Evans was as human as the next handsome man. Maybe one of these days, I'd stop letting men disappoint me.

"We need to talk, Ms. Ross."

I cringed and unloaded another bag from my cart. "Jade."

"Jade." My fake name sounded like acid on his tongue but it was better than *Ms. Ross*. "Why don't you come to the station later today?"

"Are you arresting me?"

"No."

"Then I'd rather not come to the police station. That draws attention." And I'd spent enough time in an interrogation room over the past ten months to last a lifetime.

"Then your house." He sounded smug, like he'd wanted to talk at my house but hadn't wanted to insist.

Damn. Given my hesitation to spend anymore time in public than absolutely necessary, there wasn't an alternative. But I didn't want him at the farmhouse. It was too small with him sharing my roof.

Duke's image might have dulled, but my body had yet to get the memo. Why did he have to be so freaking handsome?

"Fine," I muttered, taking the last of the grocery bags from my cart. "What time?"

"Barring any emergency, I'll be there by six."

I blew out a deep breath. "Okay. Six."

"You done?" He motioned to my cart.

"Yeah."

He dipped his chin, the nod something he seemed to do often—not that I was paying attention to his gestures. "Bye."

The wheels of the cart rattled as Duke returned it to the bin, steering it with one hand while holding his jug of milk and the rolled up magazine in the other. His shirt was tucked into his jeans. His brown leather belt was missing its badge and gun, which gave me nothing else to stare at but that ass and the jeans that molded so perfectly to his backside.

Oh, boy. I was in so, so much trouble. Because right then, I didn't really care about the bribe. I didn't really care about his moral compass, or mine for that matter. My fingers itched to dig into the rear pockets of his jeans and squeeze.

Duke must have felt my gaze because he glanced over his shoulder, the corner of that lickable mouth turning up.

Busted. I didn't bother pretending that I had been staring anywhere but at his ass. I simply shrugged, closed the hatch on the Rover and got behind the wheel.

He's just a hot guy.

He's just another hot guy.

My name is Jade Morgan and Duke Evans is just another hot guy.

I'd keep reminding myself, over and over, until it sank in.

And eventually Lucy Ross would disappear. Hopefully along with this attraction to the local sheriff.

CHAPTER FOUR

DUKE

I PARKED in front of Lucy's house and pinched the bridge of my nose. Fuck, it had been a long day. Too much had happened since I'd bumped into Lucy at the grocery store and what I really wanted to do was go home, take a hot shower and drink a beer. Put today behind me. But since I didn't have her phone number and wasn't the type of guy to no-show, here I was, sitting in my truck, trying to summon the energy to go inside and interrogate a country music star in hiding.

It was six thirty—I hated being late but it had been unavoidable. Hopefully the pizza in the passenger seat would buy me some grace. I took one more breath, the smell of crust and cheese and garlic filling the truck, then hopped out and trudged up Lucy's porch. Before I could hit the bell, the door opened and there she was.

Lucy's face was a welcome sight. One look and my bones didn't feel quite as weary. My legs weren't so tired and hard to move. One look and some of the heavy in my heart faded away.

Her black hair was piled in a knot on the top of her head. Her eyes were lined and dusted with shadow, making the green orbs appear bigger. Her cheeks were blushed and her lips glossed. I'd kill for a smile at the moment, a real smile like those she'd given me in Yellowstone. Just a little sunshine to break through the gloom of a dark damn day.

But I didn't get a smile. Instead her expression grew wary as she eyed the pizza box. "Sheriff."

"Ms. Ross. Hope you like pepperoni."

"Um . . . I didn't realize this was a dinner meeting."

I eased past her as she opened the door wider. I didn't bother waiting for her to take the lead as I walked straight through the living room to the kitchen, setting the box on the island and flipping open the top for a slice.

The first bite, I swallowed so fast the flavor barely had a chance to graze my taste buds. The second and third, I took the time to chew. And by the time I finished that first piece, I began to feel human again.

"Would you like a plate?" Lucy asked, whipping open a cupboard and yanking out two. Then she slammed the door closed and smacked the plates on the island, shooting me a scowl.

"Sorry." My mother would have strangled me for that display of missing manners. "I didn't get lunch today."

"Busy spending your bribe money already? Or was it a slammed Monday at the local speed trap?"

I bit my tongue about the money comment and matched her sarcastic tone. "No, I man the speed trap on Sundays."

The corner of her mouth quirked but she didn't give me a smile. "What happened?"

"There was an accident outside of town." Just

mentioning it was sobering. The mental image of what I'd seen today chased away my appetite.

Tomorrow morning, it would be reported in the weekly newspaper, but I suspected the details—most of which were probably inaccurate—were already riding the Calamity gossip wave.

"Oh." The edge in Lucy's voice disappeared, replaced with genuine concern. "I'm sorry. Was anyone hurt?"

I rubbed the back of my neck. "Yeah."

It was tourist season, which meant more traffic through the area. Until fall came, there were three out-of-state cars for every local on the highways. Typically, the tourists were responsible for the accidents. I didn't hold any prejudice toward them, it was just the way the stats fell. They outnumbered us.

But today's accident was the fault of a Calamity man. He'd been texting—we'd found his phone on the floor of his smashed car. He'd drifted into the opposite lane of the highway and collided head-on with a family on their way to Yellowstone.

Two kids were in the hospital with scrapes and cuts. Their father was in critical condition. Their mother had a concussion and two broken legs. The guy who'd been texting was a single guy who worked construction.

I'd pronounced him dead at the scene.

"Are you all right?" Lucy asked.

"Yep." I forced a small smile. "Just drained."

"Want to talk about it?"

"There's not much I can say until it's released to the public."

"Is everyone okay?"

"No."

Understanding crossed her gaze followed by a lance of pain. She gulped. "Was it anyone you knew?"

"I knew him. Not well, but I knew him."

He'd been from Bozeman, the nearest town of any size, about two hours away. After we'd cleared the scene, sending four people to the hospital, one body to the morgue and two cars to the scrapyard, I'd gone to the station to make the tough phone calls. I'd notified the authorities in Bozeman so they could tell the man's next of kin. Then I'd called my buddy Kase to tell him that one of his employees had died.

I blew out a deep breath. "One of my deputies was first on the scene. He's only been on the force for six months. Twenty-one years old. I'm expecting his resignation tomorrow. That wasn't a sight I could stomach, let alone the kid."

"Is there anyone who can help? Like a therapist or something?"

"We've got a good therapist in town. I called her before I came here. But still . . . it won't be the last disaster my deputy sees if he sticks with the force. He's got to decide if he can push through the nightmares. But I wouldn't blame him if he turned in his badge."

Today's scene had been gruesome. The man who'd died had been nearly unrecognizable. I could still hear the mother's screams ringing in my ears as we'd helped her out of their minivan. And those kids . . . I'd never forget the terror on their faces. Never.

Grayson, my deputy, had vomited at the scene. Once the last ambulance had driven away, he'd had a complete breakdown and been inconsolable.

"Death isn't easy to see," Lucy said in a way that made it clear she'd seen it firsthand too. "I'm sorry for your deputy. And for you."

"Thanks. I care about my team a lot. Wish there was a way to keep the shit away from them, but it's the nature of the job."

There was such kindness, such empathy in her green eyes, I wanted to cry myself. Instead, I cleared my throat and grabbed another slice of pizza. Why had I just unloaded that on her? Shame on me. She didn't need to bear my burdens. This was the woman who'd offered me money to keep a secret and make a speeding ticket disappear. A woman who, I suspected, wouldn't be in Calamity for long.

I took a bite of my pizza, remembering why I was here. "Let's change the subject. Why are you in Calamity, Ms. Ross?"

She cringed. "Jade. Please. Or Lucy. Anything but Ms. Ross."

"All right. Lucy it is." Though I'd hoped to keep it at *Ms. Ross* to reinforce some distance. And because I couldn't call her Jade, not when I knew it was a lie.

"Should we sit down?" She cast her gaze toward the dining room.

"Sure." I nodded and followed her with my plate in one hand and the pizza box in the other.

We sat at the table, facing one another, and ate in silence. The room was bright and airy, even if the table was slightly too big. The window at our side overlooked the expanse of property behind the farmhouse. It wasn't quite as stunning a view as from the front, but it wasn't ugly either.

"Do you know much about this house?" I asked.

This wasn't the conversation we needed to have, but the urgency to push Lucy for information was gone. I'd analyze it later, along with the fact that if it was anyone else sitting across from me, I probably would have come out here and rescheduled this meeting. But at the moment, I just wanted to sit and talk and think about anything other than the accident.

"Not really."

"It was owned by a widow. Everyone in town always called her Widow Ashleigh so even though Kerrigan owns the farmhouse, you'll probably hear it called Widow Ashleigh's place. She was a nice lady. Drove this huge boat of a Cadillac. Black and shiny, you couldn't miss it when she rolled through town. Mostly because she drove about five miles per hour, no matter where she was going."

"You're telling me this so I'll drive like Widow Ashleigh?"

"Yes." I chuckled. "She passed about five years ago. This house has been basically empty since. The longest anyone has lived here since has been six months."

"You say that like it's cursed."

"Might be."

She blinked, studying my face, then relaxed when she realized I was joking. "Trying to scare me away, Sheriff?"

"Tell you what. I'll drop the Ms. Ross if you drop the Sheriff and call me Duke."

"I like calling you Sheriff." She leaned back in her chair, crossing her arms over her chest, the slice of pizza on her plate forgotten. "Reminds me exactly who you are."

And I knew exactly who she was too.

Lucy arched an eyebrow, signaling she was ready for me to get on with the real inquisition. Her internal defenses were raised, her body rigid.

The idle talk was over.

"Why are you here?" I asked.

"It was time for a change."

"Try again. I'm not the kind of guy who likes vague answers."

Her stare hardened. "Doesn't my one hundred thousand dollars buy me some anonymity?"

"No, it does not."

"But—"

"None." My tone brooked no argument. "Talk."

That was the second time since I'd arrived and the third time today she'd mentioned the bribe. It was pissing me the fuck off and I was tempted to set the record straight about how this was really going to play out, but the moment Lucy didn't *have* to tell me what was going on, she'd find an excuse to clam up.

She needed to think her identity here was on the line, and I'd swallow the truth until I got the full story.

"You bought the magazine," she said. "What did it tell you?"

"I didn't read it." I had no faith that a tabloid would include anything but speculation.

"Really?" She stared at me like I'd grown a goiter on my neck. Why was it such a surprise that I'd skip the magazine? That I'd actually ask the source instead of swallowing someone else's interpretation of the truth?

"You're stalling, Lucy. What's going on?"

She shifted her gaze to the windows, looking into the distance. "I quit."

"Quit what?"

"What does anyone quit? Their job."

Lucy was a famous performer. She had the kind of life little girls dreamed of. "You expect me to believe you walked away?"

Her eyes shot to mine. They flashed angry, then her

shoulders dropped and the annoyance in her gaze morphed into something much more like sorrow. Regret. "No, not really. People don't walk away when they're at the top of their game."

Which meant something horrible must have happened to drive her away. What the hell had happened in Nashville? Maybe I should have read that magazine after all. "Then why?"

"Reasons."

Reasons. This woman was stubborn as hell and obviously had practice avoiding questions, probably from dealing with the press. I simply stayed quiet, waiting. Because I was stubborn as hell too.

"Creative freedom is one," she finally said. "I'm sure you can understand the concept of handcuffs."

"I can."

"Well, I've been wearing shackles for years and they're uncomfortable. But I've got a 360 deal with my label, Sunsound Music Group, which means they own me. They own my sound. My future. My brand." She rolled her eyes. "And I don't want to be owned by anyone. Not anymore."

"Okay. That's one reason." Not the real reason, but a reason. Disagreement with your record label didn't seem like enough motivation to give up a singing career. Maybe backtrack or change, but like she said, people at the top didn't walk away. Something else had sent her running to Montana. "What's another?"

"I can't live in Nashville. My manager, my agent, my publicist, my producer and a hundred other people are probably furious and freaking out, but I left anyway."

Clearly, this move had been on impulse. Once she came to realize that small-town Montana life didn't hold a fraction of the excitement she'd had in the spotlight, she'd race her fancy Rover straight out of town.

"And now your plan is to live in Calamity as Jade Morgan," I said.

"Yes. That is my plan."

"You'll go back."

"No, I won't."

"Bullshit." I scoffed. "I'm not sure how you're going to pull off this fake persona, because you are truly a terrible liar."

Her nostrils flared. "I can't tell the future, Sheriff. Today, the answer is no, I'm not going back. Maybe it will change one day, but for now, you're going to have to deal with the fact that I'm staying."

"Who knows you're here?"

"Everly."

"And?"

"Everly."

She'd only told one person? What about those hundreds of other people? Interesting. If that was true, her disappearance had a higher chance of success, but not by much. Eventually, people would get curious about who was living in Widow Ashleigh's farmhouse. "What about Kerrigan? How'd you rent this place?"

"I found her ad and called her. We talked for a while and I told her that I didn't believe in credit cards or checking accounts. I offered to pay her rental price plus ten percent if we could forgo the application and reference check and I paid cash every month."

I grumbled. I'd have to have a discussion with Kerrigan about background checks and being paid under the table. That was a good way to land yourself with a criminal for a tenant. Kerrigan had to know there was a story here. Maybe she'd even suspected Jade Morgan was a fake. But clearly, she was keeping her mouth shut. Besides me, Kerrigan might be the only person in Calamity capable of keeping a secret.

Lucy's story explained how she'd come here, but not why. I opened my mouth to ask more about Nashville, but before I could dive in, she spoke first.

"Why'd you pick Calamity, Duke?"

"Why do you care?"

"You've asked most of the questions so far. Humor me."

Humor her? Didn't she realize I *had* been humoring her? I'd given her the chance to tell me her story rather than research and find it out myself. But there was hesitancy in her eyes, like this innocent question was a test that she expected me to somehow fail.

I didn't fail.

"My family has vacationed here for as long as I can remember," I said. "When I was a kid, we'd come here and stay for a week in the summers. My parents stumbled upon it before I or my sister was born, and it just became our place. My dad is a cop in Wyoming, same town where I grew up. It would have been strange for us to work together, we both knew that, so when it came time for me to search for a job, Calamity was the obvious choice."

Mom and Dad's trips were usually to Bozeman, but they still loved Calamity as much as ever. They'd come four to five times a year to visit me and the friends they'd made here over time.

"Do you see your parents often?" she asked.

"They were here a couple of weeks ago to visit. My dad is talking about retiring in the next few years, and I suspect they'll move to Montana to be closer to me and my sister."

"Do you have other siblings? Or just one sister?"

"Are these questions your way of dodging mine?"

A smile tugged at her mouth. "Yep."

Honesty was a good look on her. "Just one sister. She's five years younger. Lives in Bozeman with her husband and two dogs. They're expecting a baby around Christmas."

She opened her mouth to ask another question, but I cut her off. "How about I ask you the same question? Why Calamity?"

"I liked the name. I have a thing for names."

"That's it?"

Lucy shrugged. "More or less."

I'd been getting more or less with this woman and it was wearing thin. "Let's cut to the chase. What happened in Nashville?"

Lucy held my stare and didn't speak a word.

"Ms. Ross."

"Sheriff Evans."

Christ, that stubborn streak ran bone deep. "You're going to have to tell me eventually."

"Maybe. But—"

"Not tonight, right?" I was getting the same shutdown I had the last time I'd been at the farmhouse. And I didn't have the energy to argue.

I stood from the table, taking the box of pizza and my plate. The latter was placed in the sink. The former, I closed and put in her fridge.

"You don't want to take that home?" Lucy asked, joining me in the kitchen.

"You keep it." I had a box from two nights ago in my fridge. "I assume you're avoiding public places. Now you don't need to go out for pizza."

"Thanks." She nodded, taking her plate to the sink. She rinsed hers, then repeated the process with mine, putting them in the dishwasher.

It was impossible not to stare as she moved. A few strands of hair dangled down her neck, tickling her poised, straight shoulder blades. Had I ever noticed a woman's shoulders before?

Not that I could recall. But Lucy's were the perfect size and since she stood at the perfect height, I imagined holding on to those blades, gripping them tight for a long, slow kiss.

Should have kissed her. I really should have kissed her in Yellowstone. Just once.

Lucy turned to face me and lifted her chin. I was beginning to enjoy that defiant little gesture. "Anything else, Sheriff?"

"I thought we agreed to drop the formalities, Ms. Ross."

Her lips pursed into a thin line. "I'll escort you out."

"No need." I turned and strode out of the kitchen, finding my own way to the front door.

Lucy followed, staying a few feet back with her arms crossed over her chest. Her gaze wasn't on my ass like it had been at the store this morning. "Headed home?" she asked as I opened the door.

"Not yet. I'm going to swing by my deputy's house. Drag him down to the bar for a beer and make sure he's all right."

Her head tilted to the side as she studied my face. Her eyebrows came together and formed a cute little pucker.

"What?" I ran a hand over my stubbled cheeks. Was there something on my face? The scratch of my whiskers against my palm was loud after having not shaved for a couple of days.

"You're a contradiction."

I scoffed. "There's not much contradictory about me, Lucy."

She opened her mouth to say something, but then closed it. "Thanks for the pizza. And for not pushing."

"Make no mistake, I'll get the whole story from you," I warned. "But tonight, I think we both deserve a break."

She dropped her eyes to the floor, then looked up and nodded. "Good night, Duke."

"Night." I waved and walked to my truck.

Lucy stood on her porch, watching as I drove away.

She sure was a pretty picture, standing in her bare feet in front of that farmhouse. Her jeans were torn and the flowing white shirt she wore revealed a sliver of collarbone and cleavage. She was sexy without even trying.

Lucy Ross.

It wasn't my style to let anyone off easy. To let someone dodge a question. Maybe the reason I'd let Lucy off easy was because it had been a miserable day.

Or maybe it was because the minute I learned Lucy Ross's story, I'd be out of reasons to see her again.

CHAPTER FIVE

LUCY

MY LEGS WERE ON FIRE. My lungs were burning. I was a sticky, sweaty mess.

And I hadn't felt this good in ages.

This morning, I'd woken up and the prospect of staying inside all day with the television or a book had made me nauseated. Stir-crazy didn't begin to cover how I was feeling.

I'd cleaned the farmhouse. Twice. I'd explored the boundaries of the property and peeked inside the old barn, deciding the creepy owl gawking at me from inside could live there forever. I'd cooked every meal, taking my time to do the fancy things I hadn't in ages, like garnishing my plate with parsley and shaving parmesan on my pasta. I'd baked until all that was left of my flour and sugar supply was white dust.

If I spent one more minute in that house, there was a chance I'd burn the place down. So I'd put on my tennis shoes and baseball hat, then jogged down my gravel road. I'd spent so many years working out on hotel treadmills or at the Nashville gym where Everly and I had shared a personal trainer, I'd forgotten how refreshing it was to run beneath the sunshine, huffing in fresh air.

The mountains towered blue in the distance, providing a captivating distraction from the strain in my muscles. Before I realized it, my feet hit the highway and I just kept running.

When First Street came into view, I contemplated going home. But the idea of seeing another face, even from a distance, was too appealing.

My God, I was lonely. Living like a hermit would be an adjustment. It had only been four days since Duke had come to the farmhouse with his pizza, but four days had stretched like an eternity.

Paranoia be damned. I was helpless against the charm of Calamity's sidewalks.

As I slowed my run to a lazy walk, I passed a few shop owners preparing to open. They were setting out sandwich boards and flipping signs from closed to open. Every person I passed greeted me with a smile and a good morning. Just that little bit of human contact lifted my spirits.

Every smile I received, I repaid with the same. And for the first time in years, I felt seen. Not recognized. Seen.

I wasn't *the talent*. I wasn't rich. I wasn't even pretty, not with my sweaty hair trapped under a baseball cap and a bright-red face.

I was simply a woman out for a run. I was no one. Nothing special.

The freedom was heady, so I shoved any residual fear of being recognized aside and reveled in my nothingness. I delighted with every footstep up First Street, then with those deeper into Calamity.

I wandered down random side streets, rambling on cracked sidewalks shaded beneath lush green trees. The homes in Calamity were exactly as I'd expected—simple and practical. Not one was lavish or gaudy.

They were just normal homes, organized on straight streets, with yards to mow in the summer and driveways to shovel in winter. There were no gated communities to keep people out—or in. The homes sat on the front of their lots, leaving the backyards for playtime and gardening.

It was peaceful here. Quiet. Pleasant. With every block, I fell a little bit more in love with Calamity. I could belong here, couldn't I?

Maybe when my rental agreement was up in six months, I could buy one of these lovely homes. I'd paint the front door a wild color like tangerine orange or lime green. And Jade Morgan would be someone's neighbor.

Except how was I going to buy a house? With cash? Lucy Ross had all the money. Jade Morgan would eventually be broke and couldn't exactly take on a mortgage.

And could I really let go of my real identity forever? Would I still be me if I didn't have my name?

A well of tears filled my eyes. It was a strange feeling to realize how much of your identity was wrapped up in a name, something given to you the day you were born. But I was Lucy Ross. My parents had given me that name with love, and I was the woman they'd raised me to be. Brave. Affectionate. Loyal.

Trusting.

Faults and all, at least Lucy had history. Jade Morgan had been born from a googled list of baby names. She truly was nothing. *Oh, the irony.* I'd worked my ass off for years to be *somebody*. Then I'd thrown it all away.

How many years had I chased my dreams? How much had I sacrificed for my career? How would my parents feel if they saw me now? Were they looking down at me, disappointed?

Was I disappointed in myself?

The music industry was cutthroat. There was so much more to my career than singing and touring. The contracts and the negotiations behind doors were exhausting and endless. The public scrutiny was unbearable and the negative press impossible to fight. Millions of people tried to insinuate themselves into my life just for a piece of fame and fortune.

Some more successfully than others.

I'd been sued five times by people who claimed I'd plagiarized their songs. Never mind that mine had come out years before and their claims were totally off base. It had cost time and legal resources to fight and keep my name out of the mud.

Through it all, the label had told me to *smile and wave. Protect the brand.* And Lucy Ross was happy. She was bubbly. She didn't talk about real-world issues or lawsuits or how many false, tabloid trash stories her team had smothered with cold, hard cash.

I'd been battling the media on one front while fighting the label for my creative freedom on another.

A year ago, I'd posted on Instagram how it was unfair that female, black and Hispanic artists earned a fraction of what their white male counterparts did. At the time, I'd been working on a new album and I'd begged to experiment with three songs. My sound wasn't exactly like it had been when I'd been nineteen. I wanted some flexibility to grow and try new things. My producer and the recording design team at Sunsound had balked at the idea but eventually they'd agreed to one song. One measly song. Two days after my post, one became zero.

Something about piracy and album length and market trends and consistency and blah, blah, blah. I'd gone back to smiling and waving.

Until everything had drowned in a river of blood.

My legs were suddenly wobbly, the dizziness in my head seeping into my limbs. My hands were shaking. I scanned the street, searching for a place to sit, and sagged when I spotted a park at the end of the block.

I sucked in a deep breath, checked the empty street for cars and headed toward a flat spot in the outfield of a base-ball diamond, collapsing on the grass. Besides me, the place was empty. Later in the day, no doubt the jungle gym would be crowded with kids, but for the moment, it was me, the blue sky and the occasional sparrow streaking from tree to tree.

The hammering of my heart began to fade as I breathed. Maybe running so far and then walking for an hour had been a mistake. Maybe I was spinning myself up with questions that didn't need to be answered today.

Or maybe this was my body's way of telling me to stop running—figuratively.

After a string of calming breaths, the strength returned to my legs. The fog lifted from my head and my pulse stopped racing. My fingers were steady as they splayed into the spears of grass at my sides.

Tomorrow marked one week in Calamity. The unknowns could wait another week. Another month. Hell, they could wait a year.

Maybe the life I'd known was over. Maybe it wasn't. But

for now, the only thing I wanted was to let the sunshine warm my face.

More freckles would pop up on my nose if I did this every day. Jade Morgan liked her freckles. Though, so did Lucy Ross. There was no need to choose which person I wanted to be quite yet. Since Duke was the only person here who knew my identity, I had time—thanks to one hundred thousand dollars.

Why had Duke taken that money?

Of all the questions I'd asked myself this morning, that was the one I actually wanted to answer.

My crush on him was growing with each of our encounters. Fight it as I tried, the man was endearing. I'd spend the past four days thinking about his visit and what he'd told me about that car accident.

He'd probably seen something horrific. He'd probably been through hell. Yet he'd still thought to bring dinner. And his biggest concern had been for his deputy. He'd left my porch after a hellish day and instead of retreating home, he'd gone to check on a member of his team.

Duke Evans was a good man.

Except for the fact that he'd taken my goddamn bribe.

The warmth on my face disappeared as a shadow appeared. I cracked my eyes, expecting to see a cluster of clouds over the sun. Instead, a man stood above me with a baseball bat perched on his shoulder. A glove was hanging from the handle.

"Morning," Duke said.

God, that voice. Could he sing? Because if he could carry even a mediocre tune, I wouldn't care at all about his slightly crooked moral compass. Nope. *Not. At. All.*

"Morning." I pushed myself up to a seat as he dropped to a crouch.

"Decided to venture out into public, eh?"

"How did I know you'd rub that in?"

A grin stretched across his handsome face. "Couldn't resist."

He'd shaved this morning. His skin was stubble-free and I dug my hands deeper into the grass so I wouldn't be tempted to run my fingertips over that strong jawline.

"Not working today?" I asked. It was Friday, right? The days had blurred together.

"Day off. I have a standing appointment every Friday morning in the summers."

My eyes locked on the bat. "An appointment, huh?"

He stood and held out a hand to help me to my feet.

My palm slid against his and his fingers wrapped around my hand, engulfing it in his own. His skin was warm and rough. His hand was so much bigger than mine. *Was everything about Duke large?*

I stifled a groan at the absurdity of that one but couldn't get the idea of his penis out of my mind. Seriously, *Jade?* Lucy hadn't thought about a man's, well, *manhood* in ages.

"You okay?" Duke asked.

"Yep," I lied, not letting my eyes drift across his jeans as he hauled me to my feet.

I hid the flush in my cheeks by keeping my face to my legs as I brushed the grass from my leggings. "Baseball, huh? I would have pegged you for a football guy."

When Duke didn't answer, I looked up.

Those blue eyes were glued to my ass, exactly where my hands had just been.

I fought a smile. "Duke."

He blinked, tearing his eyes away, then cleared his throat as he looked anywhere but at me. "Baseball and football. I like them both. Uh, what are you up to today?"

"Since I don't have appointments these days, I went for a run and decided to wander around town." I glanced around the perimeter of the deserted park, searching for a street sign. "To be honest, I'm not exactly sure where I am."

"First is about twelve blocks that way." Duke pointed straight ahead.

I really had gotten turned around. I would have guessed it behind us. "You don't work Fridays."

"Nope. One of my deputies has his kids on Saturdays and he needs it off. Rather than stick someone else on every weekend, I just cover Saturdays myself."

There he was, being that good guy again, making it hard for me to stay irritated that he'd taken my bribe. Maybe my standards were too high.

Even my dad hadn't been without flaws. Dad had always left the toilet seat up. He'd driven my mother crazy by never putting away his morning coffee mug. He'd loved to bicker with Mom, though I could count on one hand the number of times I'd seen my parents truly fight. Their arguing had typically been adorable, good-natured teasing laced with humor.

Duke might be taking this money to pay for a sick parent's medical bills. He might be planning a large charitable donation. Was I really going to let this bribe be a deal breaker?

It was on the tip of my tongue to ask why he wanted the money. I opened my mouth and . . . chickened out. "Is there a baseball game today?"

"Nah. Just batting practice."

"Are you a coach?"

"Something like that."

"I like baseball," I said, falling into step beside him as we walked toward the infield. "When I was a kid, I used to sing the national anthem for our local farm team. Then my parents and I would stay for the game. We'd eat popcorn and hot dogs and ice cream."

"How old were you?"

"When I started singing? Ten. At least, that's when I did it for any kind of compensation. Baseball tickets included. But I sang at recitals and events long before that. My mom used to say that I started making up songs as soon as I learned how to talk."

"How did you go from baseball fields to the Grand Ole Opry?"

"Luck."

"Luck? I don't buy it. I've heard your music. I think talent might be the better word."

I smiled, watching my feet as we walked. I'd won nearly all of the awards possible for a country music singer, but Duke's compliment gave me goose bumps. "Thank you."

"Why do you say luck?"

"I caught a break. My senior year, I made a deal with my parents. I'd take a gap year between high school and college to try music. If it worked out, great. If not, I'd get my business degree so I had something to fall back on."

They'd wanted me to stay home and live with them to save some money. I'd agreed because, besides Everly, my parents had been my best friends and I'd wanted that time with them before venturing into the world on my own.

If only we'd had that time. How differently would my life have been? I wouldn't be in Calamity, that was for sure.

The minute there'd been trouble, my parents would have collected me from Nashville and brought me home.

"I was living at home, working as a receptionist at a gym and writing music and recording demos," I told Duke. "Everything I wrote, I put on YouTube. I didn't go viral like Justin Bieber or Shawn Mendes, but I did catch the eye of a producer. Long story short, Scott is the head of Sunsound's A&R division—they do all the talent scouting and artistic development and album design. He found my videos and brought me into the label. It's never too early to sign, as they say, and I did at nineteen. Then he basically put my career on the map."

Scott Berquest had been my hero. He'd stood by my side during the worst moments of my life. He'd been in the wings, clapping and cheering during the best. He'd championed my songwriting and my singing.

Then he'd betrayed me.

Scott was as good as dead to me now.

"Do you miss it yet?" Duke asked.

"No." I missed the urge to sing and write and wondered if my love for music would ever return. But right now, I didn't miss that life.

Too much had happened.

Too much had changed.

"You're quite forthcoming this morning," Duke teased.

I laughed. "It's the endorphins. They've put me in a chatty mood." That and these were safe questions.

When we reached the chain-link barrier behind home plate, Duke set down the bat and glove, then gave me all of his attention. "I'm curious."

"Yeah, I know."

He chuckled. "Is Lucy Ross your real name? Or is it a stage name?"

"Why do you ask? Gonna look me up?"

"Maybe I already have."

I shook my head. "No, you haven't."

"How do you know?"

Because if he'd looked me up, if he'd have made phone calls to the Nashville police department, his questions would be entirely different. "Let's call it a hunch. Cops believe in hunches, right?"

"That we do."

"What's your hunch about me?"

"That Lucy Ross is your real name."

"Ding, ding, ding." I smiled. "You're correct. I considered a stage name, but because I'd had some success on YouTube under my real name, the record label didn't want me to change it."

And after my parents had died, it had become a way to honor them. I'd taken their last name and made it known across the globe. Mom especially would have loved to see my name in lights. According to her story, she'd fought Dad through her entire pregnancy for the name Lucy. Dad had wanted to name me Rose Ross, and thank God he'd had a change of heart after seeing Mom in labor for twenty-one hours.

In a way, I was grateful that Duke had pulled me over last week. It was nice to have someone in Calamity know my real name, and he seemed to prefer it over Jade.

"Well, thanks for pointing me toward First." I waved. "I'll leave you to your appointment."

"Now that you've braved the streets of Calamity, should I expect to see you around town more often?" Duke asked.

"Maybe." Though it was undoubtedly safer to stay at the farmhouse. "Bye."

He lifted an arm to wave as I eased away. The carefree grin on his face was hard to turn my back on.

I'd offered up way more personal information today than I'd planned, but it was so easy to talk to Duke. Surprisingly so, and not just because I was lonely—it had been the same way at Yellowstone. There was just something about him that felt safe. Real. Honest.

So why had he taken that bribe? From what I could tell, it was so out of character. Curiosity got the better of me and I spun back around. "Duke?"

His eyes were waiting, like he'd been watching me walk away. "Yeah?"

I opened my mouth, ready to ask, when a voice rang out across the park.

"Hey." A teenaged boy came walking through the baseball diamond, his lanky strides eating up the distance from second base to home.

Duke shifted his attention to the kid and the smile that stretched across his face was blinding. "Hey, bud."

Was this Duke's son? It had to be. I hadn't even considered that Duke might have kids. Was he divorced then?

The kid was gangly and not quite as tall as Duke, but he had the frame to grow into a tall and broad man. There was a lot of potential in those bony shoulders. It was hard to see any resemblance because he had a baseball cap on, pulled low like mine.

The kid shot me a glance, then shifted his attention back to Duke, holding out a faded white baseball. There was a glove already on his left hand. "Ready?"

"One sec." Duke stepped away from the kid—who was

giving me a head-to-toe inspection—and came over. "What were you going to ask me?"

"Oh, it's nothing." I waved it off and took a step away. "See ya, Sheriff."

"I thought we'd gotten rid of the formalities."

"Sheriff has such a nice ring to it, don't you think?"

"Then I guess I'll see you around, *Ms. Morgan.*" He smirked. "Unless you want to stay and watch, baseball fan that you are. We're practicing his fielding skills and I'll even let you critique my swing."

I was stinky and the sweat had dried to my skin, making me feel salty. There was a shower waiting for me after a long walk to the farmhouse and some baked goods that wouldn't eat themselves.

But I didn't go home.

"Sure."

CHAPTER SIX

DUKE

"WHO IS THAT?" Travis asked, his eyes glued to Lucy as she walked behind the chain-link barrier surrounding home plate.

"That's Jade." The false name tasted bitter and not nearly as sweet as Lucy. Maybe if I used it enough, it wouldn't bother me. "She's new in town."

He harrumphed and kicked at the nearly invisible chalk line to third.

I ignored the attitude, something that had been shit over the past two weeks. I'd hoped some ball would help him cheer up and remind him that I wasn't the enemy. An hour on the field usually put a smile on his face when we met on Fridays to practice, but last week, he'd been grouchy the entire time.

So far, this week was shaping up to be the same.

"Do you want to pitch first or field grounders?" I asked, tossing the ball up with my left and catching it with my right.

"Pitch."

"All right." I walked to the chain link where I'd set the

bat and my glove, casting Lucy a glance as I pulled on my glove.

Maybe it was stupid to have invited her to watch. Travis clearly didn't approve. But I hadn't wanted her to walk away. Today, she'd talked to me unguarded and it had been like speaking to the woman I'd met in Yellowstone. I wasn't ready to give her up yet, especially because I might not get this version of Lucy back.

She looked content, sitting on one of the team's benches. This field didn't have bleachers since it was used as a community field for spring T-ball and coach pitch leagues. Parents would bring their camp chairs and picnic blankets and watch from the grass.

"Have you ever played?" I asked her.

"Does Little League count?"

I chuckled. "It does here. Want to play? You can bat after we practice some pitching."

"Will you laugh at me if I whiff it?"

"Yes."

She smiled. "Well, at least you're honest, Sheriff."

Every time she called me Sheriff I found a new love for my title. That voice of hers was like warm syrup, sweet and sticky as it dripped into my ear. I wouldn't mind hearing it as a whisper as I kissed her neck.

The woman was a magnet.

When I'd come across her, sprawled on the grass, I'd had to force myself to keep on my feet. The urge to drop down on top of her and run my hands over those skintight leggings molded to her toned thighs and perfectly squeezable ass had been crippling.

I'd spent the past four days reminding myself that she was trouble. I didn't need her drama tangling up my simple, clean-cut life. She had more secrets than Alex Rodriguez had home runs, but one look at her and rational thought had flown out the window. And I was old enough to know my dick was playing a major role here.

When it came to Lucy Ross, I was at her mercy. I'd even resorted to reading that magazine—as expected, there hadn't been anything interesting inside other than the pictures.

No woman had ever consumed me like this, not even Travis's mom.

Melanie and I had ended in disaster. The same fate likely awaited me with Lucy, but damn it, there she was, sitting on that bench because I hadn't been able to send her on her own way.

"Are we going to do this or what?" Travis barked from the pitcher's mound.

I turned away from Lucy and walked to home plate, shooting him a glare. "Chill, Travis."

"Whatever," he muttered, loud enough for me to hear because he knew it would piss me off.

"Watch it." I pointed at his nose, then crouched in a catcher's stance behind the plate.

I was barely in place before he wound up and launched a fastball dead center. The sting of the pitch spread through the leather of my mitt and into my palm. When he was younger, I'd pull my hand out and shake it. Make a big deal about how much it hurt.

But at the moment, I was too annoyed to hand out praise.

I didn't need to stand to fire the ball back just as fast. It hit his glove with a sharp smack and he winced. Travis could get angry and throw the ball as hard as he wanted, but the fact was, I still had the stronger arm.

After a few pitches, Travis relaxed and we settled into a

familiar rhythm. Neither of us spoke as he worked his fast-ball. My muscles loosened and the tension in my shoulders melted away with every pitch. It was hard to stay mad at the kid. My frustration with him never lasted long, especially when we were playing ball.

"Nice." I caught a pitch and stood, giving my knees a break. "Now let's work on your changeup."

"'Kay." He caught the ball as I whipped it back and adjusted his baseball cap.

Before getting back into position behind home, I glanced over my shoulder at Lucy.

She had her face tipped up to the sky, letting the sunshine peek underneath the brim of her hat. Her eyes were closed and her lips formed a slight smile.

Beautiful. So damn beautiful. Screw the magazine photos. I'd rather stare at her on that bench for hours.

"Duke," Travis snapped.

Lucy's peaceful expression broke and she opened her eyes, dropping them to the field.

I shot her a grin, then returned to my crouch behind home plate. "What's the rush, Travis?"

"I don't have all day."

"Did you get a job I don't know about?" He'd gotten fired from his job at the hardware store last week for not showing up on time eight days in a row.

"No."

"Then relax. Throw a changeup." I held out my glove.

He gritted his teeth and threw the ball, but it went wild and hit the chain link.

Exactly in front of where Lucy was sitting.

She flinched but didn't scream or throw her hands in front of her face. It was almost like she'd expected it.

I stood and went to get the ball. "Sorry."

"It's fine," she lowered her voice, "but maybe I should go."

"Stay." Not just for me, but because Travis was going to have to learn to deal with this at some point. "Please."

Lucy nodded. "Okay."

I stalked to the pitcher's mound and held up the ball.

Travis went to swipe it from my grip, but I yanked my hand away before he could touch it.

"What's the problem?" I asked.

"Nothing. I missed."

"Don't bullshit me, Travis. That was the worst pitch you've made in weeks. You don't miss. You threw that ball exactly where you wanted, so I'll ask again. What's the problem?"

"Nothing. I just missed." His fists unclenched at his sides and his jaw relaxed. Eventually, he might be able to pull off that lie, but his eyes betrayed him. They flicked over my shoulder to Lucy.

Any other day, I'd sit him down, here and now, and have the same talk I'd had with him a hundred times. I wasn't getting back together with his mom. No matter how hard he wished for it. No matter how many times he begged.

Melanie and I would never be right for one another.

"Do you want to practice?" I handed him the ball.

"Yeah."

"Then shape up and let's play."

He nodded and dropped his gaze to the dirt as I returned to my plate.

Travis and I had been practicing here every Friday this summer. It was the one weekday morning he didn't have summer school, and it coincided with my day off. We'd spend a few hours together before he took his afternoon shift at the hardware store—except now he'd been canned.

Sports had always been our thing. Whether playing or watching a game on TV, the two of us had always had it in common. Baseball especially.

Leading into the school's spring season, I'd work with him every Sunday on his throw and swing. Then during the season, we'd play on Sundays because he wanted the extra practice while his teammates were otherwise taking the day off.

Calamity was a small town but our sports programs were solid. The community rallied around our kids, cheering in the stands and shelling out for fundraisers. Both the football and basketball teams had made it to the state championships last year. And the baseball team was constantly improving thanks to the new coach.

If Travis worked hard over the next two years, he stood a good chance at picking up a college scholarship. He had the arm and natural talent. As much as I'd miss playing on this field with him, I wanted that chance for him. I wanted him to go to college and make something of his life.

It was August and we were nearly a year away from the spring baseball season, but I couldn't wait for school to start at the end of the month. I needed the kids—Travis, especially—back in the classroom full-time. Summer school wasn't keeping him out of trouble.

I'd had some issues lately with a band of teenagers whose parents didn't give a shit that their kids were out all night. Somehow Travis had gotten mixed up with them and Melanie didn't seem to give a flying fuck that I'd caught him two Saturdays ago in my backyard after midnight.

Sitting.

That's what he'd told me he was doing when the motion light had come on and I'd cracked the sliding door to my deck with one hand, gun in the other.

He'd been *sitting*.

Yeah, sitting with the faint smell of beer on his breath. I'd been tempted to put him under house arrest.

When I was a kid, summers meant camping with friends and sneaking a couple beers along. Some of my buddies would smoke cigarettes or cigars. He wasn't doing anything I hadn't done, but that didn't make it okay.

Since he'd seemed so damn infatuated with sitting and staring at my yard last week, I'd put him to work in the evenings. I'd had him mow my lawn and trim bushes. Over my lunch break last Saturday, before I'd pulled Lucy over, I'd brought home two gallons of stain for the fence and one paintbrush.

Other than spending time with him and giving him tasks to keep him out of trouble, I wasn't sure what else to do.

We worked through his changeup and then his curveball. Then I made him do another twenty fastballs. "Good. Let's work on fielding."

Travis groaned and trudged toward short stop. When I was his age, I'd hated fielding practice too.

"You ready to show me what you got?" I asked Lucy, picking up the bat.

She stood from the bench and made her way onto the field, taking the bat and ball from me as I held them out. "Are you going to pitch to me?"

"Nah. Just toss it up and hit it. Travis will field it and throw it back."

"I'll try. Keep the heckling to a minimum, okay?"

I grinned. "No promises."

"Is he going to throw one of those fastballs at my face?"

I stepped closer, looking down at those green eyes. "If he does, I'll catch it."

There was no way I'd let her get hurt. And I didn't care if Travis was sixteen, I'd put that kid over my knee if he tried.

Lucy's gaze dropped to my mouth. "Thanks."

Don't kiss her. It was taking every ounce of restraint not to slide my fingers across the freckles on her cheek, bend down and—

"Are you fucking kidding me?" Travis appeared at my side.

I stepped back from Lucy and shot him a glare. "Watch your language."

"You cuss all the time."

"Adult." I pointed to my chest, then poked a finger at his. "Child."

"What is she doing?" He jerked his chin at Lucy and the bat.

Before I could tell him to lose the attitude, Lucy pushed between us, ball and bat in hand and walked to home plate.

"I haven't done this since I was a kid." She tossed the ball in the air two feet and caught it. Then she did it again, testing the movement. When she tossed it a third time, she gripped the bat while the ball was on the rise, took a step back with one foot, lifted the other and swung straight for the ball as she stepped through.

The ball cracked on the bat before it sailed past second base and into left center.

My jaw dropped. "What the hell?" I muttered at the same time Travis said, "Whoa."

His mouth was hanging open too.

Lucy giggled as the ball stopped rolling in the grass. "Lucky shot."

"Little League, huh?"

She shrugged. "I might have played softball until I was fifteen."

I chuckled. Everything about this woman was a surprise. I wasn't much of a guy for surprises on the regular, but damn if I didn't like each of hers.

"Hi, I'm Jade." She returned to where we were standing and held out a hand to Travis.

"Travis." He shook her hand, still dumbfounded. He looked her up and down, then to the ball in the grass.

I shoved Travis's shoulder and jerked my chin for the outfield. "Go get the ball." I crossed the gap between us, that magnetic pull of hers always seeming to drag me an inch or two closer than necessary. "Think you can do that again?"

"Probably." She winked, then sauntered back to the plate.

My eyes were glued to that ass every swaying step.

I caught the ball as Travis threw it from the outfield, then handed it to Lucy, letting my fingers brush her open palm.

The little touches, the jolts of electricity, were addictive, and each time I returned the ball for her to hit again, I made sure to repeat the chaste caress.

Lucy mostly hit grounders to Travis, who'd come back to his position between second and third. After about the twentieth hit without a single whiff in the mix, she blew out a long breath and handed me the bat. "I'm going to quit while I'm ahead. Thank you. That was fun."

"You're welcome." I set my glove aside and tossed up the ball, hitting it far into left field to make Travis run for it and keep him occupied for a minute. "Let me hit him a few pop flies, then I'll drive you home."

"Oh, that's okay. I can walk." She took a step away, waving as she walked backward. "See you around."

"Lucy," I said, her name—the sweet one—loud enough for only her to hear. "I'm driving you home."

She arched an eyebrow. "Please?"

I strode into her space, this time so close that the cotton of my T-shirt brushed against the fabric of her tank top. Close enough that I heard the hitch in her breath. "That wasn't a request."

"Bossy," she whispered. "That's a new look for you."

"And?"

"It's not entirely unattractive."

I grinned and dragged myself out of her space, turning just in time for Travis's gaze to narrow on us both.

He stomped across the infield and threw the ball to the dirt. "I'm done."

"Let's do some outfield work."

"No, I'm done." He rolled his eyes. "You're busy anyway."

"Travis." I crossed my arms over my chest. The warning in my tone was clear. If he walked away from here like this, he'd be in deep shit. I didn't hold a lot of cards when it came to serving punishments in his life, but I'd play the few I had.

He huffed and looked at Lucy from the brim of his hat. "Bye."

"Goodbye," she said.

Without another word, he turned and jogged across the park.

Shit.

"Sorry," Lucy said.

"It's not your fault. He's going through some stuff." I sighed and went to collect my mitt and bat. Then I nodded for her to follow me to my truck, parked on the street.

"How old is he?" she asked as we fell into step on the grass.

"Sixteen. Wants to be twenty-five. Acts like he's ten." Travis's lanky legs stretched as he crossed the street. "He's a good kid. He acts like a brat sometimes, but he really is a good kid."

"And you seem like a good father."

"I'm not his dad."

Lucy's feet came to a halt. "You're not?"

"No. Sorry, I forget that not everyone is from Calamity." I didn't have to explain my relationship with Travis to the locals. "I dated his mom years ago. We broke up when Travis was twelve but I stayed in his life."

Besides his grandfather, I was the closest thing Travis had to a father. He might not be mine by blood, but I loved that kid.

"Ah. Now it makes sense," Lucy said, ungluing her feet. "I'm guessing he wants you to get back together with his mom."

"Pretty much." It hadn't taken her long to peg Travis's attitude. "I've told him a hundred times it's not going to happen, but . . ."

"Kids always hope."

I nodded. "Melanie and I dated for two years. In the end, I realized the only reason I was staying was for Travis. He needed a constant and that constant was me. And even though I'm not with his mom anymore, I didn't want to lose him. So I do my best to keep up on his life. Be the guy he can count on."

She stopped walking again and stared at my profile, her eyes full of disbelief. The skepticism only lasted a heartbeat before she blinked it away and gave me a warm smile. "He's lucky to have you."

"Goes both ways."

We reached my truck and I dug the keys from my pocket, hitting the locks and opening her door, but she didn't get in. She stood on the grass, studying me.

"You keep looking at me like that," I said. "Like you're trying to figure me out."

"Maybe I am."

"I'm not a complicated man, Lucy."

"No, I think you might be the most complicated man I've ever met."

I laughed. "Give it time. You'll see I'm about as simple as they come."

She took a step closer. Her hand reached up to pick at a fleck on my shirt. Any bewilderment in her gaze was gone. Instead, there was heat. Lust. Want. My heart stuttered as she lifted her lashes, giving me a sultry smile. "In Yellowstone, in the parking lot, I thought you were going to kiss me."

Damn, I liked that she could cut straight to it. "I wanted to."

"Why didn't you?"

"I wasn't expecting to see you again."

"But here I am."

"Here you are." I lifted a hand and trailed my fingers over the bare skin of her shoulder.

"So?"

So she wouldn't have to invite me twice. I leaned in,

ready to brush my lips against hers, when a horn honked, and I whipped my head up as a familiar SUV drove past.

"Hey, Duke!" Dan, the owner of the hardware store, waved from behind the wheel.

"Hi, Dan!" I lifted the hand that had been on Lucy's skin.

Dan was a good guy. He ran a successful business and contributed a lot to our community. He'd hired Travis. And he'd fired Travis. He'd called me immediately afterward, apologizing profusely. I'd assured him it was the right decision, and had I been in his shoes, I would have done the same.

"Never a day off, huh?" Lucy asked, stepping away.

"Not in Calamity." I moved aside and held the door as she climbed in my truck.

When she was settled, I slammed it closed and took a breath, giving myself a second to get my body under control. Damn, but it was tempting to drive her to my house and strip those skintight running clothes off her delicious body.

This woman. Lucy. Jade. Lajade. Whatever she wanted to call herself, it didn't matter. She had me twisted in knots.

And at the moment, that didn't seem like such a bad thing.

CHAPTER SEVEN

LUCY

DUKE EVANS WAS as addictive as hot stage lights and a silky, Southern twang.

He'd almost kissed me. And I'd almost let him. I'd find a way to get over this bribe issue if it meant indulging my crush on the local sheriff. Sure, things would get awkward when I brought him a wad of cash. After all, maybe the reason he'd almost kissed me was for the money.

The woman who hadn't been kissed in a long, *long* time didn't care.

"What's your plan for the rest of the day?" Duke asked as he drove toward the farmhouse. He rolled down the windows and the breeze tousled the long strands of hair that had escaped his hat.

"Not much. I've been on a baking spree."

"What'd you make?" he asked, his voice low and smooth.

Duke drove with one hand on the wheel while his other arm was propped on the console between us. I hadn't really noticed a man's driving posture before, but as with everything Duke, the should-have-been-mundane details jumped out at me like fireworks. His entire demeanor shouted confidence. He was so relaxed in his skin and sexy as hell. The man was driving and I was practically drooling.

He glanced over and raised an eyebrow. *Right.* He'd asked me a question.

I faced forward and unscrambled my brain. "Cookies. Cinnamon rolls. Banana muffins."

"You've been busy."

"There's not much else for me to do. Going from a hare's speed to turtle pace has been an adjustment. At this point, I'm searching for things to do. Hence the running this morning."

"My mom's a teacher. She always says it takes her a couple of weeks every summer to slow down and transition from kid wrangler to domestic goddess." He reached into the cupholder and plucked out a packet of gum. "Want one?"

"Sure." I unfolded the wrapper and popped the sweet mint stick into my mouth as he did the same, then I opened my mouth to say something and . . . *whoa.*

We were rolling through a different neighborhood than the one I'd walked through, but instead of staring at the homes and getting my bearings, my attention was locked on the bob of Duke's Adam's apple and the flex of his strong, square jaw.

I bet he had a talented tongue. My experience with men was relatively limited—fame was a jealous lover and wanted nothing more than your undivided attention—but if a man could chew gum like that, I bet his tongue knew its way around a woman's lips.

And other places.

I gulped as a curl of lust tightened in my lower belly. It

was impossible to ignore or stifle being in this truck, surrounded by his spicy sandalwood scent.

Duke turned onto First Street and the quiet sidewalks from earlier were now teeming with people. The once empty parking spaces were full. I pulled the brim of my hat a little lower and slumped in my seat. Every tourist in Calamity seemed to be out exploring this morning, and riding in Duke's police truck drew attention.

Maybe I should have insisted on walking.

"Don't worry." He glanced over. "At least you're not in the backseat wearing cuffs."

I rolled my eyes and fought a laugh as I looked over my shoulder through the clear partition. This was my first time in a police vehicle. There was a laptop between us, the lid closed, and a radio that had a constantly blinking green light. Beneath it was an array of buttons and switches that I assumed controlled the siren and the lights on the roof.

My fingers itched to touch one of them, so I tucked my hands beneath my thighs, keeping my chin down as Duke drove down First.

"Do you know how Calamity got its name?" he asked.

"No. I just assumed it was from Calamity Jane."

"Well, she did live around here as a kid, but that's not where the town got its name. Calamity was originally called Panner City."

"Doesn't quite roll off the tongue." It definitely wouldn't have piqued my interest during those hours of internet searching for a hideaway.

"No, it doesn't." Duke chuckled. If this conversation was to ease my concerns, it was working. "It was started as a settlement during the Montana gold rush and by 1864, almost three thousand miners lived in the area."

I twisted in my seat, fascinated by the story. "More than live here today."

"You've done some research."

"A little." But not enough to have read this story.

"In the course of five months, four disasters struck Panner City. First, the mine collapsed in Anders Gulch and killed a dozen men. Then there was a heavy spring storm that flooded the area and washed out most of the smaller panning sites and claims. Then there was a fire that spread through town. And last but not least, they had a late-summer lightning storm. It caused a herd of cattle to have an honest-to-God stampede through the settlement. All in the span of five months."

"Wow."

He grinned. "Goodbye, Panner City."

"Hello, Calamity." I laughed. "Why don't they have that story on the town website?"

"The chamber thought it might send the wrong impression. That if tourists came here, they were risking their lives."

Silly. That story made this place even more rugged and attractive, like the narrator himself. "Thanks for telling me."

Duke looked over and his blue eyes ensnared me. "Welcome."

Whatever worry I'd had about being recognized had disappeared but as Duke pulled off the highway and onto my gravel road, a new thrill took hold and my stomach did a cartwheel. It was just the two of us. Alone. After he'd almost kissed me.

Should I invite him inside? Would he drop me off and leave? The dull throb in my core begged for the latter. An invitation. *Inside.*

My face flamed. Today had to be a record for dirty

thoughts. I blamed Duke for being so potent. Being around him was exhilarating and tense. It was reckless for me to be thirsting for the one person in town who knew my real identity, the person I'd bribed into silence, but my body didn't care.

Neither did my heart of hearts.

Besides the bribe, Duke was honest and kind. He didn't seem to care about my fame or fortune and hadn't once tried to exploit me for more. Most assholes would have rejected my initial offer and asked for double.

But Duke hadn't mentioned the money, had he? Why was that? Wouldn't he want to know when it was payday? The only one who kept bringing it up in our conversations was me. *Huh.*

The driveway was empty when he pulled in front of the farmhouse, because I'd started parking in the garage. Duke had barely come to a stop when I blurted, "Want to come inside for a muffin?"

He hesitated, staring past me to the house. My heart was in my throat as he silently debated my question. We both knew if he came inside, there'd be no more *almost* about any kiss. Duke finally answered by shoving the truck into park and twisting the key out of the ignition.

My mind was spinning as I hopped out. Anticipation hummed in my veins as I climbed the porch steps.

Duke wasn't far behind as I walked to the door and took the key from the small pocket in my leggings. His gaze burned a hot trail down my neck. The magnitude of his presence pinned me in place. There was no ignoring a man like Duke, not when he was within touching distance.

I fumbled the key before it finally slid into the lock. I

flicked my wrist and turned the knob, only to get a whiff of myself in the process.

Oh. My. God. I smelled like wet dog and seaweed.

The door bounced against the stop as I flung it open, practically leaping over the threshold, anything to put some space between me and Duke. Why hadn't I thought this through? I'd almost let this gorgeous, delicious man kiss me when I was a hot mess.

"Can I have ten minutes?" I asked, already racing up the stairs. "Just . . . make yourself at home. I'll be right back. Ten minutes." Twenty, max. I'd never taken a ten-minute shower in my life but damn it, today would be that day. My legs had renewed strength as I pounded up the stairs. "Muffins are in the kitchen!" I called over my shoulder, rounding the railing.

I stripped off my tank top, stiff with dried sweat, and threw it on my bed as I dashed through the bedroom. I ducked my nose to my armpit and gagged. Oh hell, what if Duke had smelled me in his truck? Was that why he'd rolled the windows down?

Shit. I collapsed on the bed, rumpling the bedding that I'd artfully made this morning, as I shoved off my leggings and kicked off my shoes. Naked, I balled up my smelly clothes, tossed them in the hamper in the closet, then hurried to the en suite bathroom.

The water in this old house took minutes to warm but I cranked it on and stepped under the cold spray, wincing and swallowing a yelp. I shampooed with fury. I conditioned haphazardly. I soaped up my shower poof and scrubbed until I no longer smelled like a man's dirty jockstrap.

I toweled off, dragged a comb through my hair and twisted it into a dripping knot. I didn't give much thought to my clothes as I slipped on a pair of denim shorts and a green tee over my favorite neon-yellow panties and matching bra.

Duke was in the living room, staring out the front window at the blue mountains in the distance, when I came downstairs.

"Sorry," I said, sweeping into the room on bare feet.

"No problem." Duke shifted away from the window and nodded to the room. The couch that used to face the window was now opposite the fireplace. I'd swapped it with the chairs and moved the coffee table to a different angle. "Looks like you've been busy."

"More like desperate for entertainment."

I'd rearranged almost every room in the farmhouse, choosing layouts that suited me best. Or that were just different for the sake of something different. Besides baking, rearranging had been my favorite pastime.

Duke grinned and his eyes held me captive. They were bluer than normal with the daylight streaming into the room. Two cerulean pools that I wanted to dive into headfirst.

Neither of us spoke. Neither of us moved. The tension grew thick and the air in the room heavy.

Maybe the fact that I'd been upstairs, naked, was the reason Duke seemed rooted on the other side of the room. Maybe I should have spent another minute in the shower thinking this through.

Except the last thing I wanted was to think. The past week, all I'd done was overthink. I'd questioned my every move.

Had running been the answer? Was I a coward for leaving Nashville?

Insecurity had been slicing through my thoughts regularly and it had taken all my energy to not let it shred me to ribbons.

Had I been too harsh? Was there something I could have done to save Meghan?

Her smile had flashed in my mind countless times in the past four weeks. Her laugh echoed in the farmhouse on the still nights. The sight of her lifeless body soaking in a pool of her own blood haunted my dreams.

I wanted to scream. I wanted to cry. I wanted to ask her why.

But she was gone.

"Lucy." Duke's voice caught my attention and I shook myself out of my head.

"Yeah?"

"What's going on?"

"Oh, nothing." I waved it off and smiled. "Sorry. I think I'm still a little lightheaded from that run. So how about that muffin?"

"Actually, I think we'd better skip the muffin. How about we sit down and talk about the reason you left Nashville and changed your name?"

"But—"

"Lucy." He used the same tone on me that he had on Travis. "Sit down."

I groaned. "It's been such a nice morning. Let's not ruin it. Please."

He fisted his hands on his hips. "Lu—"

"You took the bribe. You agreed to keep my secret. So can we just drop this? Whether I tell you my story or not, you'll still get your money." The words sounded trite and repetitive. I cringed, regretting my outburst instantly as his face turned to stone.

Duke strode out of the room, blowing past me on his way to the door. "Good luck, Ms. Ross."

Damn it. What was my problem? "Wait," I said, my throat hoarse.

The door flew open and Duke stepped onto the porch, not slowing.

"Wait." I raced after him. "Please."

He stopped and turned his cheek, giving me one ear and maybe five seconds. The silhouette of his body took up nearly the whole doorframe.

"I'm sorry. That was . . . I'm sorry."

If he left today and never returned, I wouldn't fault him. What gorgeous, devilishly sexy, single man needed my kind of drama in his life? Especially when I kept reminding him of that insane bribe.

It was only money. I had plenty to spare. Maybe Duke wanted to use the cash for Travis's college education. Maybe he was hoping to help fund his parents' retirement. Maybe—

"I don't want the money." He shook his head and turned. "I was never going to take it. Should have told you no from the start."

I blinked. "What?"

"I'm not taking your bribe."

No. My heart plummeted and my mouth went dry as panic set in. "I can get more money. I just need some time. Please, please don't tell—"

"For fuck's sake, Lucy. I don't want your goddamn money. I'm not going to tell anyone who you really are, just because you asked me not to."

I gulped and dropped the hands that had been flailing in the air. "You aren't?"

"No."

"But . . ." This seemed too good to be true. "But why did you agree to the bribe?"

"Because I need to know why you're here. I need to know what I'm dealing with. For your safety. For the town. For me. The easiest way to keep you from slamming the door in my face was to make you think you owed me something. Figured you'd be more willing to talk if I was on the hook. Turns out, you just keep throwing it in my face."

"You don't want the money."

"No." His jaw clenched. "For the last time, I don't want your fucking money."

"Then what *do* you want?"

"Nothing."

"That's not how the world works."

"Maybe." He sighed. "But this is Calamity."

A world of its own. A world where good men existed. Where I wouldn't be exploited or betrayed or despised.

The knot in my stomach unraveled. My heart soared.

Duke was the quintessential, unprecedented good man. I'd been denying it, scared to trust in his decency. But deep in my heart, maybe I'd already known the truth.

"Thank you," I whispered.

He nodded. "Take care, Lucy."

I was surprised when he left, but it still hurt to watch him descend the porch steps.

The urge to cry nearly drove me to my knees but I put a hand on the wall and held fast, then bit the inside of my lip to keep the tears at bay.

I'd lost Duke. I'd lost someone I hadn't even had, and *fuck*, I was tired of losing people.

This time, I couldn't blame a drunk driver or a razor-sharp kitchen knife.

This loss was on me.

"Actually . . ." Duke stopped on the bottom stair.

I blinked my eyes clear, pushing off the wall. "Yeah?"

"I do want something." He spun and stalked up the stairs, each step deliberate. He pinned me with his piercing gaze as he crossed the porch.

My breath was lodged in my chest. When he stood before me, I tipped my chin up to hold his eyes. I was frozen, unable to contemplate what this meant as he leaned in so closely that his nose was inches from mine.

"I want something." His whisper caressed my cheek.

"What?" *Me.* Let the answer be me.

"A kiss."

My knees wobbled.

Duke lifted his hand to my cheek. "You gonna stop me?"

"No."

He flashed me a smile before dropping his lips to mine, stealing my senses with the touch of his soft lips.

Duke's kiss was firm. Steady. Then his tongue licked the seam of my lips and we melted into one another. I opened for him and let him sweep inside as his arms banded around my shoulders.

My hands ran up his torso, skimming over the soft cotton of his T-shirt to feel the hard, rippled grooves of his stomach. I stretched up onto my toes as my hands ran up the wide and solid plane of his chest. Our tongues tangled and I looped my arms around his neck, pulling myself closer as his hold on me tightened.

Duke was a wall of muscle, a tower of strength. He held me at his mercy.

He tasted like man and spice mixed with the sweet, cool mint of his gum. My heart thundered in my chest as he devoured me, leaving no corner of my mouth untouched. The strength of his arms was a marvel. He held me effortlessly, my toes dangling above the wooden boards of the porch.

A hum came from deep in Duke's chest and the vibration pebbled my nipples.

I tightened my grip on his neck and wove my fingers into the short strands of hair at his nape. The kiss took on a whole new heat as he angled his head to dive deeper. I nipped at the corner of his lip. He fluttered his tongue against mine, a move I wanted to feel against the swell of my breast. Against the swollen bud between my legs.

I'd underestimated Duke. The spark between us hadn't just been a sizzle. It was a raging wildfire that was going to incinerate, not singe. At the moment, I didn't care how dangerous this might be. I was too consumed by the blinding need for more.

Duke growled against my mouth. His arousal was thick and heavy where it pressed into my hip.

More.

But instead of hauling me inside and using that tongue on my naked skin, he tore his mouth away. I didn't loosen my hold and his arms stayed tight at my back. He held me, my toes still off the floor, staring into my eyes as we both panted.

His gaze darted to my swollen, wet lips and his jaw ticked. Was that a good tick? Bad? I'd have to spend more time around Duke to figure out how to read them. I was willing to put in the time, especially if at the end of our conversations he kissed me like this.

The corner of my mouth turned up. "Not bad, Sheriff."

"Hope that earned me your vote in the next election," he teased.

I giggled as he set me on my feet.

Duke held on to my elbow until I steadied my legs, then he ran his thumb over my bottom lip.

I waited for another kiss but he sucked in a deep breath, took one step away, then turned and jogged down the steps before I had a chance to object.

"What? That's it?"

He kept moving. "No, that's not it."

"Then where are you going?" I walked to the top stair and put my hands on my hips.

"Think it's better if I leave now," he said, reaching his truck.

Seriously? "But you didn't get a muffin."

Lust flared in his gaze and his feet stopped. He dropped his head and rubbed the back of his neck. Then he looked at me like it was torture to walk away.

Good. It was torture to watch.

"If I step inside that house again . . ." He didn't need to finish that sentence.

If he stepped inside this house, everything would change.

There'd be no more guarding my secrets. Or my heart.

"Come inside, Duke."

His eyes darkened at the sound of his name. He stalked up the stairs until he stood in my space, one step lower so we were closer to eye level. "You sure?"

Was I? This was out of character for me. I'd met Duke just one week ago—he was practically a stranger. I didn't have sex with strangers.

He ran a hand up the bare skin of my forearm. His tongue darted out, pink and hot and my mouth watered, desperate for a longer taste.

The breeze caught Duke's scent, dragging it to my nostrils and forcing me to take a long breath. I wanted that smell on my sheets.

So I shut off my brain, shoved my nerves aside to fist the hem of Duke's T-shirt.

And dragged him inside.

CHAPTER EIGHT

DUKE

THE MOMENT LUCY pulled me across the threshold, my mouth was on hers. My hands roamed her body as she clung to me, kissing me with as much fervor and raw lust as I had racing through my veins.

Christ, this woman could kiss. Her tongue did this little swirl that sent all the blood rushing straight to my cock.

I kicked the door shut and broke away from her lips long enough to whip her shirt over her head and toss it to the floor.

"Up," I ordered.

She jumped.

With one arm under her ass and the other around her back, I held her to me as fiercely as she held me, her lips seeking mine as her fingers dove into my hair.

Lucy moaned, angling her head so I could devour her mouth. I nipped and sucked and licked, arching into her center as her legs circled my waist. Her nipples were pebbled beneath her bra, begging for my hot mouth.

The heat from her core spread through her shorts to my

jeans and I was seconds from tearing them off her legs. If I didn't get her to a bed, I'd fuck her on the couch. I'd save that for later.

I tore my lips away again and blinked the haze from my vision as I started for the stairs.

Lucy dropped her mouth to my neck, latching on to my pulse to suck.

"Fuck," I groaned, picking up my pace. My cock throbbed beneath my jeans and my heart slammed against my sternum. "Where?" I asked at the top stair.

"Left."

I hit the landing and moved straight for the bedroom door. It was bright inside, the sunlight streaming from the window onto the plush white bed.

Lucy unwound her legs, dropping those bare toes to the carpet, and her hands pounced on the button on my jeans.

"In a hurry?" I teased, reaching behind my neck to yank my T-shirt over my head before kicking off my boots.

"Jeans off, Sheriff."

Christ, it was sexy when a woman wanted to order me around.

I swatted her hands aside, but instead of stripping my own jeans, I dropped to my knees and worked free the button on her shorts, tugging the denim and the brightest pair of panties I'd ever seen free from her body.

Her skin was like sweet cream, smooth and silky. The sight of her glistening folds made my head spin, and her scent . . . *fuck me*, she smelled good. Like cherries, sweet and rich, with a hint of warm vanilla.

The smart thing to do would be to slow this down. Savor her. I hadn't been with a woman in a while, but my body wasn't listening to any mental commands. *Want. Need.*

Take. The words pulsed through my veins with every heart-beat. But we'd do slow later. There was no doubt in my mind that I'd have her once and need her again, over and over.

Lucy was addictive.

Her fingernails scraped my scalp as she dragged her hands through my hair, tugging and teasing it beside my temples.

I gripped her hips and jerked her to me, earning a little yelp. Then I dropped my mouth to that beautiful, bare pussy, dragging my tongue through her slit and flicking my tongue against her clit.

"Duke." Her breath hitched.

Her taste exploded on my tongue, cherry sweet. One day, I'd feast on her, let her hold on to my hair as I devoured her, but not today.

I placed a kiss on her belly button, working my way up her stomach and ribs to the center of her breasts. Worshipping. Savoring. When I was back on my feet, I flicked the clasp of her bra and stripped it from her arms.

She stood there, her eyes closed, waiting for my next move.

"You are . . . breathtaking," I whispered, my fingers trailing down her collarbone to a rosy nipple.

Her lashes fluttered open and the look in her eyes nearly dropped me to my knees. It was vulnerable. Pure and open. No pretenses. No need to stroke egos or fake a reaction.

Lucy's gaze flicked to my jeans and the straining bulge beneath. Her index finger rose to my chest. Starting with one of my nipples, she trailed across my skin from one pec to the other before letting her finger drop down my sternum.

My abs bunched when she hit the valley between the

muscles. She skimmed my stomach and her featherlight touch made the throb spike.

If she kept going, I'd never last. So I moved like lightning, picking her up and tossing her on the bed.

She laughed as she bounced, then sat up on her elbows to watch me strip. My cock bobbed free and a drop of cum beaded at the tip.

She licked her lips.

"Fuck, you're killing me here."

"You're"—she gulped—"big."

I wrapped a fist around my shaft and stroked.

The flare of heat in her eyes was my invitation into the bed. I came down on her, settling into the cradle of her hips and positioning at her entrance, ready to thrust home, when that fucking good conscience of mine sent a siren blaring in my ear.

"Condom." Fuck. I didn't keep them on me because hookups weren't my style.

"Ugh," Lucy groaned and slapped a hand over her eyes. "I don't have one."

This would be the worst case of blue balls I'd had in my life. I pushed up to get the hell off this bed but she grabbed my bicep and stopped me.

"I'm on the pill. I, um . . . I haven't been with anyone in a long time."

"Same. I got my annual physical three months ago. I'm clean."

She sighed and that sultry smile was back. She opened her legs wider.

"You sure?"

"Fuck me, Duke."

Okay, she could definitely order me around. I didn't hesitate. I dragged the head of my cock through her wetness, then slid deep with one stroke.

Lucy gasped, her back arching off the bed as her hands came to my shoulders. Her nails dug in hard as she breathed, adjusting to my size.

I waited, giving her time. "Good?"

She nodded and circled her hips. "So good."

I grinned and dropped my lips to her neck, peppering her smooth skin with kisses as I eased out, then thrust forward, earning another gasp when I pushed as deep as I could go.

My palm came to one of her luscious breasts, letting it fill the cup of my hand. I ran a thumb over her pink nipple.

She quaked beneath me as I moved, in and out, over and over. A pink flush spread across her chest. Her freckles had darkened from a morning in the sun.

Lucy Ross was magnificent. This Lucy. It was heady— powerful—knowing that I was included in her secret. The rest of the world expected the blond and glitter. But I had black hair spread on white cotton. Eyes like water-clear emeralds.

I dropped a kiss to the corner of her mouth as I drove inside her tight body.

She turned her cheek, taking my mouth. She sucked on my bottom lip before slipping her tongue between my teeth.

We were lost in one another, moving like old lovers, not new. And I moved in steady strokes, taking us both higher and higher until she whimpered, pulling away from my mouth.

Her eyes squeezed shut, her grip on my shoulders fell away, and her body writhed.

"Duke," she whispered right before she exploded, crying

out and shaking in my arms as her inner walls pulsed and clenched around me.

I kept going, faster and faster, until the pleasure was too much. The pressure in my spine hit and I was done. I shot long and hard, collapsing on top of her as my orgasm broke, wringing me dry and leaving me boneless.

I'd expected sex to be good, but this? This was beyond comprehension. The best I'd ever had.

Lucy's hold on me tightened and she giggled. "Damn."

I eased out and rolled to the side so she wasn't bearing all my weight but kept her pinned with our legs tangled and her cheek resting on my chest. I stared at the ceiling until the white spots faded from my vision, then I kissed the top of her head. "How long does it take you to get ready?"

"Usually an hour. Why?"

"Good." She'd have plenty of time. There was a lot for the two of us to talk about. A lot of shit to figure out, especially now.

Sex with her had changed everything.

I kissed her again, then slid free and climbed out of bed. I tugged on my boxer briefs, then my jeans, covering my still-hard dick.

"Uh . . . where are you going?" Lucy asked, sitting up, completely naked and not trying to cover up.

I didn't answer as I shrugged on my T-shirt.

"Duke," she warned.

Damn, but I loved the way she said my name. Smooth and smoky, like expensive whiskey.

"Are you seriously leaving?" Her hair had fallen out of its tie. It was wild and damp as it draped down her shoulders. Her cheeks were flushed and that delicious bottom lip of hers was puffy.

She'd never looked more stunning.

"Yep. Get ready." I planted a knee in the bed, bent down to kiss the corner of her mouth, then walked to the door. "Be back at seven."

"Back for what? And what do you mean get ready?"

I kept walking.

"Duke!" The covers rustled and the bed creaked as she hurried to chase me down.

But I was already jogging down the stairs. "Seven o'clock."

When I started my truck, she appeared on the porch, draped in a white towel she must have snagged from the bathroom. The terry cloth was blinding in the afternoon sun. There was a scowl on her face as she watched me drive away.

I liked that scowl too.

I liked all things about Lucy Ross.

It was a good thing she was hell-bent on staying in Calamity.

Because I wasn't ready to let her go.

———

"THIS PLACE IS . . ."

I chuckled as Lucy's eyes widened. "Interesting?"

"That's one word."

"Come on." I tightened my grip on her hand and led her through Calamity Jane's bar.

"Are you sure this is a good idea?" She ducked her chin as a man passed us by. "I'm trying to keep a low profile here."

"Trust me."

She sighed. "Okay."

No hesitation.

This woman. Things were about to get really fucking complicated.

Maybe they already had.

I spotted an empty booth against the wall and walked over, ignoring the many faces staring our way. I held out an arm to one side of the booth, waiting for her to slide in, then I took my seat opposite her, grinning as she tucked a lock of hair to hide her profile.

"I don't like this," she said.

"Been thinking about it. You'll create more gossip if you hide away at that farmhouse. People in a small town are nosy. They'll want to know about the gorgeous recluse in Widow Ashleigh's place."

"But what if someone recognizes me?"

"They won't."

"How do you know?"

"Because right now, they're more curious about why you're in here with me than who you are."

She arched an eyebrow and I couldn't help but laugh.

"Hiya, Duke." The waitress appeared at our table, tossing down two cardboard coasters.

"Hey, Kelly."

"Can I get you guys a drink?" Her eyes wandered to Lucy, who was trying to stare a hole in the table.

"Beer for me. Whatever IPA you've got on tap."

Kelly nodded, waiting for Lucy to order. I nudged her foot under the table and her gaze whipped up.

I smirked.

She frowned, then forced a smile up at Kelly. "I'll have the same. Thanks."

"Menus?" Kelly asked.

"Nah." I tapped my temple.

"Be right back." She turned from the table but cast a glance over her shoulder at Lucy.

"See?" Lucy hissed.

"That's not about you. It's me."

"Why?"

I leaned in closer. "Because I walked in here with your hand in mine. Because I didn't sit at the bar like I normally do. Because I haven't brought a woman to dinner at Jane's who wasn't my mother or my sister in four years."

"Oh." She blushed.

"Yeah. Oh." I leaned back and slung one arm across the booth.

The bar was noisy tonight. Fridays usually were. Which was why I'd decided to bring Lucy here.

She wasn't the only one invested in keeping her secret.

What I needed right now was time. Time with her. Time to learn more about her past and what had happened to bring her to Calamity. Time to figure this out.

And at the moment, my gut was telling me I didn't have much time. That before I was ready, she'd be headed to Nashville. We were on a countdown headed to zero.

The last thing I needed were people asking around about the woman holed up in Kerrigan's latest rental property. They'd get curious. The quilting guild would show up at her front door with a pan of cinnamon buns and a slew of questions, and those ladies were hard to dodge.

But if Lucy was seen around town—specifically, if she was seen with me—the questions would take on a different tone. The gossip wouldn't be about a single woman, but rather the woman who'd captured my attention.

"Hi, Duke." Jane came to the table with two pint glasses, foam nearly overflowing the rims.

"Hey, Jane. How are ya?"

"Bar is packed. Can't complain." She turned to Lucy and stuck out a hand. "Jane Fulson."

"Jade Morgan." Lucy smiled, the fake name rolling off her tongue with the same ease as always.

"Nice to meet you, Jade. You're living out in Widow Ashleigh's place, right?"

I fought a grin at the momentary flash of surprise in Jade's eyes. Maybe she'd thought a week was too short a time to have been noticed. She'd learn soon enough that tabloids and paparazzi had nothing on the Calamity gossip mill.

"That's right." Lucy nodded. "It's a beautiful house."

"Kerrigan sure fixed it up nice." Jane looked at me. "You showed her your house yet?"

I grinned. Jane didn't ask where Lucy had come from. She didn't ask what Lucy did for a living. No, she was more curious about how serious this relationship was. Exactly as I'd hoped. "What's your burger special tonight?"

Jane shot me a playful sneer, knowing full well I'd evaded her, then jerked her thumb over her shoulder toward the chalkboard behind the bar. "Classic cheddar with fries."

"Still trust me?" I asked Lucy, earning a nod. "We'll take two specials."

Jane whipped a notepad from her apron pocket, scribbled down our order and disappeared to the kitchen without another word.

"Jane owns the bar," I told Lucy. And she was one of the reasons I'd chosen tonight to bring Lucy down.

Jane was in her fifties, her white-blond hair always tied up in a messy twist. She had kind brown eyes and a leathery tan, and though she was thin, her stature packed a punch. When Jane Fulson aimed her pointer finger at someone and told them to get the fuck out of her bar, only idiots made her say it twice.

"She's a little intimidating," Lucy said.

"Comes with the job. But Jane's a good woman. And she knows most of Calamity's secrets."

"Does she keep them?"

"Depends on the secret. Some she'll leak when it's for the greater good."

Jane heard all there was to hear around town—expected, considering her occupation. Tending bar all day, people gravitated to her when they had a problem to vent.

"If I ever need to know the street gossip, Jane's is my first stop. In all my years working here as a cop, she's never once let me down. There have even been a few times when she's called *me* with tips about things that she could have just let fly."

"Is that why you brought me here?"

"It's one reason. If Jane knows you're with me, she won't press for information."

"And the other reason?"

I took a sip of my beer. "Cold beer and greasy cheeseburgers."

Lucy giggled, then sipped her own beer, and the two of us sat in comfortable silence, taking a look around the dark bar.

I caught some eyes and gave some waves, but otherwise people—bless them for trying—did their best to not outright stare.

"This is quite the place." Lucy's eyes were everywhere, taking in the tall, wooden ceilings and the excess of tin and aluminum signs on the forest-green walls. The lighting was dim. Tables filled the center of the room and booths hugged the walls. The bar itself was on the far wall, the mirrored shelves jammed full with liquor bottles.

Lucy kept scanning, oblivious to—or just ignoring—the people looking her way. When her eyes landed on the taxidermic bison bust beside the stage, her expression flattened. "A buffalo. Great."

I chuckled, shaking my head as I drank my beer.

With her inspection over, Lucy gave me her attention, leaning her forearms on the table between us. The high-backed black vinyl booth blocked our conversation from prying ears. That and the jukebox was blaring. Still, she lowered her voice. "So . . ."

"So."

"You took off on me earlier today, Sheriff."

"Did that on purpose."

"Why?"

"Because I assumed you'd want to talk."

"Don't you think we should?" She blinked. "Casual sex is—"

"That was not casual."

Her breath caught. "It wasn't?"

I leaned in, holding those green eyes. "I knew you'd want to talk and probably downplay what happened between us, so I left. Gave you some time to think and freak out."

Her expression read guilty. She'd definitely freaked.

"We aren't casual, Lucy."

She dropped her eyes to her glass.

It would shock the hell out of me if she wanted casual. I wasn't going to agree so it didn't matter, but still, my heart stuttered as her silence lingered. Lucy had to know that whatever was happening here wasn't casual.

"Okay," Lucy whispered, lifting her gaze.

I let out the breath I'd been holding. "Glad that's settled."

The corners of her mouth turned up in a shy, sexy smile. "When was the last time you dated?"

"I've been on some dates. Nothing serious. Last long-term relationship I had was with Travis's mom. You?"

"No one serious since high school. If you can call a high school boyfriend serious. A year ago I dated Blake Ray for about two minutes but he's a tool."

"And his music sucks."

She burst out laughing, covering her smile with her hand. "You just made my night. We were both with the same record label and everyone was always blowing smoke up his ass. But he's consistently pitchy and can't remember the lines to his own damn songs."

"Who are your favorite singers?" I asked, wanting to learn everything there was to know about her. I didn't press for any information about Nashville. We'd discuss it eventually, but tonight I only wanted her relaxed and at ease, talking about nothing.

We talked until our burgers arrived, then we ordered another beer and ate, soaking in the noise of the room and the good company.

I was finishing off her uneaten fries when the house band arrived and began to set up on stage. "They have a band every Friday and Saturday night. They're good."

"Mind if we stay for their first set?" she asked.

"Not at all." We could stay as long as she wanted

because when we left here, we were going to the same place —her bed.

The band started right after Kelly swung by to collect our empty plates and bring us each a glass of water. As long as I'd known the guys who played at Jane's, they'd never given themselves an official band name. Two of the guys were Jane's nephews, and besides the occasional wedding, they only played at their aunt's bar. Everyone just referred to them as Jane's band.

Despite that, they were good. They had toes tapping beneath tables and by midnight, the dance floor would be packed with people doing the two-step and jitterbug.

Lucy seemed lost in the music, a soft smile on those perfect lips. When the band announced they'd been working on something new, she whispered, "Dear Fool," before they'd even finished the first bar.

It was one of her songs—my personal favorite. It wasn't the most popular of her hits, but it was fast-paced and the lyrics were funny.

"I love this song," I said.

Her eyes lit up. "You do?"

"Did you write it?"

She nodded. "On a bus driving from Tallahassee to New Orleans."

The room was into it and energized. After tonight, the guys would add it to their regular set list.

Lucy didn't hum as the band played. She didn't drum her fingers on the table or move her head to the beat. She just listened with a proud tilt to her chin.

She wasn't the only proud one at our booth. My chest swelled and my eyes were locked on her, honored to be sitting across from this talented woman.

"Well?" I asked when the band wrapped up her song and took a break. "How'd they do?"

"I approve."

"You ready to get out of here?"

Her eyes flashed and her tongue darted out to her bottom lip. "I'm all yours."

Music to my ears.

I dropped three twenties on the table and slid from the booth, holding out a hand to help her out. Her dainty fingers curled, soft and gentle, around the callouses of mine.

Jane waved goodbye. I nodded to a table of Jane's regulars in the middle of the room who were watching us leave. And when we stepped outside, the parking lot was dark, lit only by the bar's lights, neon signs and the moon.

"Do you think anyone recognized me?" Lucy asked as we strode to my truck. "Those guys were staring as we left."

"They're just wondering who the hottest woman in the bar was tonight and how I got to her first."

She smiled, leaning her temple into my arm. "Thank you. For tonight. I'm starting to like being Jade Morgan."

We reached my truck and I pushed her against the cold metal, bending low so my breath whispered against the shell of her ear.

Her hands came to my sides, gripping the starched button-up shirt tucked into my jeans and belt.

"In public, you're Jade. But behind closed doors, you're—"

"Lucy?" she breathed.

I shook my head. "Mine."

CHAPTER NINE

LUCY

"I GOTTA GO." Duke dropped his lips to mine.

"Not yet." I latched on to his roped triceps, holding him before he could leave, and dragged my tongue across the seam of his lips.

He growled, dropped the bag he'd been holding and framed my face in his hands, taking the kiss to the next level.

I melted into him, wishing the sun weren't up and he didn't have to go to work.

Duke tore his lips away and dropped his forehead to mine. "Tonight. My house. I'll text you the address."

I panted. "Okay."

"And we're going to talk."

I held back an internal cringe and nodded.

He kissed me once more, then swiped up his backpack and walked across the porch, jogging down the steps as I watched from the doorway.

I waved as he reversed his truck out of the driveway and down the gravel road.

My lips were raw. I was sore in places I hadn't been sore

in a long time. And I was unabashedly sated. This would be the perfect Thursday morning if not for the growing pit of dread in my stomach.

"Because Duke wants to talk," I muttered, closing the door.

And I most definitely did not.

Sex had been an excellent way to avoid conversation this past week.

That or maybe Duke sensed I needed a reprieve and wasn't ready. He'd given me time and so many orgasms I'd lost count, but his patience had been waning over the past few days.

Maybe if I showed up at his house wearing a coat and only a coat, I could buy myself just one more day.

Probably not.

Tomorrow was his day off and the one-week mark to our relationship. We hadn't gone to his house yet, but I suspected he was going to trap me there until he knew everything there was to know about my past and why I'd come to Calamity.

I went to the kitchen for another cup of coffee, then took my mug to the living room, curling up in the couch and looking out the front window. Sunbeams streamed through the glass. Birds chirped, welcoming the new day.

Sleep had been sparse the past week thanks to Duke, and my eyes were heavy. He'd stayed here every night since the bar. He'd go to work during the day, then come here for dinner and spend the night exhausting me into a dreamless sleep. Despite the coffee, I'd been falling asleep in this exact spot every morning, indulging in a pre-breakfast nap.

One of the hidden gems in this whole run-away-from-your-life-and-create-a-fake-identity scheme was that I had nowhere to be. My habit of being perpetually late had cured itself thanks to the circumstances.

I closed my eyes, savoring nature's peaceful morning song, and was ready to snooze when my phone rang in the pocket of my hoodie. I jolted up, sloshing a dollop of coffee onto my lap.

"Damn." I blotted it with my sleeve.

Duke hadn't learned about another one of my habits, that I spilled on myself constantly. That I'd made it through a cheeseburger and fries at the bar unscathed had been a miracle—though I'd refused to go anywhere near the ketchup bottle.

I dug out my phone, not surprised to see Everly's name on the screen. The device only had two contacts, hers and Duke's.

"Hey." I smiled as I answered.

"You're not dead. Then you'd better have a good explanation for not calling me yesterday or answering my texts last night."

Oh, shit. "Sorry. I was, um . . . preoccupied."

Everly and I had agreed to keep contact to a minimum, at least while I was getting settled and the media storm around my disappearance was blowing over.

I'd promised to check in every Wednesday, something I'd forgotten yesterday because apparently regular naps and sex were not only a good way to avoid conversation but also to forget you hadn't called your best friend.

"Preoccupied?" she asked. "With what? Last week you said you were bored out of your mind."

"About that. I sort of found something"—*someone*—"to fill my time. Do you remember Duke?"

"The hot cop from Yellowstone? Yeah. His face is a hard

one to forget. Wait. Did you leave Montana? Are you in Wyoming?"

"No, still in Montana. It turns out he's the sheriff here in Calamity."

"No. Way." She laughed. "Only you. So I assume you two are hooking up? You were getting laid last night, weren't you? That was why you didn't answer my texts."

I giggled. "I was most definitely getting laid."

"Bitch. How do you go into hiding and land a hot cop the first week? You and your lucky breaks."

Everly was teasing but that didn't stop the twinge of guilt from hitting hard.

When it came to my career, I'd had lucky break after lucky break. Everly and I had both wanted to be singers. As little girls, we'd sung together while playing on the swings or combing our Barbies' hair. I'd found my way to the spotlight, thanks to luck. Meanwhile, she was chasing the same dream, and luck had given her the cold shoulder. But she hadn't let it get her down. She worked her ass off and wasn't giving up.

Maybe if I wasn't there to catch the breaks, they'd fall into her lap instead.

I hoped so. Everly was a talented singer. She had the pipes and the natural talent. She wasn't into songwriting like I was, but she loved to sing, and if she found a song to take her to the top, she'd soar.

And the horrors I'd survived, the ones she'd witnessed firsthand, would keep her from making my same mistakes. From trusting the wrong people. From letting the world turn so upside down that her only choice was to run.

Run far. Run fast.

I was lucky though. I'd run straight into the arms of a good man.

"There's more," I said. "He, um, knows who I am."

The line was silent. I pulled the phone away from my ear waiting for the—

"What?" she shrieked. "How could you tell him? That went completely against our plan. What were you thinking?"

"I didn't tell him. He pulled me over the day I got here."

"Christ, Lucy. Running late?"

"Yes." My best friend knew me well. "Duke won't tell anyone."

"How do you know? He could be feeding you to the tabloids for a check. Do you have an exit plan? What are you going to do if a bunch of reporters shows up in Montana?"

"No, I don't have an exit plan. But Duke isn't like that. He won't tell."

"Are you sure?"

"Yes." There wasn't a sliver of doubt in my mind.

Duke wouldn't betray me.

"He doesn't know what happened yet," I told her. "But I'm planning on telling him." Tonight, unless I could barter orgasms for more time.

She blew out a deep breath. "I don't like this. I'm not trying to be mean here, so don't get mad at me for what I'm about to say."

"What?" I braced.

"You're too trusting."

She meant Meghan. And she wasn't wrong. I had been too trusting.

Everly had never liked my assistant. I'd chalked it up to best-friend jealousy because Meghan and I had been close, but I should have listened.

I opened my mouth to tell her that Duke was different,

but no matter how much I defended him, Everly would still worry. "I'll be careful."

"Don't be mad at me."

"I'm not." I sighed. She was only looking out for my safety. "Anything else happen lately?"

"Nothing new. I'm still getting calls from reporters and I'm just sticking to the story." The story that we'd invented together on our living room couch—I'd moved out and Everly wasn't sure where I'd gone. "I don't know if people are buying it but eventually they'll get sick of the same answer."

"Sorry for making you deal with it."

"I don't mind. You've dealt with enough," she said. "Scott called. Five times."

"He can go to hell."

She laughed. "Funny. That was exactly what I told him too."

"Ev. You can't do that."

Scott wasn't her producer, because she wasn't with a label, only singing freelance at the moment, but he was famous in Nashville. And he could crush her career, black-listing her at any label with a single email.

"I don't care. If Scott wants to try and sink my career, I'll tell the world what he did. And I'll call his wife."

Something I wish I had the guts to do. Instead, I'd taken the high road to Montana.

"Have you looked on social media?" she asked.

"Once." I'd ventured onto Twitter Monday, and after reading seven speculative threads, I'd closed the app. "Apparently I'm either in rehab or I had a mental break. One troll posted that I had to quit because Meghan had been the actual singer and I was only lip-synching her stuff."

"People are assholes."

"Truth. It doesn't matter. I'm Jade Morgan now."

"And how is Jade doing?" There was genuine concern in Everly's voice. "Are you holding up okay?"

I glanced out the window, taking in the spectacular view of towering mountains in the distance and rolling fields of green and gold in the valley. "I think I found the right spot."

It had only been a week, but I felt more at peace here than I had in years in Nashville. Maybe it was the lighter schedule. Maybe it was the quiet. Maybe it was Duke. Whatever the reason, Calamity was making its mark, gathering up the little pieces of my soul that had been shattered. Day by day, those broken shards were knitting together, forming a new me.

Jade.

"I miss you," Everly said.

"I miss you too. Tell me what's happening with you."

We talked for an hour about the album she'd been working on for months. Next week, she had time in a studio to start recording. She hummed the melody to one of her favorite songs, then gave me a couple of options for a hook and asked me which I liked best. I listened, rapt, ignoring the piece of my heart that longed to be in her place.

I still hadn't been able to bring myself to think about music yet. For years, I'd open my mouth and the first thing that escaped was music. For weeks, since Meghan, there'd only been silence.

After Everly and I said our goodbyes, I skipped my nap and wandered upstairs for a long shower, then spent the day tidying the farmhouse.

And fretting.

Everly's concern had come from the heart, but it sent my head into a tailspin. Was I too trusting? *Yes.* Should I have an exit plan? I couldn't imagine leaving Calamity at the moment. But what if reporters did show up looking for a story? The farmhouse was secluded and isolated. One of the reasons I adored it was because it was nice to have space. But if a news truck pulled into my driveway, I'd be stuck.

Once the cleaning was done, I pulled out my laptop and logged in to each and every one of my social media accounts. Without checking them, I deleted all my notifications and messages just in case.

Then I sat in front of the TV, not paying any attention to the sitcom on the screen as one hour passed into two. The paranoia I'd had my first days in Calamity had returned. I drew the blinds over the living room window to hide. To worry about what was to come.

Tonight, Duke would ask the questions I didn't want to answer. I'd relive the fear and pain of the past six months, something I wanted to avoid, even if it only lasted minutes.

I knew him well enough to predict his reaction. He'd get mad. He'd want to step in and help. And I'd have to beg him to leave it be. I only wanted it to disappear.

My phone dinged, a text from Duke with his address and a note to come over whenever I was ready.

Stalling would only make this harder, so I shoved off the couch and walked out the door, taking my purse, which I'd stocked with a few things to spend the night, and driving across town.

My fingers drummed on the wheel, my anxiety spiking, as I followed my navigation app. I'd pictured him living in town, nestled in a quiet neighborhood, surrounded by the community that he loved so much. But Duke's house was on the edge of Calamity, where neighbors had space from one another. The properties on this road were bordered by open wheat fields.

Duke's turnoff was marked with a boulder, his house number etched into the stone. I nudged my Rover off the street and onto a driveway lined with trees. Beyond their trunks was a lush and sprawling lawn. The gravel crunched under my tires as I drove past tree after tree, the towering branches and green leaves providing a canopy down the straight lane.

Then his house appeared and a wave of surprise shoved my worries aside. His home was not at all as I'd expected.

This was no bachelor pad. This was a home. A family's home. I parked in front of a three-car garage with a sturdy basketball hoop standing in the cement pad beside the third bay. Two whiskey barrels with potted petunias bracketed the hoop's base, the yellow and white blooms in desperate need of deadheading.

Opposite the garage was the house itself. The brick on the rambling rancher had been painted white. The cedar shutters had been stained a chocolate brown that matched the pillars on the front stoop.

Who knew my boyfriend was so trendy?

The front door opened as I hopped out of the Rover. Duke stepped out, still wearing his olive-green sheriff's shirt tucked into a pair of jeans, but he'd taken off his boots and was standing barefoot on the welcome mat.

He looked so domestic and relaxed. His arms were crossed over his chest and he leaned against the door's frame, his lazy stance belying the sharp eyes eating up every one of my steps across the sidewalk.

I'd opted for a pair of skintight jeans and a tank top with thin straps that crisscrossed at my shoulders.

No bra.

He'd soon find out I hadn't bothered with panties either.

"Nice place, Sheriff."

He grinned as I stepped in close and stood on my toes, waiting for him to come the extra inch.

Duke unfolded his arms and took my face, kissing me much like he had on my own threshold this morning, leaving me breathless and smiling and aching for more. He boggled my mind and tangled up my heart in the best possible way.

Never in my life had I longed to be with a person the way I craved Duke's presence. I'd take him every minute of every day. I was hoarding our moments together, locking them deep in my heart.

Just in case it all came crumbling down.

"How was your day?" I asked when he let me go.

"Fine. Normal. I did paperwork all day and fielded three phone calls from city council members who were checking in after last week's crash. They wanted to make sure Grayson was doing all right."

"Aww. That's nice."

He shrugged. "Just how things are in my town. We look out for one another."

My town. Someday I wanted to call it my town too. Maybe it already was.

"How is Grayson?"

"Doing all right. I'm keeping a close eye." Duke took the purse from my hand and slung it over his shoulder. Then he gripped my hand and led me into his house.

The smell of garlic filled my nostrils as I stepped inside. Past a rug in the entryway and a line of empty coat hooks, hardwood floors led us to the kitchen. A large window overlooked the sink, which was probably where

Duke had been standing when he'd spotted me coming down the drive.

An island in the center of the kitchen made the room a horseshoe. The cabinets were white, the countertops a speckled granite. My fingers begged to run themselves over the glossy surface. "This is beautiful."

Duke set my bag in a small nook beside a tall cabinet I assumed was the pantry. "I bought this place years ago and have been slowly fixing it up."

"Did you do this yourself?"

"Nah. Kase, my buddy who owns a construction company in town, did all of it. He did the design stuff too, so don't give me any credit. My only requirement was that it was updated, comfortable and functional. I didn't really care to pick through paint samples and carpet swatches, so I recruited my sister and she worked with Kase to design it all."

"Ah. Well, your sister has lovely taste."

"I'll pass that along."

Two things melted me in that moment. One, that Duke would talk about me to his sister. That I was significant enough for him to share with his family. And two, that Duke had created a *home*. A sanctuary to live in, not show off.

I'd been surrounded by material people for years. Everything was about the size of their house and the model of their car. The label hosted an annual Christmas party and I'd walk in the room and be instantly sized up. People who needed to up their social status would bring me glasses of champagne and compliment me on my dress. Those who thought I was beneath them would turn up their nose and snicker at my lack of jewels.

Duke's humble roots were winding around my ankles and I was loving their firm grip.

"I'll give you the tour later," he said. "The main floor's been done for about two years. But be warned, the basement is still the original eighties style because the only thing down there is my home gym and I don't care much about the wallpaper when I'm working out."

"Now I can't wait to see it."

He grinned at me and jerked his chin to the fridge. "Water and beer are in there. I picked up a bottle of red if you want that instead."

I spotted an amber beer bottle beside the sink so I helped myself to the same. "Can I help?"

"No. You just relax."

"That's all I've done today." That and worry. But I stayed on my side of the island, sipping from my beer as he threw a towel over his shoulder and dug out a cutting board and knife. Then he started pulling vegetables and a bundle of lettuce from the refrigerator. "What are we having?"

"Steaks are ready for the grill. Potatoes are in the oven. Thought I'd whip up a salad too."

"You can cook?"

"I can cook," he said as he began slicing a tomato. Judging by the smell of the potatoes roasting, dinner would be delicious.

He chopped in his bare feet, looking sexy and charming and completely at ease in the kitchen. Knowing that he was king of this house like he was king of the town was a total turn-on. One day, if the music returned, I was absolutely writing a song about this man.

Duke Evans deserved one hell of a song.

I wanted to immortalize him into lyrics. The same way I'd done for my father.

"My dad cooked," I said. "Not all the time but often. He loved coming home early from work a few days a week and beating Mom to the kitchen. He'd strap on her floral apron and go to town, make something fancy for us."

"What was your favorite thing he cooked?"

"Tacos. They weren't fancy but Mom loved tacos. And Dad loved Mom so we ate a lot of tacos."

I smiled, thinking about how he'd pull out her chair and drape a napkin over her lap. Then he'd bring her a plate of tacos and act like it was escargot.

"My parents had this silly little thing," I continued. "My dad was the master of cheesy, over-the-top gestures. If there was a chance it could make my mom blush and giggle, he'd do it. Then afterward, he'd ask her if it was cheesy enough. She'd rate him on a scale of cheddar at best"—I raised my hand above my head, then lowered it past my waist—"to American singles at worst."

"Because that's not really cheese."

"Exactly." I pictured Mom's smile when she broke the news that his efforts were mediocre mozzarella. And heard Dad's laugh when he scored the elusive *holy swiss*.

Duke set down his knife and braced his hands on the counter. "What happened to them?"

"Car accident. It was about three months after I moved to Nashville. They went out to a movie one night and never came home."

He dropped his head. "I'm sorry."

"It was a long time ago."

"I shouldn't have told you about the accident." His jaw clenched. "Probably brought it all back. Fuck, I'm sorry."

"No, it's okay. I was happy to listen."

He shook his head, pinning me with his blue eyes. "It's time, baby."

"For the potatoes?"

"No." He came around the island and put his hands on my shoulders. "Time for you to tell me what's going on."

"Oh," I muttered.

"Gotta know what I'm dealing with here." His thumbs stroked my skin. "I wanted to give you some time. Give *us* some time to just sink into this thing. But I don't like that I'm walking through a minefield with a blindfold on."

"Okay." I took a deep breath, ready to launch into it from the beginning, when the doorbell rang.

Duke's eyebrows came together and he dropped his hands, tugging the towel off his shoulder. He tossed it behind him to the island, then he strode from the room, leaving me and my beer with a short reprieve.

Why was I so nervous about telling him my story? When I'd told Everly that I trusted Duke, I'd meant it. There was no way that man would betray me. But a part of me wanted to keep my secrets locked up tight. Maybe I feared he'd think less of me.

Yes, I'd been stupid. I'd given up too much control to the wrong people. A woman was dead and it was because of me.

But it hadn't been my fault. None of it had been my fault. At least, that was what I'd been telling myself for weeks.

So why did I feel so guilty?

"You walked here?" Duke's voice carried down the hallway, echoing before his footsteps. He came around the corner from the entryway but he wasn't alone.

Travis followed behind him. "Mom grounded me from the car."

"Why?"

"Because I—" The second he spotted me in the kitchen, Travis's face turned to stone. He must not have realized it was my car in the driveway. I doubted he'd make that mistake again.

"You remember Jade?" Duke nodded to me as he went back to his cutting board.

"Yeah."

"Hi." I smiled and waved, hoping a friendly face would thaw the boy a bit.

It didn't.

He scowled at me and then glared at Duke. "Is she here for dinner?"

Duke answered with a hard glare. Had it been aimed at me, I would have dropped to my knees and begged for sweet mercy.

Travis wasn't fazed. Without a word, he spun around and stormed out of the house, marking his exit by slamming the door.

I jerked and, when the sound stopped reverberating through the house, looked at Duke. "I'm sorry. I don't want to come between you two."

"Don't apologize. He's going to have to deal."

"Okay," I muttered, feeling like a wedge driving a boy and his role model apart.

Duke returned to cooking and though he didn't admit to it, Travis's attitude dampened his mood. He chopped the salad toppings with a bit too much force, squishing the tomatoes with every slice. He yanked the pan of potatoes from the oven to give the spuds a turn, almost rolling one onto the floor.

And the conversation from before Travis had arrived was over.

It was probably for the best. It would be hard enough to tell Duke when he was in a good mood. Grumpy Duke would freak the fuck out.

When Duke went outside to grill the steaks, I followed him to the deck. "Would Travis normally have stayed for dinner?"

He nodded. "Yeah. He comes over once or twice a week. We eat. Play hoops or watch a game."

The comfort and ease with which Travis had entered the house spoke of how many times he'd come here. "I'm sorry."

"Hey." Duke came over and wrapped me in his arms. "Don't. I want you here. Travis will come around."

"But—"

"Lucy, it's fine." He let me go long enough to drop a kiss to my lips. "Let's forget about it. Have dinner. Go to bed."

"Are you going to ask me to stay?"

"Wasn't planning on asking but you're definitely staying."

I smiled. "Good thing I brought my toothbrush."

Sex would take his mind off Travis.

And buy me one more day to avoid the inevitable conversation.

CHAPTER TEN

DUKE

"LUCY," I called, closing the front door of the farmhouse behind me. We were going to have words about her leaving it unlocked while she was home alone.

"Upstairs!"

I kicked off my boots and unholstered my gun, leaving it and my badge in the backpack I'd brought along. Sooner rather than later, either she was going to have to start spending more nights at my place, where I had a gun safe, or I was buying one to leave here.

I jogged up the stairs, turning for the bedroom. It was bright, smelled like laundry soap and . . . empty. "Where are you?"

"I'm in the bathroom."

I crossed the room and there she was, standing in front of the mirror, wearing rubber gloves with a plastic bottle of black in one hand. She dragged the pointed tip through a sharp part in her hair, squeezing the dye into her roots to cover the blond that had begun to peek through.

"You left the door unlocked."

"Because I knew you were coming over and my hands are a little busy at the moment to answer the door."

"I'm having a key made tomorrow."

"There's a spare in that wooden bowl in the kitchen. Just take it."

No hesitation. No serious conversation about exchanging keys and *where are we headed*.

Because she knew, like I did, that this wasn't going away.

"Want some help with the back?" I came into the room, bending to drop a kiss on the sliver of skin showing past the thick towel covering her shoulders.

"Sure." She met my gaze in the mirror and smiled. "That would be great. Want the gloves?"

"Nah. You keep them." I didn't want her delicate fingers marred with stain. And if my fingertips were black, it would just be a reminder that she'd let me help.

There was something intimate and trusting about helping her color the blond roots. About lifting sections of her long hair and placing them here and there.

Did she trust me?

I'd been trying not to pressure her into telling me her story. At dinner the other night, she'd had this look of dread, of fear, on her face right before Travis interrupted us, and after that, I just hadn't pushed. I didn't want to go into my normal interrogation mode and make her feel like I was grilling her for a confession.

But damn it, it was killing me not knowing what had happened. My thirst for answers had nearly driven me to the internet over the past week, but I'd held back. I'd waited.

"Done." I handed her back the empty bottle after hitting the last section of hair, following her instructions.

"Thank you." She put the bottle down and twisted up

her hair, pinning it at the crown of her head before stripping off her gloves. She read the back of the dye box and nodded. "Thirty minutes."

"Do you like the black?"

"It's different. Not horrible." She shrugged, meaning she didn't really like it at all. Lucy would be beautiful with any color hair—blond or black or brown or blue. She hopped up on the counter, her bare legs dangling and feet swaying. "How is Travis?"

"Mad. Confused." I sighed. "Sixteen."

After Travis had shown up at my place for dinner and run out like he had, I'd wanted to spend more time with him. So yesterday on my normal Friday off, I met him at the park to practice ball. Then the two of us ran errands around town, doing stupid stuff that didn't matter, except it did because we were together. We gassed up my truck. Cleaned it at the car wash. Took some cardboard to the recycling drop and stopped by the grocery store to buy his grandma some flowers for her birthday. Then I took him to dinner at the café and we came back to my place to watch a movie.

His attitude through it all had been a roller coaster. Mostly he'd been happy to hang out. He grumbled about summer school and bitched about his Spanish teacher being too hard. Any time the name Jade came up, his mood would plummet. But what worried me the most was that he'd gone quiet and tense as I'd driven him home.

"Something is going on with him but he's not talking. Maybe it's his mom. Maybe it's his grandparents or his friends. I don't have the first damn clue. So I'm just trying to be there if he decides he does want to talk."

"You're a good man, Duke."

I stepped into Lucy's space, running my hands up the

smooth skin of her thighs. I'd missed her in my bed last night. It was the first we'd spent apart since the bar. "How was your night?"

"Lonely." She plucked at a button on my shirt. "I was thinking maybe I need to get a cat."

"You mean a dog."

I expected a laugh or a smile. Instead, her eyes filled with such sorrow I wanted to say fuck the hair dye and my shirt, then take her into my arms and hold her until that sadness was gone. "What?"

She sagged. "I had a dog. She was killed about two months ago and I miss her a lot."

"Shit. I'm sorry." Yet another time I'd shoved my foot down my throat because I didn't have the faintest clue what the fuck had happened in Lucy's past.

"It's okay." She kept her chin down, staring at her fingers as they toyed in her lap. "Her name was Spot. I know, very original. But she had this perfect brown circle on the bridge of her nose, and I couldn't *not* name her Spot."

"How'd she die?"

Lucy lifted her chin and met my eyes. "Can dogs be murdered?"

What. The. Fuck. "Yes."

"Then she was murdered. By the same person who drove me out of Nashville."

I took a step back and bent low so we were eye to eye. "Trying not to push, but baby, you gotta tell me what's going on. I can't take not knowing. Worrying. I know I'm asking a lot, but you can trust me."

"I know." She fitted her palm against my cheek. "Let's get my hair washed out and then take a walk."

We waited until the dye had set, then I helped her rinse

it out in the sink. She twisted it up in a knot before we went downstairs so I could pull on my boots and she could slide into a pair of flip-flops.

She opted to stroll down the gravel road that led toward the highway. I fell into step beside her, not rushing as we walked under the evening sun.

"It's truly beautiful here." She took a long breath of air, holding it in like she was pushing the clean molecules into her cells. Then she blew it out and reached for my hand, lacing her fingers through mine. "This is a long story."

"I've got nothing but time for you."

She stroked my knuckles with her thumb. "I guess the best place to start is with Scott."

"Your producer?"

"Yes. I'm surprised you remember."

"Occupational hazard." I made sure to remember names and relationships because they were often the key to a crime. Plus when it came to Lucy, I'd memorized every detail.

"The minute Scott got involved, everything in my life changed. I moved to Nashville—Everly came with me—and it was full steam ahead on my first album. My parents . . . they were so excited. They'd call me every day and check in. Mom had Scott's number in her favorites. They loved that he'd taken me under his wing and was watching out for me. And when they died, he was there. He and Everly pulled me through. That, and my music."

From the disappointment in her tone, I could tell that I was going to end up hating Scott.

"I threw myself into the music. It was how I coped with my grief, going as fast and hard as I could every single day. I didn't have time to be sad. Scott said my dedication to the music was unparalleled. Really, I was just desperate to stop feeling so heartbroken."

"I'm sorry about your parents." I was thirty-three, and losing my parents would be devastating. She'd only been nineteen.

"Me too." She gave me a sad smile. "My first album dropped and I went on a whirlwind press tour. Three of my songs landed in the top hundred and the label wanted my face and music everywhere. They hired me a manager, Hank. His real name is Cameron but he changed it because Cameron wasn't country enough. He's a douche."

I chuckled. "Sounds like it."

"They booked me to open for some major headliners. Lady Antebellum. Keith Urban. Luke Bryan. And in between the big shows, I was playing small gigs in Nashville and doing radio spots. All while the label had me recording a second album. Things were coming at me so fast that I couldn't keep up. So Scott hired me an assistant too."

I remembered hearing about her assistant's death on the radio but didn't interrupt.

"Meghan Attree was with me from the beginning. The label found her and she handled everything. My schedule. My wardrobe. My bills. When things got crazy enough that we needed more assistants, she managed them too. And through it all, she was there for me. Every day. Meghan was more than my assistant. She was my friend."

We walked for a few yards without Lucy speaking. Her flip-flops smacked against her heels. My boots ground into the gravel. But she never let go of my hand.

"About eighteen months ago, I started getting death threats."

My entire body jolted. "What the fuck?"

Lucy tugged my hand so I'd keep walking. "They'd actually been coming for a year before that but Meghan and Scott and Hank and everyone else *assigned* to me had decided it wasn't a big deal. They didn't want me to quit doing performances, so no one told me that once a week Meghan ripped up a letter that arrived in my mailbox."

This was fucked. Completely fucked. "That's not okay."

"No, it wasn't."

"How'd you find out?"

"Meghan caught a cold and we didn't want her around me because I had a big show coming up and couldn't risk having something happen to my voice. She'd arranged for another one of my assistants to get my mail, but Everly was home. We'd always lived together. She took Spot for a walk and grabbed the mail on her way inside."

Lucy sounded so calm about this, almost robotic. Me? I was seething. How could they have kept something like that from her? For years? If Lucy wasn't angry, I sure as fuck was on her behalf.

"It all came out after that. I demanded to know all about the letters. Turns out, I had a stalker. A persistent one at that."

Damn it to hell. So that was why she was here. That was why she was so desperate to stay hidden. She was dealing with a psychopath. I'd thought this new identity had been crafted to escape her record label. To figure out a way to quit. No, she'd been driven out of Nashville by fear.

We kept walking, Lucy's pace picking up to match the beat of my racing heart. "It was right about the time I learned of the letters that the stalker escalated. First it was two letters a week. I made Meghan bring them to me. Then it was emails. Then it was emails with photos. About six months ago, I started getting texts. No matter how many times I changed my number, I'd get texts."

"What were they? More threats?"

"No, mostly they were just pictures. Sometimes with a caption or a short text. But it was always a photo of me in public. I'd be at a restaurant and get a text with a picture of me at my table in that exact moment. It was so scary that I stopped going out. Unless I was at a concert or performance, I didn't leave my house."

"What about the cops?"

"I brought them in along with private security. For the most part, I felt protected. I asked to stop doing concerts but the label said no. I was at their mercy and they kept telling me how they've seen this kind of thing before. How it's never serious. I mean, I know other artists who would say the same thing. And since I didn't go anywhere alone, I didn't push. I had around-the-clock surveillance. Still, there's something horrifying about knowing someone is watching you and you don't know who they are or what they want."

"There were never any demands?"

"Not at first. The detective on my case thought it was a mind game. That the stalker's goal was to freak me out and ruin my life. To drive me into seclusion. Which worked, at least when I wasn't performing."

"But then the demands came."

"About three months ago." She nodded. "What does any crazy person want from a rich and famous singer?"

"Money."

"Send me five hundred thousand dollars and I'll stop. Send me six hundred thousand and I'll stop. Every day the number went up until we hit five million dollars. Then it went quiet. Completely quiet for three weeks."

"Why?"

"Detective Markum thought that it was all an escalation. That since I wasn't giving in and wouldn't pay, maybe the stalking would stop. I stayed on alert. I didn't let up on security. But after months and months of fearing the ding of my phone, when the texts stopped, it was so . . . peaceful. Normal. I changed my number. Nothing new came through and I let down my guard."

"Spot."

A sheen of tears filled her eyes. "I let her out the back patio to potty. It was by the pool. I went back inside because I was watching TV with Everly. She was such a good dog. We trained her to bark when she was ready to come inside. And that's what she'd do. She'd bark once, then sit patiently and wait."

"She didn't bark."

Lucy shook her head. "I thought she was out there playing. I didn't think a thing of it until it started to get dark and we hadn't heard her. So I went outside and found her dead in the pool. Her throat was cut and the pool was red."

I cringed. The hand not linked to hers balled into a tight fist. "Where was Detective Markum at this point? Did he have any leads?"

"He was baffled that no matter how many times I changed my number, it always leaked, so he'd been digging into my staff."

"Meghan. Meghan was the leak." It made sense given how full her access would have been to Lucy's life. But if they were friends . . . "Why?"

"I don't know," she whispered. "She was my friend. I loved her. And I don't know why she did that to me."

And she never would, now that Meghan was dead.

The news reports about Lucy's assistant's death had come in this summer. I remembered exactly where I'd been when I'd heard the story on the satellite radio. I'd been in my truck, parked outside Melanie's house at 5:32 in the morning.

I'd made note of the time because I'd calculated the hours it had been since I'd seen Travis the evening before.

Ten. It had taken him exactly ten hours to leave my house after dinner, hook up with his friends and spend the night chasing all over town until I'd gotten a call from dispatch that the night-shift deputy had hauled three kids in for breaking into school property and drinking beer on the football field.

I'd come down to the station fucking pissed and hauled Travis home. Then I'd just gotten angrier because when I'd woken Melanie up, returning her kid, she hadn't even known he'd been gone.

On my drive home, the story had come on the radio about how Lucy would be postponing the rest of her tour dates. The only reason it had stuck was because she'd been scheduled to come to Bozeman and my sister had gotten us all tickets for the show.

My heart had gone out to her then.

Lucy had been a stranger. A shining star halfway across the country.

Now she was here. She was mine and more than I could have ever imagined. She was real and honest. Grounded. Kind. She didn't deserve this torment and heartache.

"I found her." Lucy's fingers slipped out of mine as she spoke, but not to let go of my hand. Instead, she clutched it. "I fired Meghan. Obviously. It was a mess. I had to change everything. Bank accounts. Passwords. Another phone number. The day she died, I was meeting with Detective Markum to talk about whether I should press charges. I left the police station and went to the Apple store. I bought a new laptop, brought it home, ready to start over, and found Meghan in my bed. She'd slit her wrists in *my* bed."

Christ. That particular detail hadn't made the news.

On a different day, I'd find some pity for the woman. Clearly, Meghan had been troubled. But not today. What a bitch. To screw Lucy over, then kill herself in a way that would haunt Lucy forever? Fuck that.

My molars could turn diamonds to dust with how hard I had them clenched.

"That was six weeks ago," she said. "Things unraveled so fast. I learned that Scott, my mentor, had known for months that it had been Meghan slipping information to my stalker."

"Wait. What?" My boots ground to a halt. "He knew?"

She nodded. "According to him, it had been a one-time thing. He thought Meghan had just messed up. Done it on accident."

"No fucking way."

"It's a lie." Her lip curled. "He knew and he didn't do a damn thing about it because he'd never taken the stalking seriously. Oh, and he was screwing Meghan. He didn't want to lose his side piece because he knew I'd have fired her had I found out."

"He was fucking her?"

"Yep. Nice, huh? He tried to explain but it was just a string of excuses."

"Did he get fired?"

"No." She sighed and nodded for me to keep walking. Something about it seemed to soothe her, so I unglued my boots and shortened my stride to match hers. "I should have blown the whistle, but it wasn't like I had proof. The label would have taken his side. And he's a greedy, selfish asshole. I was more worried about getting out of there than getting revenge."

So the fucker had thrown Lucy under the bus and gotten away with it.

"He keeps calling Everly," Lucy said. "He's trying to track me down. He's probably wondering when I'll write my tell-all story. She told him to fuck off."

"Good."

"It is tempting to send his wife a note."

"Say the word. I've got a stamp in my wallet."

She smiled. "That's it. That's why I left. I didn't feel like I had any control and the label was pretending like everything was fine. I was scared every single day. Nothing about my life held appeal. Between Scott and Meghan and the stalker, I didn't want to be Lucy Ross anymore."

"I'm sorry, baby."

"It's okay." She took in another long breath, lifting her chin and turning her face to the sky. "This is where I need to be."

In Montana. With me. Damn, she was strong.

"I think I would have gone crazy in Nashville, hiding in my apartment, just seeing things over and over again in my mind," she said. "After finding Meghan, all that blood . . . you don't forget images like that."

"No, you don't."

"I had nightmares for the first week. The same thing happened after Spot. But then there's just this deep sadness. You remember that life is so fragile. I wish there had been a way to prevent everything. I wish I could ask Meghan why and understand. I wish she hadn't ended her life."

I bent and pressed a kiss to her temple.

She leaned into my side and I let go of her hand to wrap an arm around her shoulders and pin her close. "The reason I asked you not to call me Ms. Ross was because Meghan always did. She was in charge of my entire team and she had this rule that everyone had to call me Ms. Ross. Even her. Isn't that strange?"

"Maybe she was just being respectful." Or maybe—

"Or maybe she was keeping me at a distance," Lucy said, plucking the words from my head. She looked up at me, her eyes full of worry. "I feel guilty. So, so guilty. I feel like this was somehow my fault. When I fired her . . . it was bad."

"What happened?"

"I was cold. I don't know if I've ever been that harsh to another person before. It's not me."

No, it wasn't. Lucy was anything but cold. She was as warm as this evening's breeze. As gentle as the slope of the hills rolling up to the mountains. She was a treasure. "It's not on you. Don't go looking in the mirror if you need someone to blame."

"Yeah," she muttered, facing forward. "You're right. But it's been bothering me and, well, you're the only one who knows the truth now. Except Everly and Detective Markum."

"Talk all you want. I'm here to listen."

"Thanks." She slowed her steps and moved out of my hold. "Let's go back. It's my turn to cook dinner and we can relax and forget all about this."

"In a minute." While we were here, airing it all out, I had some questions. "The stalker. What happened there?"

"It's done." She turned and started for the house, leaving me in her literal micro cloud of dust.

"What do you mean, it's done? Did Markum track the guy down?"

"No. I mean, it's done because without Meghan, it's not hard to hide. Lucy Ross is a ghost."

"Hold up." I gripped her elbow and spun her to face me. "This changes everything, Lucy. Your stalker is still out there. I thought you were here to hide from the media and quit the label, but this . . ." This was serious shit. I mean, the fucker had killed her dog.

"I know. That's why I've been so careful. Only two people know that Jade Morgan is really Lucy Ross. You and Everly. As long as that doesn't change, I'm safe here."

Maybe, but fuck. What happened if someone recognized her? Why the hell had I taken her to the bar? I should have kept her locked up at my house, hidden behind an arsenal of firearms.

"Don't worry." She stepped closer and pressed her palm against my heart. "I trust Everly. And I trust you."

I wrapped my arms around her, pulling her body close. What-if scenarios were spinning through my mind, going from bad to worse to totally fucked. But I shoved it all aside, because no matter what, I'd protect Lucy. I'd be her shield if this clusterfuck came to Calamity.

"You can trust me," I whispered into her damp hair. "With your life."

CHAPTER ELEVEN

DUKE

"HEY, BABE."

"Hey." I grinned into the phone, loving the way *babe* sounded in Lucy's voice. "I was gonna pick up pizza on my way over. What do you feel like?"

"Is there like a meat medley or something?"

"Christ, you are perfect."

She giggled. "I'll make us a salad."

"I need to swing by Travis's house. If I can convince him to come along, would you mind?"

"Not at all."

"'Kay. See you in a bit." I ended the call and put my phone aside as I parked in front of Melanie's house.

It had been two days since Lucy's confession. Yesterday, I'd remained close, spending most of Sunday in bed with her since I hadn't had to work. Truthfully, I was scared, and letting Lucy out of my sight this morning had been hard. But I couldn't avoid the station today, so I'd made her promise to keep the doors locked. Then I'd texted her constantly to check in.

She'd been a good sport. She'd teased me about being overprotective when I hadn't let her stand in the doorway like she normally did and wave goodbye. But she'd still closed it while I stood on the other side, waiting to leave until the dead bolt had clicked.

Slowly, I'd come to terms with my fears, especially now that I knew what I was up against. If Lucy couldn't be by my side every minute, at least she was safe at the farmhouse while I worked. And while I checked on Travis.

I rang the bell at Melanie's, hoping Travis would answer. These days, Mel and I rarely talked without it ending in an argument, but as the footsteps came my way, lighter than those of a growing sixteen-year-old boy, I braced for my ex.

"Hey, Duke." She crossed her arms over her chest after opening the door. "What's up?"

"Hey. I just wanted to see how Travis's doing."

"Fine. He's upstairs in his room. I guess his Spanish teacher gave him a bunch of homework today."

"Mind if I go say hi?"

She shook her head, standing aside to let me in.

"Thanks." I headed straight for the stairs, hoping this would be the end of my exchange with Mel. But before I could escape, she stopped me.

"Heard you've got a new girlfriend."

Damn. So close. "Yeah. Travis tell you?"

"No. I heard it from Jane on Saturday."

Of course she'd heard it from Jane and not her own son. Part of Travis's problem was that his mother didn't talk to him—and vice versa. Melanie didn't seem interested in developing a bond with Travis, maybe because she'd never been close with her own parents.

Mel and Travis coexisted and I didn't doubt that she

loved him. But there was no underlying friendship like the one I had with my parents. Melanie didn't confide in Travis, and therefore, he didn't confide in her.

Travis was bothered by the fact that I had Lucy. But instead of telling his mother about it, he bottled it up inside.

"Her name is Jade, right?" Melanie asked.

I nodded. "Yeah."

"And she's new in town?"

"Yes." I was sure she'd gotten the whole story from Jane. Melanie often went dancing on Saturday nights at the bar whenever Travis was sleeping over with her parents.

"I thought you preferred blondes."

No, Melanie was blond. And the woman I'd dated for a few months before Mel had been blond. Yes, technically Lucy was blond too, but I didn't give a shit about her hair color. I was attracted to her heart and personality.

"Can we not do this?" I asked.

"I'm just being polite."

"Uh-huh," I deadpanned.

Melanie and I'd had a bad breakup. She hadn't wanted to call it quits. I hadn't been in love with her but had loved Travis. She'd refused to let me see him for two months after the breakup. She'd called me every name in the book and had spread rumors at the bar that I'd cheated.

Eventually, she'd apologized and come around with Travis, but even after we'd built a civil relationship, she'd been jealous of the few women I'd dated. Hell, she'd even gotten annoyed when I'd taken Kerrigan Hale on one and only one lunch date at the café.

Melanie wasn't a bad person. She wasn't a bad mother. She had a good job, worked hard and had a lot of friends in town.

She just wasn't the woman for me.

"Jade's a nice person, Melanie, and I really like her. We've got something serious brewing. Let's just leave it at that."

Her face flashed with irritation but then she shrugged, turning and walking away. "Travis's upstairs."

"Thanks," I muttered and jogged up to the second floor.

I knocked on his door and turned the knob, expecting him to be playing video games or on his phone. I didn't expect to find him with his headphones on and a vape pen in his mouth. "What the fuck?"

He leapt off his bed, blowing out a puff of vapor and hurrying to shove the pen in his pocket, but he wasn't fast enough.

I flew across the room and yanked the pen from his hand. "What is this?"

He pulled his headphones free. "It's nothing."

"Bullshit. Where did you get this?"

He clamped his mouth shut and gave me that defiant, blank stare he'd perfected over the past year. Where had the sweet and loveable boy who wouldn't have dared speak back to an adult gone?

"Travis, you either tell me here or I haul your ass down to the station and you can tell me there."

"You can't arrest me."

"Like hell I can't." I turned my gaze to the door and bellowed, "Melanie!"

It didn't take her long to come up. She knew exactly how I sounded when I was hot and at the moment, I was molten.

"What?" She looked between me and Travis.

"Did you know he was vaping?" I held up the pen.

"Travis." Melanie shook her head. "Seriously? What about baseball? You'll get kicked off the team."

"Who cares?" He rolled his eyes. "It's not like I'm going pro or something."

"You're grounded." She planted her hands on her hips. "Again."

"Not good enough." Grounding Travis hadn't worked in two years. He'd sneak out anyway. I glared down at Travis and jerked my chin to the door. "Outside."

His face paled. "You're arresting me?"

"What?" Melanie gasped at the same time I said, "Yep."

"But—"

"Travis Reid, you're under arrest for the possession of contraband as a minor."

Being in possession of the pen wasn't exactly against the law. Kids under twenty-one weren't allowed to buy tobacco products or e-cigarettes in Montana, but I doubted he knew the technicalities. And this was more about proving a point.

I recited his Miranda rights as I took his elbow and escorted him downstairs.

"Duke, please." Melanie rushed after us. "Don't. He's going to get kicked off the baseball team."

"Guess he should have thought of that first."

"Duke," Travis pleaded, giving me those big dark eyes that I'd fallen for when he'd been younger.

Goddamn, it was hard to punish him. But I forced one foot in front of the other, not stopping until we were at my truck. I opened the back door and pointed for him to get in so he was behind the screen, then slammed him inside.

"What are you doing?" Melanie hissed, dragging me by the arm away from Travis's window.

"Trying to get through to him. When's the last time you went into his room? When's the last time you asked him how he was doing?"

"Don't make this my fault. I love my son."

"So do I." I raked a hand through my hair. "I'm doing this because I love him too. He's spiraling, Mel."

The Travis I knew wasn't a kid who vaped or drank. He wasn't one to fail a class and have to retake it in summer school.

"I know." Melanie closed her eyes, the anger in both of us deflating. "I'm trying. I don't know what to do to get through to him."

"Neither do I."

Fuck, I'd just thrown the closest thing I had to a kid in the back of my truck. I'd read him his rights. If that hadn't scared him, I didn't know what else to do because it sure as hell had scared me.

"I'm never going to jeopardize his future. But he has to see that this"—I held up the pen—"and sneaking out and doing stupid shit is not the way."

"Do I need to call a lawyer?"

"No. I'm going to take him for a drive. When I bring him back, sit down. *Talk* to him."

She nodded, and I walked away, climbing in the truck and slamming the door so hard the whole vehicle rocked.

My hands strangled the wheel as I spoke to the rearview mirror. "Swear to God, if you were my son—"

"But I'm not."

"No, I'm not your father. Doesn't mean I don't care."

"Whatever," he mumbled.

Travis's father was a mystery.

Melanie had gotten pregnant from a one-night stand in college. She'd partied too much her freshman year and after telling the guy, he'd told her to make it go away. Instead, she'd just come home to Calamity to live with her parents and raise Travis, then finished her degree online. She worked as a loan officer at one of the banks in town.

I revved the engine and pulled away from the curb. All I could do was try to teach him. And it was up to him to learn.

Travis sat perfectly still and silent in the backseat, his eyes glued to his lap.

I drove across town to the station without a word, and the silence was punishing—for us both. When I pulled into the parking lot and parked in my usual space, I twisted to speak through the steel grate in the clear partition between the back and front.

"Travis."

His shoulders were hunched forward and he wouldn't look at me.

"Hey," I said gently. "Look at me."

He glanced up and his eyes, glassy with unshed tears, were so full of remorse it broke me.

"What is going on with you, kid?"

"I don't know."

"How long have you been vaping?"

"Couple months." He shrugged. "Everyone does. It's not like I'm smoking."

"It'll ruin your lungs all the same."

"Are you arresting me?" His gaze bounced between me and the station.

I counted six heartbeats, making him sweat it out for a long moment, then I reversed the truck and drove us to the pizza place. When I parked, I sent Lucy a text.

Had some trouble with Travis. Gonna be late.

Her reply came as I was opening the back door for Travis to get out.

Take your time. I'll be here. The door is locked.

God, she was incredible. The sheriff before me, my predecessor, had told me once to find a woman who'd understand the long days and crazy situations. A woman who'd roll with the punches and was strong enough to take the ones that didn't bounce off.

Lucy was stronger than any person I'd met in my life.

"I promised L"—fuck—"*Jade* pizza," I told Travis as we stood in line to place our order. That was the first time I'd fumbled her name.

His jaw clenched. "'Kay."

"I asked her what she wanted and she said the meat medley." That was Travis's favorite too. "Then I told her I was going to invite you along to the farmhouse. See if you wanted to eat with us. Hang out for a while."

"I have homework."

"You get your grade today?" I asked and he nodded. "What was it?"

"D." He looked at the floor. "I suck at Spanish."

He was so smart. It wasn't that he couldn't understand the language, it was that he didn't try. That was why he was in summer school in the first place. Because he'd flunked Spanish and this was his chance to fix his grade so he could earn the credits to graduate. That and to play sports. He'd be off the baseball team if his GPA didn't improve.

But he was distracted. This anger in him was growing and unless we figured out how to deal with it, we'd sink further and further down this rabbit hole.

"What can I get you guys?" The clerk waved us forward

and I placed our order to-go. Then Travis and I stood in the waiting area, both silently letting go of the fumes, until we had our box of pizza and were outside.

But instead of driving us both to the farmhouse, I popped the tailgate, hopped on and flipped the lid open on the pizza, diving in for a slice.

"Want one?" I offered up the box.

He sat beside me and took a piece, devouring it like he hadn't eaten in days. It had probably been an hour.

Then we each ate another and when he started in on his third, I set the box behind us in the bed of the truck and leaned my elbows onto my thighs. "All right. Let's talk."

He groaned. "Fine."

"First up. Jade."

He groaned again.

"She's important to me. I'd appreciate it if you gave her a chance, simply because I'm asking you to. One day, you'll meet a woman who'll be important to you. And when that happens and you bring her to meet me, I'll be respectful. I'll do my best to get to know her because she means something special to you. Think you can give me the same?"

He sighed and nodded. "Yeah."

"Next. Vaping." I reached behind us and smacked the back of his head.

"Ouch."

"That's for being a dumbass."

Travis glared at me and rubbed the spot where I'd smacked him. "I'm sorry."

"Take care of your body, kid. You only get one."

"I won't do it again."

"Hell no, you won't. I catch you vaping again, I'll make jail seem like a summer vacation. Got it?"

"Got it."

"Now what's going on at home?"

"Nothing."

"Don't lie to me."

"Nothing. I'm just . . . I don't know." He blew out a long breath. "I can't explain it."

"Okay." The kid was sixteen. He was adjusting to new hormones and figuring out where he fit. I'd cut him some slack as long as he wasn't causing himself any harm. "Make me a deal. When you can explain it, come talk to me. Day or night. All right?"

"Yeah."

I held out my hand and shook his, then grabbed the pizza box from behind us. "Another?"

We each ate another slice before hopping down from the tailgate and getting in the truck. Travis seemed glad to be in the passenger seat, not even glancing behind us through the partition.

Melanie was sitting on the porch stoop when we pulled up and she shot to her feet, jogging to the sidewalk.

Her forehead was furrowed and her eyes were red from crying.

"You owe your mother an apology."

Travis nodded and pushed the door open as she rushed down the sidewalk to meet us. "Sorry, Mom."

Melanie stopped in front of him and swallowed hard. "You're in *so* much trouble. Go inside."

She waited for him to sulk past her before she looked at me and mouthed, "Thanks."

I held up a hand, then drove away.

Maybe I'd scared him enough to shape up. Maybe not. For tonight, I'd say a prayer that Melanie could get through to him while I pushed my worries aside and unwound at Lucy's.

I pulled into her driveway and took the pizza inside, using my key to unlock the door. I'd brought a spare toothbrush to leave behind and some clothes so I didn't have to keep hauling a change with me.

"Baby, I'm here," I called, toeing off my boots.

There was a rustling noise upstairs, then footsteps, but she didn't answer.

"Lucy?"

Still no answer. I took the pizza to the kitchen, tossing the box on the island, then hustled upstairs.

What I saw from the door of her bedroom made me freeze.

Lucy was racing between her closet and the bed, where a suitcase was splayed open. Clothes had been shoved inside and some had toppled over the edge, spilling onto the floor.

For the second time tonight, I walked into a bedroom and asked, "What the fuck?"

She flinched, her hand slapping to her chest as she spun from the closet, where she'd been stripping clothes from hangers. "Oh my God, you scared me."

"What is going on?" What had happened to the calm, cool woman who'd wanted the meat medley and salad for dinner?

Her eyes were overflowing with tears. Her chin quivered as she crossed the room, dropping another armful of clothes onto the pile. "I'm glad you're here."

"What's wrong? What is all this?"

She sniffled and dried her cheeks. Then she looked at me and my heart broke in two. "I was worried you wouldn't make it here in time."

"In time for what?"

"In time for me to say goodbye."

CHAPTER TWELVE

LUCY

DUKE'S FACE changed from shocked to *fucking pissed* in a snap.

"I'm sorry. I'm so sorry." The fresh onslaught of tears blurred my vision. "I'll come back."

Maybe. Hopefully. I wasn't ready to walk away from Duke.

He crossed the room in two long strides, towering over me. But he didn't touch. He crossed those strong arms over his chest—arms that held me so gently as I drifted off to sleep —and bored down on me with a look so cold, so stony, I had a new understanding of the term *intimidating*. "Explain."

I blinked and swallowed hard, choking down the fit of hysterics that threatened to break free. "I have to leave. I have to get back to Nashville. Tonight."

Duke's jaw ticked. I'd been around him enough to recognize that one as *really, really mad*. It had done the same when I'd told him about my stalker. "Why?"

Why? Because I didn't have a goddamn choice. Because I was never going to be free. Because I'd been so fucking selfish, running away from my life and responsibilities, that all I'd done was draw a target on Everly's back.

I spun to the bed, sifting through the pile of clothes on top.

"What are you doing?" Duke put his hand on my shoulder. "Lucy."

"I can't find my phone."

"Who cares about your damn phone?"

"Me!" And there were the hysterics. "I need my phone! If I show you, you'll see."

His mouth pursed in a thin line. "Where did you have it last?"

"Downstairs. In the kitchen." The words were no sooner out of my mouth than I was barreling past him and racing for the stairs.

Duke's footsteps followed close behind, and when I found the phone on the counter, its hot-pink cover blinking like a strobe light, he watched over my shoulder as I swiped it up and unlocked the screen.

My hands were shaking. My fingers trembled as I pulled up the email and held the phone up for him to see.

"What am I looking at here?"

"That's Everly."

"Yeah?"

"It's from the stalker."

He studied the screen, unblinking, until he must have memorized every detail.

I hadn't needed to memorize it. One look and my heart had jumped into my throat. I'd known exactly what I was staring at.

Everly was on the balcony of our apartment.

After Spot and Meghan, the two of us hadn't wanted to

stay in the house I'd bought after the money had come rolling in. So we'd moved into an apartment with a doorman and a security guard stationed outside the one and only elevator.

I'd lived in that apartment for just weeks, but Everly had returned after leaving me in Montana. In the picture, she had a guitar on her lap and was singing. It hadn't been taken from the street, eight floors below, at an upward angle. It had been taken from the building across the street. The light and angle were perfect, like the photographer had been watching her for days, waiting for a beautiful photo opportunity.

Everly's long brown hair was braided over one shoulder. One of my neon-orange coffee mugs was on the little electric blue table beside her. She wore a pair of silk pajama pants in a deep olive green. Her tee was hanging loosely over one shoulder and she had this smile on her face, like she wanted to be nowhere in the world at that moment but sitting in that white outdoor lounge chair.

This was exactly how the pictures of me used to pop onto my phone and ruin a good day. The photos were faultless. If I hadn't known better, I might have confused them with a candid photo shoot. Whoever was behind the lens knew exactly when to click the shutter to encapsulate exactly how I was feeling at the moment.

This picture of Everly had the same style. The same coloring. And a single word photoshopped in faint letters in the lower right corner.

Sweetheart.

"I won't let him come after her too," I whispered.

Duke ground his teeth together, then he took my hand and led me to the living room, nodding for me to sit on the couch as he took up a perch on the coffee table. His elbows came to his knees and he leaned in close. "All right. Let's talk this through."

Gone was the hard man from upstairs. The calm in his voice instantly put some of my fears at rest because while I was here with him, I was safe.

And that was the problem.

"How do you know it's the same guy?" he asked.

"That's the same type of picture I'd get in my emails and texts. I was always sent a picture of me doing something fun. Always in a moment when I thought I was alone. I'd get one of me reading a book by the pool with Spot lying at my side. One of me in my car at a stoplight, singing along with the radio. One of me exactly like this, playing the guitar with my morning coffee."

After enough photographs, the private sanctuaries I'd carved out for myself had all been ruined. Every peaceful retreat, save for my own bedroom, had been stripped and stolen away, picture after picture.

And then Meghan had claimed my bedroom with her suicide, taking that one last safe place.

"You're sure?"

I grabbed the phone that he'd balanced on a thigh and reopened the picture. "See this word? Sweetheart? Everything to me was labeled sweetheart. The photos. The emails. The letters."

A growl came from his chest. That handsome jaw I would miss kissing so much ticked again. "How'd it land in your inbox? I thought you said you started from scratch. Was that an old email address? Or a new one?"

A chill crept down my spine. "It's one I used personally. I haven't checked it since coming here but I was waiting for you tonight and decided to just clear it out quickly. I expected a ton of junk. That's usually all there is because I only use it for online shopping."

"Did Meghan have access to it?"

I shook my head. "No. It's from when I was in high school. It's ancient."

"Is this the first email that's come to that one?"

"Yes. All of the other emails were to accounts that Meghan monitored. Or texts."

"Okay." Duke rubbed his jaw. "Not a bad thing. That means he doesn't have your phone number."

"Is there a way to get a number if you open an email?" My heart dropped. "Oh my God, what if there's like a virus or something in it?"

I tossed my phone aside like it was poisoned. What if my Calamity hideaway was no longer secret?

"I have no idea if that's possible but we'll find out." Duke put his hand on my knee, his thumb drawing circles on the denim of my jeans. "But right now, we're not going to overreact. That includes packing up your stuff and going to Nashville."

I closed my eyes. "This is about me. Not Everly."

"Exactly. This is to draw you out, which means you've done a good job of disappearing."

"Duke, she could be in danger. I can't leave her there to deal with this alone."

"You're not going to Nashville." His voice was gentle but firm. Calm. Except I didn't need calm. I needed to help my friend and I needed him to let me go.

"I have to."

"No, you don't."

I shot off the couch and walked for the stairs. There was packing to do.

"Lucy." Duke gripped my elbow, stopping me at the mouth of the living room. "You are not going to Nashville."

"I have to!" I threw my hands in the air, shaking him off. "She's my best friend. She's in danger."

"No." He stepped around me and blocked my path to the stairs. "Let's calm down. Talk about—"

"What if it were Travis?"

He held up his hands. "But it's not."

"No, it's not." I sidestepped, trying to slip past him, but he moved too quickly. "Duke."

"You're not leaving like this."

"Yes, I am. Get out of my way." I tried once more to get by, but with one fast pivot, he'd cut off my steps. "Duke."

"Lucy, look at me."

I shook my head, staring at the staircase. "Move."

"Lu—"

"Move!" I screamed, on the verge of tears again. "I won't lose her."

"And I won't lose you," he whispered.

My anger fell away along with the strength in my legs. I was about to crumple to the floor, curl into a ball and cry for days, but before my knees could give out, Duke swept me into his arms and carried me to the couch.

This time, he didn't sit on the coffee table. He tucked me into his chest and cradled me on his lap.

"You can't go, baby. It's not safe."

I leaned back and looked into his eyes. "It's not safe for Everly either."

"The stalker never made a physical move on you, right? Never tried to hurt you?"

"Me, personally? No. It was more of a mind game. But my dog is dead. What if Everly is Spot all over again? I wouldn't be able to live with myself if something happened to her."

"Let's start by getting ahold of her. Does she know about what happened?"

"Yes, she knows everything."

"Good," he said. "We'll start with her. Then we'll get in touch with Detective Markum."

I worried my bottom lip between my teeth. "But . . . then that means he'll know where I'm at."

Maybe it had been foolish not to trust the cops. Well, that cop. I trusted the one holding me with my life. But it was different with Detective Markum. He was a nice man and had done what he could to help me. But I didn't want my name in a database. I didn't need Jade Morgan listed as an official alias.

The minute someone other than Everly knew I was in Calamity, no matter how much they promised to keep my secret, the plan would fall apart. And I wasn't ready for my peaceful, country life to end.

Duke blew out a deep breath. "Do you trust him?"

"Honestly, I don't know if I trust anyone at the moment."

He took my hand from my lap and pressed it against his chest. "Me. You trust me."

"You." I dropped my forehead to his. "I don't want him to know where I'm at. I think the reason my stalker got my number all those times was from Meghan. But what if it wasn't? What if there's a dirty cop involved?"

"Then we'll tell Everly to get in touch with him."

"What about the email? He's going to want to see it."

"We can get it to her and she can pass it along. But as long as she's willing, she's the middleman."

I sighed. "I don't want her in the middle."

His arms wrapped around me tighter. "Fact is, baby, until we find out who this is, we're all in the middle."

"I didn't want to bring this into your life too. I'm sorry."

"Hey." He hooked his finger under my chin and tipped it back so I had to look at him. "Never apologize."

"Your life was a lot simpler before I showed up in Calamity."

"My life was lonely before you showed up in Calamity. These past few weeks, it's been the best time I've had in years. Maybe ever."

My heart melted. "Me too."

His blue eyes caught the light from outside, making them shine like jewels. But it wasn't the color that stole my breath. It was the affection, the protective comfort and sheer confidence we'd figure this out, that made it hard to breathe.

"Okay," I whispered. "I won't leave."

"Good." He kissed my lips, soft and sweet. Then he stood up in a flash, depositing me on my feet. "Call Everly."

An hour later, my phone was on the butcher block island because I'd had enough of her yelling directly into my ear.

"This is fucking bullshit," Everly snapped. "You know this is a trap, right? To get you back here? You're staying right where you are."

Duke chuckled from where he was leaning against the counter.

"Hi, Duke," Everly said.

"Hey, Everly."

"Don't let her come to Nashville, okay?"

"I'm not going to Nashville," I told them both.

"Good," Everly said. "And I'm going to keep living my life. Singing on the balcony. Drinking coffee from one of your ugly-ass mugs."

"You can't ignore this, Ev."

"Like hell I can't."

"We need to get Detective Markum involved," Duke reminded her.

"I'll call him as soon as we hang up."

"And the security company."

"And the security company," she mimicked.

Duke pushed off the counter and braced his hands on the island. "If the stalker is watching closely, which I suspect is the case, an increase in security activity and a visit to see Detective Markum are probably going to tip him off that you two are talking."

"Okay. But the alternative is not to hire security or talk to the police."

"And I'm not suggesting that." He gave me a sad smile. "I don't like that you two talk once a week. He's going to know you two talk. And if I was digging into phone records, trying to track you down, I'd wonder who called Everly every Wednesday. I doubt he's found a way to crack into phone records yet but let's be proactive, just in case."

"I bought my phone from a Walmart in Omaha," I said. "It's a Nebraska number."

"I know, baby." He put his hand on my shoulder. "But it's bouncing off a tower in Montana."

My heart sank. "We can't talk?"

"What if we got new phones?" Everly suggested.

"I'm good with that," Duke said. "In a month. Lucy wanted to disappear. Well, let's make that actually happen and see what shakes loose. I have no idea how far this stalker has gone, but if he's listening and watching closer than we realize, I think a few weeks of radio silence would be prudent. Let's get Markum on the case and see what happens. Then you can get a new phone with a new number. And the only people who will have it live in Calamity."

Fucking prudence. How was I going to not talk to Everly? We'd grown up talking to each other.

"Well, this sucks," she muttered.

"I agree."

"What if I need to talk to her?" Everly asked. "What if it's an emergency?"

"Go buy a disposable phone and you call me," Duke answered.

My eyes dropped to the floor. I didn't want to cut myself off from Everly but if doing so would end all this, I'd do it.

"What if things get worse?" I asked Duke. "What if the stalker gets angry and this sets off another explosion? What if my absence and disappearance bring havoc to Everly's life? That's not fair."

"None of this is fair. And I don't care," she said. "I say . . . bring it on, asshole."

"Ev—"

"I know what I'm dealing with here, Luce. I was there, remember?"

"But—"

"I'm not scared."

I could see her jutting out her chin. Squaring her shoulders. Everly took life head-on. In everything, she was courageous. She was tenacious and fearless. When she hadn't scored one of my lucky breaks in her career, it hadn't gotten her down. She'd just kept singing.

That was what I was worried about.

Everly would be so dead set on walking forward, she

wouldn't notice the guy sneaking up behind her and clubbing her over the head.

"Please, be careful. Don't downplay this."

"I won't."

"Got a pen, Everly?" Duke asked. "I'll give you my number."

"Okay," she said after he rattled it off. "Miss you, Luce."

"I miss you too."

"Don't worry about me. I'll be fine. You just go and be Jade Morgan."

"Thanks. I'll talk to you . . . soon. It's only a month." That sounded like an eternity.

"Exactly. It's only a month. Easy peasy, lemon squeezy."

I laughed, already missing the dorky sayings she spouted because they made me smile. "Bye." I ended the call and slumped forward. "It's not fair."

"No, it's not." He ran his hand down my back and when I stood, his arms were waiting.

It was hard enough not talking to her every day after coming to Calamity. Now to go so long and not know if she was in danger? My stomach twisted and I gripped Duke tighter, drawing from his seemingly bottomless well of strength.

"What's her real name?" he asked.

I leaned back. "How did you know it's not her real name?"

"Didn't." He grinned. "But I do now."

"Fell for that one, didn't I?" I poked him in the ribs. "Her first name is Everly. That wasn't a lie. But her last name is Christian. Sanchez is her mother's maiden name."

"Hmm." He shook his head. "Doesn't ring a bell. Would I recognize any of her music?"

"Probably not. She's amazing and has a beautiful voice. But . . ." There were hundreds of other amazing women with beautiful voices in Nashville, all trying to make their mark.

Duke held me for a few more minutes, then let me go and flipped open the pizza box he'd brought over. "Hungry?"

"No." I closed the box and put it in the fridge for later, but not before noticing there were quite a few slices already eaten. "What happened with Travis?"

He groaned and gave me a summary of what had happened earlier, giving me a much-needed change of subject.

"He's failing Spanish?" I asked.

Duke nodded. "Yeah."

"Hmm. I took Spanish all through high school and spent three weeks in Barcelona the summer between my junior and senior year. I could tutor him."

"Appreciate the offer." He dropped a kiss to my forehead. "More than you know. I'll tell Melanie. But . . ."

"I get it. He doesn't like me much right now. And that's okay. If he wants help, the offer stands. It would be a nice distraction and I need one of those right now. Maybe I should take up knitting? Or gardening?"

"Or I can think of another distraction." Duke slid in closer, his hands finding their way into my hair, massaging my scalp.

I moaned, letting him erase some of the tension from the past couple of hours. "That feels amazing."

Duke's touch was everything I needed in that moment. Comforting. Grounding. Safe. He was the metronome, the steady beat, keeping my song in time.

What would have happened had Everly and I picked

another hiking trail? Or if I'd found any other place to run but Calamity?

I wouldn't have missed him. Somehow, eventually, our paths would have crossed. I wasn't dealing with this alone, because he'd been meant for me to find.

"Do you believe in destiny? Because I was just thinking . . . I've caught a lot of lucky breaks. My career, mostly. But this one, finding you here, doesn't feel like luck. It feels like something bigger."

His gaze softened, the crinkles at the corners of his eyes deepening. "It sure does."

"That was your chance to get rid of me, Sheriff."

"Too bad I missed it." He snaked his arms around me, pressing his hard body into mine.

"Yeah." I ran my hands up and down the roped muscles of his back, then dipped into the back pockets of his jeans as he pressed his growing arousal into my belly. "Too bad."

CHAPTER THIRTEEN

DUKE

"SORRY I'M NOT MUCH HELP," Blake said.

"It's okay." I sighed. "Appreciate it anyway."

"Want me to keep digging?" he asked. "I'd have better luck if I took a trip to Nashville."

"Maybe. But not yet. I need to talk to Lucy first."

Sending my friend to Nashville would undoubtedly lead to some answers, but it would mean contact with Detective Markum too. Maybe we could spin it and say Everly had hired him as a private investigator, but before we took that step, I wanted to run this by Lucy.

Blake worked for a security firm in Los Angeles. We'd gone to high school together and when I'd gone to the academy, he'd gone into the military. I'd always expected Blake to be a lifer in the Army, but after his last deployment, he'd returned to the States and reentered the civilian world. I wasn't sure what had happened, and I hadn't asked. My gut told me it was a sensitive—classified—subject.

He'd returned to our hometown in Wyoming, and I'd bumped into him on a trip to see my parents. I'd offered him my guest bedroom if he'd wanted to visit Calamity and explore the area. He'd taken me up on it. I'd been a deputy then and had more free time. The two of us had squeezed in a few hikes around the area and a couple in Yellowstone, including the trail where I'd found Lucy. Then a few months later, he'd called and told me he'd gone to work for a company in California.

We'd kept in touch and he'd told me about some of the jobs he'd taken. It seemed exciting and risky, and once, he'd asked if I'd consider moving. Though the money was good—it would cost me a fortune to send him to Nashville and investigate Lucy's stalker—I much preferred my small-town life. Six months after he'd asked me about moving, I'd been elected sheriff.

Since Lucy's wasn't officially a Calamity Sheriff's Department case and I knew Blake was one of the best investigators around, I'd phoned in a favor.

After a week of beating my head against the wall trying to find anything on Lucy's stalker, I'd realized I needed help. It actually made me feel better that Blake, with all his legal and not-so-legal resources, hadn't found anything in his week of digging either.

The news on Lucy's stalker was nonexistent. It hadn't caught the media's attention. Mostly, the reports as of late had been in regard to her assistant. I'd looked into Meghan Attree and found a spotless record. Everly Christian's background was more of the same.

Lucy would be pissed at me when I told her I'd pulled info on her best friend, but at this point, my suspect list included every name she'd ever given me. My instincts said Everly was honest and fiercely loyal to Lucy, but I wasn't taking any chances.

Garrison, the company Blake worked for, had access to systems that I did not, and he wasn't bound by my oaths and rules. However Blake got his information was his deal and I was turning a blind eye because I was desperate to solve Lucy's stalker problem. I'd offered to pay Blake but he'd refused. If Lucy agreed to send him to Nashville, I would insist.

"Keep me posted," Blake said.

"I will." I pinched the bridge of my nose. "Tell me this. How's Markum? Any reason I should worry he's not doing his job?"

"From what I can tell, he's good. He's dealt with a lot of stalking cases, which is probably why his captain put him on Lucy's. The problem is, whoever he's dealing with is better."

"Lucy doesn't want to tell him she's here. That makes me nervous." If she didn't implicitly trust the cop, I sure as hell didn't.

"For a stalker to be this imbedded, he's either got hacking skills or personal connections. There could be a leak."

"Yeah," I muttered. "That's what I'm afraid of."

"He was definitely connected to her assistant," Blake said. "I've got all the emails sent from Meghan Attree's personal account. I didn't pull her texts, but unless there is a pile of them out there, it looks like mostly she communicated with the guy over email."

I sat up straighter. "Anything there?"

"No. She'd send phone numbers. Schedules. No commentary. Just logistics."

"Damn. What about the email recipient?"

"Dummy accounts, and they changed every time. My guess is the stalker would send her a text or deliver a physical note with the new email address and Meghan would send the next dump of info on Lucy. He was probably watching Meghan even more closely than your woman."

Which would explain the suicide. If Meghan had been as scared as Lucy was and had been maintaining closer contact with whoever this guy was, it might have pushed her to the brink. Then when Lucy had fired her, it had been the final shove over the edge.

"You've got me interested in this case," Blake said. "I'd be happy to spend a week in Nashville. No charge."

"Thanks, but I'm paying you."

He chuckled. "We'll see."

"I'll call Austin." His boss would probably decline too, but my chances were better.

"Good luck. I told him about this earlier and he's on board to send me. He likes Lucy's music."

"Let me talk to her," I said. "Thanks again."

"No problem. See ya."

I set the phone aside and swiveled my chair, taking in the wall of bookshelves behind me. I'd built those shelves myself a few years ago. I'd wanted something other than a painted cement wall to stare at when I turned around.

There weren't any exterior windows in my office. There weren't any exterior windows in the station, period, not even beside the front door. This building had been erected for function, not beauty, and the cement cube served its purpose.

The station was divided almost exactly in half—the front half for the staff, the rear half the jail. Next to my office, there were three interrogation rooms, then a small kitchen with a refrigerator, sink and industrial coffeepot. All function. No frills.

When I turned around and faced my desk again, Carla

was weaving through desks, headed my way. Across from my desk, I had an interior window that overlooked the bullpen. I usually only lowered the blinds when I was having a confidential meeting with a deputy. Otherwise, they were up so that even if my door was closed, my team knew I was here, working on paperwork alongside them while the others were on patrol.

Carla reached the door and pointed to the handle, mouthing, "Can I come in?"

I waved her inside.

"Got a sec?" she asked.

"Always. What's up?"

She whipped out the notepad she'd tucked under an arm, sat across from me and started firing off questions. Carla was a hell of a deputy but preferred dispatch to fieldwork. She'd also claimed the title of unofficial station manager since out of all the staff, she spent the most time in the building. We worked through her list, then she left me to tackle the work on my desk.

When six o'clock rolled around and my stomach grumbled, I realized I'd missed lunch. So I grabbed my keys, waved goodbye to the evening shift and left.

My truck was stuffy from a day in the sun. The first week of September had been as hot as the last of August. The school year had kicked off with little fanfare and I was glad to see the decrease in traffic around town.

Not that I didn't appreciate the tourists who came through every summer and helped support our small economy, but I loved these weeks, when nine out of ten cars parked on First Street had Montana plates. When the faces I saw each day were familiar. When the smiles and waves were from neighbors and friends.

This was the Calamity I wanted to share with Lucy, except I wasn't sure how.

Someone might recognize her. Someone might blow this entire thing to pieces. I couldn't keep her locked away at the farmhouse or my place forever. Lucy seemed to be enjoying the slower pace, but how long would that last?

She was a social person. Sooner rather than later, staying home each and every day was going to drive her nuts.

But I still made sure she locked up behind me every day. When she needed groceries, I insisted on going with her to the grocery store. We didn't go out to eat. We didn't go to the movie theater.

Ever since she'd told me about her stalker, I'd been plagued with the nagging sensation that danger was coming. We were on the precipice of a hurricane, and I wanted the windows boarded up before it hit.

I drove through town with the air conditioning cranked, heading straight for the farmhouse. I'd called Lucy earlier to see if Travis had shown up for his tutoring session. He hadn't.

After Lucy had offered to tutor him, I'd pitched the idea to Melanie. Travis had barely passed his summer school class and much to my surprise, Melanie had accepted the tutoring idea immediately. Then she'd all but ordered Travis to meet Lucy at the farmhouse after school.

There had been disappointment in her voice when she'd told me he'd stood her up. I think she'd wanted the tutoring not only to build a relationship with a kid who was important to me, but also because she was going crazy at home. She was lonely and after two weeks of not talking to Everly, it was starting to get to her.

Maybe tonight I'd get over my own shit and we'd go downtown for dinner. Take another chance at the bar.

The front door was locked when I got to the farmhouse. I let myself in with my key as I did most nights, then tugged off my boots. I opened my mouth, ready to call through the house to let Lucy know I was here, when the faint sound of music drifted my way.

The soft notes of the guitar and the sweet croon of Lucy's voice lured me to the kitchen's back door, which she'd propped open with a wooden wedge.

She was sitting in a chair on the patio. Her legs were stretched out and only her toes were in the sun. Otherwise, she was shaded from the roof's peak as she sang to the fields. In the distance, Widow Ashleigh's old barn sat abandoned and weathered in a field of swaying grass—a classic rural Montana scene. With Lucy singing, the whole thing made a pretty picture.

I hadn't heard her sing. Not a note. Not a hum. Nothing since we'd met. It had made it easier to forget she was a country music superstar. But right here, as my stomach plummeted, I knew.

She was Lucy Ross.

There was no way I'd keep this woman in Calamity. She had greatness pouring out of her soul, and trapping her here would smother this woman who'd consumed my life.

Lucy's hair was up, revealing the long line of her neck. She was in those tattered denim shorts I loved so much, the ones that showed the smooth skin of her long legs. Her feet were bare and she'd applied a new color to her toes today. Neon orange. She loved her neon. Panties. Bras. Nail polish.

It was as bright as the music coming from her lips.

I hovered in the doorframe, staying quiet as I watched.

Feeling like I was about to lose her. God, she could sing. She was meant for the radio. She was meant for the stage.

She was meant to make music.

The tune she played wasn't fast but it was cheerful. It wasn't one I'd heard before and when she hit a lyric about a small town in Montana, I knew she must have written it lately. When she got to a line about a potbellied chief of police with a comb-over, I couldn't keep the laugh inside.

The sound of my chuckle caused her to turn and glance over her shoulder, but she didn't stop singing. She just winked at me and repeated the chorus for one final round, ending with my applause.

"Well?" she asked, standing from the chair. "Do you think it's a hit?"

"A little farfetched in some places but . . ."

She giggled and set the guitar aside, coming over and standing on her tiptoes to give me a kiss. "I didn't want to write about a sexy sheriff who can pull off an olive-green shirt like nobody's business. The last thing I need are all these single women moving to town and making this a competition."

"Oh, I'd say you've already won." My undivided attention and my heart.

"What do you want for dinner tonight?" she asked.

"Feel like heading to the bar? It's ladies' night. Might make some new friends."

"No, thanks."

"I've been monopolizing you."

She ran her hands up my chest. "Really? I thought it was the other way around."

I wrapped her in my arms, pulling her to me as I dropped my mouth to hers for a taste of that cherry sweet. We'd never really been much for inhibitions when it came to the physical stuff, but any hesitancy from either of us had vanished over the past weeks. She was as comfortable with my body as I was hers, and we held nothing back.

We made every kiss count. Every touch.

When we finally broke apart, she had a pretty flush to her cheeks and a puff to her lips. My cock was hard and if not for the hunger pangs, I would have said screw dinner and taken Lucy instead.

She collected her guitar, then brought it into the house, taking it to the living room.

"I didn't realize you had a guitar here," I said as she set it in the corner beside the fireplace.

"I had it in the guest bedroom." She stared at the instrument as she spoke. "My dad gave it to me for my birthday when I was ten. It was too big for me but he promised I'd grow into it."

"What made you take it out today?"

She shrugged. "I don't know. After everything that's happened, I didn't feel like playing. I needed a break. Then today, I just felt . . . ready."

"When did you write that song?"

"Today," she said, like it was no big deal.

Amazing. I'd never been around anyone with such talent. She had more in her fingers than I did in my entire six-foot-two body.

Lucy's gaze stayed fixed on that guitar, like if she stopped looking at it, the thing might disappear.

I walked up to her and put my hands on her shoulders. "You okay?"

She nodded. "When my parents died, the music saved me. But this time . . . singing was something so ingrained in every part of my life. After Meghan, seeing her dead like that, the music was just gone. It was like someone took an eraser and rubbed it from my heart."

It was that son of a bitch stalker. "I'm sorry, baby."

"It's okay." She blew out a long breath and turned, falling into my chest. "I think I just needed time to grieve. Does that make sense? I needed some time away from the music so I could say goodbye. Then today, I was sitting in the living room, waiting for Travis, and it was so warm and sunny. I closed my eyes and took some deep breaths. And there was this song. It was funny and light. So I hummed it out and went straight for the guitar."

Goddamn, it was going to hurt when she left. I'd known it all along, hadn't I? But I'd let myself believe that she'd stay. She'd seemed so determined to make this her home and I'd turned a blind eye and a deaf ear. Lucy had come here to get back on her feet. She'd come here to lick her wounds.

But when they stopped gushing, she'd return to her life. The life where she belonged.

"I missed it," she whispered. "I don't think I realized until today just how much."

Every heartbeat was pained. "It's a part of you." A part I wouldn't hold her back from.

Lucy was a shooting star. Vivid. Mesmerizing. Her voice and her abilities weren't made for small-town life. Sooner rather than later, she needed to stretch her wings. When they weren't bruised any longer, she'd fly home.

"I need to talk to you about something." I took her hand and led her to the couch.

"That look on your face isn't making me feel warm and fuzzy."

I let go of her hand and laced my own fingers together in

front of my knees. "Since that email came in, I've been trying to get caught up on your case." Something I hadn't told her about.

"Okay," she drawled.

"As expected, there wasn't much to find in the media. What I did, fit with everything you told me about Meghan. But the stalker . . ."

"None of it was released to the press."

"Right. And without alerting Markum, there's no way I can get looped in on the case. Even then, he might tell me to fuck off. So I called a buddy of mine who works in private security."

"What does that mean? Won't he find the same information as you?"

"Not necessarily. I'd hoped he might find something else because he's not bound by the same rules."

"And did he? Find anything?"

"No, but he offered to go to Nashville. And I think we should take him up on it."

She hesitated. "Why?"

"Because he might have better luck at finding your stalker."

"Better than the police?"

I shrugged. "Maybe. Maybe not."

Lucy rubbed at a small stain on the hem of her shirt, probably from a dollop of spilled salsa. "Okay."

"Good." I breathed. "When you go back to Nashville, the threat needs to be eliminated and I think Blake's our best bet."

"When I go back to Nashville?" Her forehead furrowed. "What are you talking about? I'm not going back."

"Baby, we both know you'll never be happy living here forever. You need—"

"No." She flew off the couch. "Have you not heard me? Have you not listened to me? I'm not going back there."

"But your music."

"I grieved that part of my music. And today, I realized I can have it. Here. In *this* life." She shook her head. "Duke, I'm not leaving."

"Lucy—"

"I'm not leaving!" She threw her hands in the air. "Please, hear me. *I'm not leaving.* Nashville is not my home. Not anymore. I live here. In Calamity. I told you, you had your chance to get rid of me."

"I don't want to get rid of you."

"Then don't try to shove me out the door. I'm not going anywhere."

"You might change your mind."

"Duke," she whispered. "I'm staying."

Fuck me. She was staying.

I flew off the couch, sidestepping the coffee table as she raced my way. We collided, lips and hands and gasps and *want.* Then I swept her into my arms and carried her upstairs to the bedroom, stripping off her clothes to worship her body and feast on her pussy until she came.

When I buried myself deep inside her, our gazes locked, I made a silent vow to hold tight and cherish this woman for as long as she'd have me.

Lucy had asked if I believed in destiny. I hadn't, not until her.

We made love, hot and passionate and all-consuming, until we were both spent and darkness had fallen outside.

"Things are going to change," I whispered into her hair as she rested on my side.

Lucy lifted and propped her chin on my chest. "Like what?"

"How attached to the farmhouse are you?"

"I like it here. But I'm not attached. Why?"

"Because I'm attached to my house."

"Are you asking me to move in?"

"When you're ready."

She laid her cheek on my sternum, her ear pressed to my heartbeat. "I don't want to bail on my lease with Kerrigan. How about when it's up?"

"Fine by me." I grinned as my stomach growled.

"We missed dinner."

"I didn't."

Lucy laughed and sat up, holding the sheet to her chest. Her black hair was draped over her creamy shoulders. Her freckles complemented that beautiful smile on her face. "I'm going to go get us some snacks—"

The sound of shattering glass followed by a loud thud made her yelp and flinch. Her hands covered her ears as I jerked and scrambled out of bed.

I swiped up my boxers and stepped into them before grabbing my gun from its holster still attached to the belt on my jeans. "Stay here."

"Duke—"

"Stay here," I ordered and strode out the door, gun raised.

The sound of a dirt bike's engine filled the air. I leapt down the stairs, two at a time, hoping to get a closer look, but froze at the mouth of the living room. Shards of glass littered the floor, their jagged edges catching the light coming in from the kitchen. Lying beside one of the coffee table's legs was a gray rock twice the size of my fist.

The cool evening air blew through what had once been the picture window, raising the hair on my bare skin. And beyond, a single taillight flew down the gravel road.

"Son of a bitch." I lowered my gun and jogged upstairs.

Lucy had pulled on a T-shirt and her shorts. "What's going on?"

"Someone threw a rock through the front window."

"What? Why?" She gasped and her face paled. "Do you think—"

"No." I pulled her into my arms. "This is about me, not you. I saw a dirt bike race outta here like its wheels were on fire and I'm pretty sure I know who was holding the handlebars."

"Was it . . ."

Travis?

That boy had better not have had anything to do with this. I grabbed my jeans and tugged them on. Lucy helped button my shirt.

"Do me a favor," I said, taking the keys from my pocket and twisting off the key to my house's front door. "Get some shoes on and pack stuff for a couple of nights. Then head over to my place."

"Where are you going?"

My shoulders sagged. "To arrest a kid."

CHAPTER FOURTEEN

LUCY

I HUMMED as I drove down First Street.

In Nashville, I hummed constantly. I'd hum a song stuck in my head. I'd hum a song I was trying to write. I'd hum to the radio.

Then I stopped.

As a habit, it should have been something I had to force myself to stop doing. But it had taken no effort. No conscious thought to *not* hum. The music had just been . . . gone.

It was returning again. Slowly. And there was no question that part of the reason was Duke. If he hadn't come into my life, the music might have been silenced forever. But I was falling for him, a little bit more each day. Those emotions, the beginning of what felt a lot like love, were healing a lot of wounds.

So I kept humming, smiling as the music purred from my throat, as I eased the Rover into a parking space near one of the banks downtown. The sidewalk was shaded by a tall cottonwood, the limbs still green even though autumn was chasing the summer heat away.

Fall was going to be spectacular in Calamity, an orange and yellow and evergreen kaleidoscope. If we had more chilly temperatures after dark, the leaves would soon turn. Last night had felt especially cold, though that was likely because I'd spent most of it alone in Duke's bed, curled under the covers, missing his body heat.

After I'd dressed and packed a bag for a couple nights' stay, he'd led me downstairs and past the wreck in my living room. I'd wanted to gawk and linger and mourn my broken window, but Duke had kept a firm grip on my elbow, not slowing a beat as he walked me out the door. But even with only a quick glance, the destruction was fresh in my mind.

It was just glass. I'd been telling myself all night and all morning that it was just glass. One broken window and a rock on the floor. Except it was familiar. The broken window was an attack on my sanctuary, like my stalker's texts on my phone. The letters in my mailbox. The emails that had made me fear the ding of an incoming message.

The stalker had never damaged my property though. That was probably the reason I hadn't freaked out. I could compartmentalize the events in Nashville as something entirely different from some shattered glass.

The reason I'd spent most of the night awake had been less about fear and more about worry.

For Duke.

He hadn't admitted it was Travis who'd thrown that rock, but as far as I knew, no one else in Calamity hated Jade Morgan.

Why did Travis dislike me so much? Duke hadn't dated his mother in years. Maybe Melanie and Duke had been more serious than Duke let on and I was missing a piece of the puzzle. Did Travis actually think coming after me would drive Duke back into his mother's arms?

Complicated creatures, teenage boys.

When Duke had finally come home after four this morning, he'd collapsed into bed and wrapped me up tight. Wordlessly, we'd both drifted off to sleep. Then this morning, he'd snuck out.

He'd gotten up, showered and dressed for work while I'd slept through the whole routine. The sun had been streaming through the bedroom window by the time I'd finally forced myself out of bed. In the kitchen, I'd found a note beside the coffeepot.

Went to work. Call me when you wake up.

We hadn't talked long when I'd called because I could tell there were people around him. He'd told me that a deputy was at my house cleaning up the glass. His friend Kase was heading to the farmhouse later today to get measurements for a replacement and board up the hole with a piece of plywood. Duke had rattled off logistics, then asked me not to go home until we could go together.

I'd agreed, something I would have protested had I been properly caffeinated.

Five hours later, his laundry was done, his kitchen was clean, and I hadn't heard a word about Travis. Rather than sit and spin myself into a tizzy, I'd decided to brave First Street to kill an hour or two. Maybe an afternoon of window shopping would settle my nerves.

And keep me from calling Everly.

My fingers itched to dial her number on my new phone. But we were both holding to the agreement. I hadn't called or texted in two weeks. Whenever I reached for my phone,

I'd slap my own hand as a reminder that emails and calls were off-limits.

Was she okay? God, I wanted to know. She hadn't contacted Duke, which meant there weren't any emergencies, but she was also incredibly stubborn. And our definitions of what constituted an emergency were on opposite ends of the severity spectrum.

Be okay. I sent up the silent wish, then got out of the Rover to walk off my anxiety.

I was wearing Duke's green ball cap, the same hat that he'd worn when we'd met in Yellowstone. I'd stolen it from his house this morning and wasn't planning on giving it back. It was mine now. Along with the man. Along with this town.

Calamity was mine, and it was time to stop hiding. Maybe someone would recognize me. Maybe not. But if they did, Duke and I would deal. Together.

There'd been such relief on his face yesterday when I'd assured him that I was staying.

His fears had been justified. I hadn't made it abundantly clear that I wasn't going back to being Lucy Ross, country music superstar. Because there'd been a part of me, deep down, that hadn't been wholly ready to say farewell to my former life. The small part that loved the music almost enough to deal with the gruesome politics and the label's bullshit and the endless rehearsals and the ruthless media and the crazed stalker.

But yesterday in the living room, when Duke had spoken with a goodbye in his voice, I'd known I was done.

I'd satisfy my love of music another way, even if that meant writing songs to sing on my patio for no one other than myself. Nashville was history.

I chose Calamity.

I chose Duke.

Eventually, we'd have to make some decisions. Who was I going to be? What color did I want my hair? Could I stay in hiding forever?

Realistically, I knew the answer was no. But I pushed those worries aside and continued my stroll. My problems would wait until I was ready to solve them.

Downtown was quiet today. There were fewer tourists and more empty parking spaces. My footsteps were unhurried as I walked, smiling at shop clerks through their front windows. The baristas in the coffee shop weren't scrambling to make lattes, instead laughing with one another as most of the tables sat empty. The neighboring jewelry store had left their door open and a dog lay in the threshold, napping. And for the first time, the small art gallery wasn't swarmed with people.

The featured painting in the window display lured me inside. It was of a buffalo, the oil paint done in chunky, bright strokes on the canvas. The reds and oranges and blues and browns were so striking, my eye wasn't sure which color to love first.

Before Yellowstone, I would have purchased it immediately. Now, it was a firm maybe.

"Hello," the receptionist greeted, adjusting the rim of her black-framed glasses as I stepped inside the gallery. "Is there anything I can help you find?"

"No, thank you. I'm just browsing." I smiled, my eyes struggling to make contact because they were so drawn to the paintings on display.

There were animals—a wolf, a deer, a rainbow trout—spaced between stunning landscapes. I walked slowly along the walls, taking it all in, but stopped when I came to the one and only portrait on display. A painting of a girl.

The style of the piece was the same as the others, chunky paint dried thick on the canvas in bold, rough strokes. This must be an artist's personal gallery because all of the paintings were signed with the same black smudge in the lower right corner.

But this girl was different from the animals. The colors were muted with the exception of her eyes. They were so brilliant, so vivid a deep blue, that violet tinted her irises. Pale hair framed her face, its color white and shimmery like beams of the morning sun.

It was an eye-catching piece. Breathtaking and heart-breaking. The girl wasn't smiling. She wasn't frowning. Her expression, like most of the colors, was blank. She looked . . . lonely. I wanted to reach past the paint and give her a hug.

I turned to the receptionist. "How much—"

"It's not for sale." A man appeared at my side, reaching past me to tap the small golden placard underneath the portrait I hadn't noticed.

Display Only. Not For Sale.

"Oh. Sorry." I took a step away, feeling like I'd intruded on his personal space. "I didn't notice."

He studied me in a way that made me feel like my face would be on the next canvas.

Was this the artist? It had to be. He had that tortured, brooding vibe rolling off his broad shoulders.

He was handsome. Not Duke-level hot, but definitely attractive with a tall and strong physique. His eyes were a deep blue and his sandy-blond hair was buzzed short. The sleeves of his Henley were pushed up to his elbows, revealing a tattoo on his left forearm that was nearly as colorful as his artwork. He'd be a lot more good-looking if he lost the scowl.

Maybe he thought I was a tourist. Maybe he'd lighten up if he realized I was a resident too.

"Hi." I held out my hand. "I'm Jade Morgan."

His eyes flicked to my hand, but his arms stayed firmly crossed over his chest.

Jerk.

"Sorry, Hux." The receptionist appeared with a panic-laced smile, stepping between me and the man. She waved, motioning me to step away with her.

Their customer service could use some improvement. If that painting was so precious and guarded, why have it hanging for the world to see? I'd buy my art online. I spun around, ready to leave, and ran into a solid wall of man.

A familiar wall.

Duke's arms steadied me. I relaxed. He must have gone home and found me missing, then spotted my car on First.

"What are you doing here?" he asked at the same time he moved me to his side and away from the receptionist and angry artist. He'd asked a question but wasn't waiting for an answer.

"What do you want, Evans?" Hux barked.

I looked between the men, who glared at one another.

The receptionist ducked her head and muttered, "Excuse me," before disappearing.

I inched away, ready to follow. "I was just doing some window shopping. But we can go."

Duke's attention was locked on Hux and he didn't make a move.

Ah. He wasn't here for me.

"Stay," he commanded. "This involves you too."

"It does?"

Duke nodded but spoke to Hux. "Last night, your daughter threw a rock through Jade's window."

Daughter? I thought it had been Travis.

Hux's jaw ticked. "Do you have proof?"

"Prints on the rock she used. An eyewitness—me—who saw her riding off on a dirt bike. And her confession."

"Fuck." Hux ran a hand over his short hair. Hair just a shade darker than the paintings. She had to be his daughter.

Why would his kid come to my house? Why would she vandalize my property? I swallowed my questions, sensing that I was here strictly to observe.

"How much trouble is she in?" Hux asked, letting some genuine concern slip into that cold front.

"That's up to Jade," Duke said.

Hux's eyes snapped to me and the glare was gone. In its place was a pleading look. "I'll pay. I'll get the window replaced. Kase'll do it."

"He's already got a new one ordered," Duke said.

"I'll call him. Get him to send me the bill. We'll get the window replaced and forget it. Okay?"

"Uh . . . okay?" Was I supposed to agree? Or protest? I looked to Duke but he was no help. We'd have to talk later about him clueing me in *before* the confrontation.

Duke blew out a long breath. "She's getting desperate, Hux. She wants out of that house and thinks if she gets hauled into the station enough times, I can make it happen. But there's only so much I can do. Only so many times I can cut her a break. She pushes me too far, then I have no choice but to talk to the county attorney and she's going to end up in juvie. Call your daughter. Be the father she fucking needs. And get her out of that goddamn house."

I was getting whiplash looking between the two men. What house? What was happening?

"No one's going to give her to me." Hux spoke through gritted teeth. "I tried. For years. Remember?"

"Yeah, I remember. And I remember you giving up."

"I can't win this one." There was a hopelessness to Hux's words. "No matter what I do, it won't be enough."

Before Duke could speak, Hux turned and disappeared down a hallway I hadn't noticed.

"Damn it," Duke muttered before taking my elbow and steering me away. He jerked his chin at the receptionist as he escorted me out the door. It was only after we were in the sunshine and the door's chime had faded behind us that his stiff posture relaxed. "Fuck."

"Okay, Sheriff." I put my hands on my hips. "What is going on? Who is that?"

"That is Reese Huxley. His daughter, Savannah, is the same age as Travis. She's one of the kids I *don't* want him hanging around."

"Because she throws rocks through people's windows."

"Yeah." He sighed. "Among other things."

"What other things? What does she do?"

"It's more like, what doesn't she do? She hangs out with older guys who buy her beer. She rides a dirt bike around town even though it's not street legal. I'd bet a year's salary she was the one who gave Travis the vape pen. Spray-painting trees. Out past curfew. Whenever I've got trouble with a group of teenagers, she's in the thick of it. And it's all to get Reese's attention."

"Why?"

"It's a long story. But the short of it is, her mom is worthless, and her stepdad is a rotten piece of shit."

So that was the house she wanted out of. Her own home.

"Come on." Duke snatched my hand, leading me past the edge of the gallery so we weren't in view of the receptionist inside. "April is Savannah's mother. She and Hux grew up around here and from what people have told me, they were just kids when they got together. Got married right after high school. Both worked minimum wage jobs. Hux got into some trouble gambling, trying to make some extra cash. Cheated and got caught. The guy he cheated came after him and the two got in a fight. Hux beat the hell out of him. Put the other guy in a coma. The judge didn't like Hux, said it was beyond self-defense and sent him to prison for two years."

I blinked. "Wow." The man inside had been intimidating but I wouldn't have pegged him as an ex-convict.

"April didn't even tell him she'd had his kid. He came home, on parole, and hadn't heard from her except for the divorce papers she'd served him while he was inside. I'm not sure how he didn't hear about it, but I guess he didn't have contact with many while he was in prison. He came home and learned he was a dad."

I glanced at the window to the gallery, to the beautiful bison behind the glass, and my heart squeezed for Reese Huxley. For his daughter too, even though she'd vandalized my home.

She'd been crying for help.

"So she threw a rock through my window because . . ."

"Because my truck was parked out front. She knew it would take me all of five seconds to realize it was her. When I pulled up to her house last night, she was on the dirt bike, just waiting for me to haul her in. Because the fucking hell of it is, jail is better than home."

"What's wrong with her home?"

"April is . . . well, she's a bitch." He raked a hand through his hair. "You can't believe a word that comes out of her mouth. If she can step on you to gain something, she won't think twice. And after Hux, she married a lawyer in town. Wanted the money and the prestige. The guy's a monster. Beats the hell out of April behind closed doors and they both get off on it. Has Savannah trapped there while he's doing it too."

"Does he hit Savannah too?"

"I don't know. If he does, she won't admit it. I've asked her about a hundred times. Hell, I even made Travis ask her, hoping she'd confide in him, but she just clams up."

My stomach twisted because we both knew the answer. "Can't Hux get custody?"

"He tried. When he came back from prison, he tried. April's husband might be garbage, but he's a damn good lawyer. And Hux is an ex-con. He doesn't even get visitation with Savannah."

"That doesn't seem right."

"It's not." Duke shook his head. "She'll run away from home and show up on Hux's doorstep. April will call the station and I'll have no choice but to take Savannah home. She screams and cries the entire way."

"Oh my God."

"Hux finally just gave up, which pisses me right the fuck off. But I get it. You get kicked enough, have your heart broken enough, you put up walls around yourself. Savannah's not the only one screaming and crying when I have to take her away."

My heart broke for all of them.

It was so incredibly unfair that bad parents were allowed to keep their children.

"I don't want to make things worse for her," I said. "If she was acting out, grasping for something, I don't care about the window."

"I figured you'd say that." He touched the brim of my hat, giving me a sad smile. "I called Kerrigan and she said that as long as you don't want to press charges, she only wants the window fixed."

"Okay, good." I stepped in closer, wrapping my arms around his waist. Duke leaned into me instantly and I was happy to shoulder some of his weight. "How are you?"

"Wiped." His face was covered in stubble because he hadn't shaved this morning and his eyelids looked heavy.

"I have a confession. This was not the story I expected you to tell. I thought it was Travis who broke the window."

"No. Thank fuck." He chuckled. "I would have had to strangle him."

"I'm glad it wasn't." Maybe there was hope that Travis didn't completely hate me. "Is there anything I can do for you?"

"Keep me company for the rest of the day."

"You're in luck," I said, letting him go. "I happen to have a wide-open schedule today. And tomorrow. And the day after. Should I follow you to the station?"

"Actually, I'm headed out on patrol. Needed to get out of the station for a while. Feel like doing a ride along? Though I'll warn you, it'll probably be boring."

If that was all I could do today, just take his mind off things and stick close, I'd call it a win.

I wagged my eyebrows. "I don't mind boring. Especially if you let me hold your radar gun."

CHAPTER FIFTEEN

DUKE

LUCY DUCKED her head to hide her smile.

"What?" I nudged her shoulder with mine.

She looked up, taking in the football stadium. "I love this. It's exactly what I pictured. The lights. The green field. The bleachers." She rapped her knuckles on the silver bench. "It's perfect."

The stadium lights were on full blast, though the sun hadn't quite set. But in an hour, when darkness crept over Montana, those lights would blanket the crowd gathered tonight to watch the Calamity Cowboys in their first home game of the season.

It had been two weeks since the incident with Savannah, and the only shiny thing to come out of the situation was the new window at the farmhouse. Savannah was back at home with her mother and stepfather. Hux, as far as I knew, hadn't tried to intervene. And for the time being, the clusterfuck that was Hux, April and Savannah was on hiatus.

It wouldn't last but unless something changed, my hands were tied.

So we'd done our best to move on, and tonight, we were at the high school football game.

Besides our first dinner at the bar, it was the only social outing I'd had with Lucy. When I'd mentioned the game, she hadn't hesitated about coming.

She was tired of hiding, so here we were.

"This will be fun." I put my arm around her, pulling her into my side so that her thigh was smashed against mine. She was wearing a long-sleeve gray T-shirt and jeans. Our coats were tucked beneath the bench, waiting for the sun to set and the temperature to drop.

"Hey, Duke." Grayson appeared at my shoulder from the row behind us. "Thought I'd come down and say hello."

I twisted to shake his hand. "Hey. Glad you did. I'd like you to meet someone. Gray, this is"—*my Lucy*—"Jade."

"Hi." She smiled up at him and shook his hand. "Nice to meet you."

"Same. Welcome to Calamity. Duke said you're living out at Widow Ashleigh's place?"

"I am. It's a lovely home."

"I've always liked that place," he said. "Well, I just wanted to say hello and introduce myself. Enjoy the game." Grayson left with a wave, returning to his seat.

Others around us must have been waiting because after Grayson broke the seal on introductions, we were inundated with person after person coming to say hello and meet *Jade*.

Her smile didn't falter. If she was nervous about meeting people in town, it didn't show in her voice, but her leg beside mine bounced almost constantly.

"Don't worry, baby," I told her. "No one recognizes you."

Especially since she'd stolen my favorite green hat and

apparently claimed it as her own. With the cap, fresh face and black hair, she simply looked beautiful.

"I know. It's not that," she whispered.

"Then what?"

"I just want them to like me. I don't want people to think your girlfriend is a dud."

My heart skipped.

I was in love with her.

The chance that someone would recognize her was slim, but if they did, it would likely mean a media onslaught and potential targeting from a crazed stalker. But here she was, not nervous that her secret would be blown, but that people wouldn't think she was good enough for me.

The truth was, I didn't know what I'd done to deserve her. My father always introduced my mom as his better half. I'd always thought it was just a saying, but I was beginning to understand he was simply stating a fact.

She was his better half.

I wanted Lucy to be mine.

"Don't worry." I kissed the top of her hat. "They'll love you."

The crowd began to settle and focus their attention on the field.

Lucy smiled at Kerrigan, who'd turned from her seat three rows down to wave.

"I heard yesterday that Kerrigan bought a shop downtown," I said. "It's been vacant for a while."

"Yeah, I guess she's going to turn it into a workout studio."

"Huh? How'd you know that?" How did she have the one up on me with town gossip? Lucy rarely left the farmhouse.

She shrugged. "When I called to tell her that the new window was in, we started talking. Actually, I talked. She was gracious enough to listen. I think my lack of conversation with Everly has made me a little needy. Kerrigan indulged me and then, when she could get a word in edgewise, she asked my opinion on the gym idea. She wants to focus more on classes for women's fitness and I told her it was brilliant. I'm the first member."

"It's not open yet."

"Doesn't matter. I'm still number one."

I chuckled. "Good job, baby."

Kerrigan saw a need and was going to be the one to fulfill it. There was only one gym in town and it was mostly frequented by men. Since I had my gym in the basement, I'd never joined, but Grayson and a couple of the other deputies were members. They had some boxing and martial arts classes but very few women were members.

"Kerrigan Hale is going to run this town one day," I said with a chuckle. "Just watch."

Lucy smiled as the announcer came on the loudspeaker and welcomed everyone to the game.

The student section cheered, their whoops and hollers echoing over the field. The grass was as green as it would get all year, the chalk lines bright white and fresh. A thrill of excitement raced through my veins as the team captains took their positions for the coin flip.

"I played on a field a lot like this when I was in high school," I told Lucy. "It's fun to be in the stands, cheering these kids on."

Most of the kids I'd known for years. I knew their parents and their grandparents. This was what our small town was all about—gathering together, supporting one another and looking out for each other.

If the town did know that Jade Morgan was actually Lucy Ross, I suspected there were a few who'd make a big deal out of it. The assholes. But the others, the majority, would do everything in their power to shut those few up.

When we pulled someone into the fold, they were in it for life.

And based on the welcome reception she'd gotten at this game, she was in.

The small pep band began playing the Cowboys' school anthem and she looked past me to where they played and smiled.

"When I was a sophomore, my dad arranged to have our school's marching band play 'Happy Birthday' to my mom," Lucy said. "My school was a lot bigger than this and it wasn't at a game or anything. Just after school. I made up a story about having a club meeting so Mom would have to come late to pick me up. Dad knew the band director and they'd set it up so that the band was waiting at the front of the school. She was so embarrassed. That was one of the last times he earned a cheddar for his cheesy gestures."

The longing and the love in her eyes made my heart ache. I'd have to start taking notes about her stories. Make some cheesy gestures of my own.

"You okay?"

"Yeah." She looked up at me and smiled. "I'm glad we're here."

"Me too." I tucked a stray lock of hair behind her ear and into the band of the hat.

I beamed with pride as the Cowboys kicked off, not just because of my community, but because sharing this moment with Lucy was special. It was a beginning. We had hundreds of Calamity events in our future. Of nights together, sharing moments under the stars. There'd been a lot of moments lately. I'd only be satisfied with a lifetime more.

She was special and I wasn't letting her go. Maybe I'd known since Yellowstone that Lucy was the one.

The Cowboys were up by ten as halftime approached, and the concession stands would be a madhouse soon.

"Want a hot dog or nachos?" I asked Lucy.

"Both. With a Diet Coke, please."

"Okay." I squeezed her knee. "Be back."

I made my way through the stands, returning waves and nods and keeping one eye on the game until the field was out of sight. The lines were already forming at the concession booth, and I spotted a familiar face in the farthest row.

"Hi, Travis." I clapped him on the shoulder. "First night of freedom?"

"Yeah." He gave me a sheepish grin. "Let's see if I can go a week without getting grounded again."

"How about we aim for a month?" I chuckled. "Good timing. I'll buy you dinner."

"Mom gave me money."

"I got it." We shuffled forward in line one place. "Are you at home this weekend or with your grandparents?"

"Grandma and Grandpa. Mom was meeting some 'friend.'" He rolled his eyes with the air quotes. "Which means she'll be out all night."

Was Melanie seeing someone? If she was, that would explain Travis's attitude. Too much was changing on him, including his body. He looked an inch taller than when he'd come over earlier this week to mow my lawn in exchange for twenty bucks of gas money.

"You're, uh . . . you're here with Jade?" he asked though he already knew the answer. I'd spotted him in the student section earlier, looking our way.

"Yes." I nodded. "Which means it's the perfect night for you to give her an apology for missing Spanish lessons."

Lucy had spent each of her Wednesday afternoons the past two weeks waiting for Travis to stand her up. He'd been consistent.

He groaned.

"Someday, you'd better learn that you don't leave a woman waiting. And when you do, you apologize."

He hung his head. "I don't need a tutor."

"Your grades say otherwise." So far, he'd flunked his first two Spanish quizzes.

Travis grumbled something under his breath about the teacher.

"One session. You meet with her for one session and I'll give you an extra twenty bucks."

Yes, I was bribing him. But if I could just get him in front of Lucy for an hour, he'd fall for her. Just like I had. That was worth a twenty.

"Fine," he grumbled.

"And the apology. Tonight."

He nodded. The only reason he was this agreeable was because he was probably running short on spending money and his lawn mowing income was about to get snowed on.

We finally reached the concession window and I ordered our food. Travis helped me carry it to the bleachers, clutching our haul close as we squeezed past the opposing flow of traffic exiting the stands.

Lucy was chatting with Kerrigan, who stood a few rows down. When the pair spotted us, Kerrigan waved goodbye and Lucy's smile widened. As her gaze shifted to Travis, she sat up straighter.

Her determination was showing. Lucy wanted Travis, more than any other person in Calamity, to like her.

"Thanks, babe," she said as I handed her a tray of nachos and pop. "Hi, Travis."

"Hey." The seat beside me was taken so Travis had no choice but to sit beside Lucy.

I leaned forward, arching an eyebrow in a silent reminder that his twenty bucks had to be earned.

"Sorry," he muttered to her. "For standing you up."

"Thank you." Lucy cast me a glance and winked.

"I'll, uh, be there on Wednesday."

"Then so will I." She dunked a chip in the nacho cheese and popped it into her mouth, chewing with a grin.

Travis surprised me by sitting with us while we ate. He devoured three of the seven hot dogs I'd bought, plus a boat of nachos.

"Want another hot dog?" Lucy offered. "I'm only going to eat one."

"Sure." He shrugged and took it from her, eating it at normal human speed this time.

We'd all finished by the time the team came back on the field and the stands were again full of spectators.

"You don't play football?" Lucy asked Travis.

He shook his head. "Not my thing."

Someone caught Travis's eye and I followed his gaze, spotting Savannah walking along the bottom aisle with a group of girls. She looked up and gave him a smile. Then she shifted her gaze to me and stuck out her tongue.

Brat.

She had her troubles at home so I gave her a pass on

some of her behavior. But she also courted some of her problems. Savannah was wild. I suspected that spirit of hers was much like Hux's had been before prison.

Travis made a move to stand but I reached behind Lucy and put my hand on his shoulder, forcing his ass back to the bench.

"Don't even think about it."

"What?" he asked, feigning innocence.

I scowled. "You know exactly what."

"She's my friend."

"She's a bad influence."

"Come on, Duke. Savannah's not that bad."

"Tell me the truth. Did she give you that vape pen?"

Guilt flooded his expression, saving him from answering.

"That's what I thought," I muttered.

"She's my friend," he said, quietly this time, without any defense.

"Be her friend." Lucy nudged his shoulder with hers. "Help her make good choices."

He gave her a solemn nod and shifted his attention to the field just as Lucy mumbled, "Son of a bitch."

"What?" I asked.

She pointed to her lap where a glob of red ketchup clung to the denim on her thigh.

I chuckled and handed over a napkin from the extras I'd brought for just this reason.

"I spill," Lucy told Travis as she cleaned her jeans. Then she popped the last bite of her hot dog in her mouth, focusing on the game just as a ref blew his whistle and threw a yellow flag.

The stands erupted in cheers—the penalty was for the visiting team.

"It's about time." Lucy clapped. "That kid's been holding all night. Good of the refs to finally notice. It only took until the third quarter."

I blinked.

Travis stared at her with an open mouth.

Damn, there was something sexy about a woman who knew football.

"What?" She shrugged. "My dad liked football. He taught me the rules when we watched on Sunday and Monday nights. And I used to go to a lot of Titans games."

Probably to sing the national anthem.

"I like the Titans," Travis said. "Except Cal Stark seems like a dickhead."

"Oh, he's a massive dickhead." Lucy laughed. "But he wins football games, so he gets to keep being a dickhead."

"And make millions of dollars."

She nodded. "This one time, I saw him freak out because he stepped in his own gum. His. Own. Gum. He spit it on the concrete at the stadium, got stopped by a reporter and forgot that he'd been too lazy to find a trash can, then stepped in it. He blamed the reporter. Douche."

Travis laughed, then launched into something he'd heard on ESPN, never realizing that the reason Lucy knew so much about Cal Stark was because she likely knew him personally.

I grinned, listening to the two of them rip Cal to shreds as the game played on.

Travis stayed through the beginning of the fourth quarter until he finally loaded up a pile of garbage and stood. "Thanks for dinner."

"Welcome," I said.

"See you Wednesday," he told Lucy, then shuffled down the row and disappeared back into the mass of students.

"He's going to like me," she said, leaning into my side. "He's going to like me."

"Yeah, baby. He's going to love you."

"Yes." She fist-pumped in her lap.

We watched the rest of the game, cheering as the Cowboys won. There was no rush to leave the stadium and we hung back, moving with the lumbering crowd to the parking lot. In a sea of glow-red taillights, we waited our turn and inched toward the exit.

We met Travis's car at the end of a row. He waved from behind the wheel. Savannah was in the passenger seat.

"Where's his father?" Lucy asked.

"I'm not sure. Melanie didn't know him well. And it wasn't something we talked about much."

"He's lucky to have you. What did you have to give him to get him to agree to meet me on Wednesday?"

I chuckled. It shouldn't surprise me she'd known there was something at play. "Twenty bucks."

"And four hot dogs." She giggled, then her expression turned more serious. "I wish . . . never mind."

"Wish what?"

She slumped into her seat. "This was the first time I had to hold myself back."

"From what?"

"From who I am. I wish I could have told him the reason I know Cal Stark is a dickhead is because he dated Everly for a hot minute a few years ago. That I could get him tickets to a Titans game if he ever wanted to go because the owner's wife is a huge fan of my music. I just . . . tonight, I wished I didn't have to be Jade."

"I get it." I wished she could be Lucy too.

"I created this entirely new person, but she doesn't have any memories. She doesn't have a past or a family or friends. It's strange, stepping into her shoes. When we're together, I'm Lucy. And the closer I get to other people in Calamity, the more I want to be Lucy with them too. I've been back and forth on the Jade Morgan thing. I feel stuck in the middle and I'm not sure which way to go."

Because she didn't have options. She wasn't really free to decide, not with how things were at the moment.

I reached across the console and took her hand off her lap, then threaded my fingers with hers. More than anything, I wanted her to be free. I wanted to stop reminding myself before we went anywhere to call her Jade. I wanted to stop worrying about the lurking, invisible threat.

The only way to do that was to find this stalker.

"The only way you get to be you is if we end this for good. Let's give Blake some time. When I talked to him last, he said he was wrapping up a job in LA, then he'd get to Nashville."

She turned and stared out her window, taking in the dimly lit streets of Calamity as we made our way down First. "I hope he finds something."

"Me too."

"And I want to call Everly."

"Lu—"

"Please. I need to know that she's okay. Maybe I'll never be Lucy Ross again—at least, the Lucy Ross I was—but I'm not going to give up the people I love. If that brings this entire disappearance thing crashing down on our heads, we'll deal with it."

We. It wasn't her tackling this alone. She knew without

needing me to remind her that we were in this together. Not that it made me feel any better about her re-forming that tie to Nashville.

"It's a risk," I said.

"If we both have burner phones?"

"Mitigates it some, but I don't know . . . I feel uneasy about it. Can we wait until after Blake gets there and does some digging?"

"That could be weeks and it's already been a month." She sighed and lifted my hand, bringing my knuckles to her lips. "I want to call her."

And I wanted to keep her safe. But not at the expense of her happiness.

"Okay." I nodded. "I'll get in touch with Everly. Get her your new number."

Despite the warning light flashing in the back of my mind.

A storm was coming. I just wasn't sure when or how hard it was going to hit.

CHAPTER SIXTEEN

LUCY

"MORNING." Duke slid his arms around me and dropped a kiss to the bare skin on my shoulder.

"Morning." I leaned back into him, absorbing the heat from his chest as the coffeepot brewed, filling the kitchen with its drip and buzz. Duke's scent filled my nose and I held it in, savoring that scent of spice and soap.

He'd been in the shower when I'd woken up so I'd snuck in to brush my teeth, then come downstairs to start the coffee. I was still wearing a pair of silk pajama shorts and matching camisole, the color a lavender shade so light it was nearly electric white.

Duke kissed me again, this time his lips lingering longer, and a smile stretched across my face as I closed my eyes. "Wish I didn't have to work today."

"What would we do if you had the day off?"

"Fuck in every room of the house."

My breath hitched and an ache twisted in my lower belly. "Call in sick."

"I can't." One hand traveled lower and his fingers dipped

beneath the elastic of my shorts. "But we can cross off the kitchen."

I nodded, spinning around so quickly it forced his hand out of my shorts, then I stood on my toes, my lips seeking his.

Never would I get enough of this man.

He crushed his lips to mine as he gripped me by the hips, picking me up so the tips of my toes skimmed the wood floor. Duke set me on the island while his tongue dove into my mouth, plundering and claiming.

My hands roamed everywhere. Over his broad shoulders covered by the stiff, starched cotton of his shirt. Down his muscled arms, which strained to be rid of his sleeves. My palms traveled up his rock-hard chest to his face, where I cupped his cheeks and angled my head so his kisses could go even deeper.

Duke licked and sucked until my core was drenched and I was perched on the edge of the butcher block. My legs were spread and my center throbbed for him as he pulled away and started undoing the buttons on his shirt.

"Off." He jerked his chin at my cami.

I whipped it off, my breasts bouncing free.

His eyes zeroed in on my pebbled nipples. His tongue darted out and ran across his lower lip as he worked the buttons even faster.

"Hurry." I yanked at the hem of his shirt, needing to feel his skin on mine.

Over the past week, something had switched with us. We were just as hot for one another as we had been from the start, but ever since the football game, there'd been this want. This insatiable hunger. Neither of us could get enough and we were frantic to be connected all the time.

Maybe because we both feared there was a change

coming now that Blake was investigating in Nashville. Or maybe we were using sex as a way to tell one another how we felt when we hadn't yet shared the words.

I was in love with Duke.

And I wanted to take a chord out of my parents' symphony and tell him that at just the right, epically cheesy moment. Like maybe I'd write it in a song. Maybe I'd wait until we had a date night. Maybe I'd bake a cake and write the words in frosting.

I wasn't sure exactly how to say it yet, so for the time being, I was showing his body my affection.

Duke seemed to be doing the same. The minute he got to the farmhouse after work, we were clawing at each other. The two nights that I'd spent at his house this week, we'd been ravenous.

He'd said he wanted to fuck me in every room of the farmhouse, except he already had. This was the beginning of lap number two.

And I was not complaining.

I shoved at the sleeves of his shirt, helping to pull them off those roped and corded arms. The minute it was off and on the floor by his bare feet, his hands were on my breasts, kneading and tugging at my nipples. The pinch was a mixture of pleasure and pain that turned the heat in my veins to a raging fire.

"I need you." I reached for his jeans, palming his erection through the denim.

He rolled his hips, pressing into my touch. "Shorts."

I nodded and let him go, planting my hands behind me so he could pull the shorts from my legs.

They sailed to the floor to join his shirt as he worked his jeans open, revealing his long, thick shaft.

I panted as he pulled my ass to the edge of the counter, using a fist to drag the tip of his cock through my soaked folds. Then with one marvelous thrust, he was inside, stealing my breath.

"Duke." I closed my eyes and gripped his shoulders, digging my fingertips into the taut skin.

"You feel so good, baby."

"So good." I hummed and widened my legs, letting him ease out to slam inside again.

He knew exactly how I wanted it. Every time, he took his cues from my gasps and my moans. I'd spent weeks learning his sounds and the expressions on his face so I could give back as good as he gave.

Duke's hands came to my thighs, his fingers digging into the soft curves as he pumped in and out, the rhythm slow at first, until I'd adjusted to his size. Then he worked in fluid strokes, each one building me higher and higher until I was trembling.

"Touch yourself," he ordered.

I nodded but kept my eyes closed as I brought one hand to my clit. I rubbed and circled the hard nub, matching the speed of his strokes until I felt an orgasm seconds away.

"Open your eyes."

I obeyed, finding his blue gaze waiting. It was dark and full of lust. The deep blue pools were mine and mine alone.

Duke's focus dropped, watching as he disappeared inside my body beneath my fingers. "Baby, that is hot."

I hummed my agreement, biting my lower lip as heat licked my skin.

"Faster."

My fingers shook and I followed his gaze, watching us together. It was erotic and dirty and beautiful. The sight pushed me over the edge and on a cry, I shattered. The orgasm took me over in crushing waves, pulse after pulse, as I clenched around Duke. White spots broke over my vision as the explosion continued its relentless assault. My legs shook as they dangled from the counter, my torso jerking with each clench.

My body was completely out of control, putty in Duke's hands.

"Lucy." He groaned, then erupted, fucking me even harder until we were both spent and limp.

The aftershocks of my orgasm were still coming as I fell forward, giving him my weight.

He dropped his head into the crook of my neck and breathed as we found our equilibriums.

"Don't go to work," I whispered. We could do this all day. Because no matter how many times I had him, it wasn't enough.

"I have to."

I wrapped my arms around him. "I know."

"Tonight." He pulled away and pushed a stray lock of hair away from my cheek. Then he studied my face, like there were words he wanted to say too.

But it wasn't time for him either.

"Do you want another shower?"

He shook his head, his hand cupping my cheek. "I want to smell you on me all day."

I leaned in and gave him a slow, sweet kiss, then he slipped free and helped me off the counter.

A drop of his cum leaked down my leg.

Duke bent to pick up his jeans and saw it. When he stood, there was a sexy, cocky grin on his face.

"Like that, do you?" I smirked.

"More than like." There was a seriousness in his expression that made my heart skip.

More than like. He wasn't talking about that drop.

Duke got dressed while I filled a travel mug of coffee for him, not bothering with my own clothes.

I moved around the kitchen naked and followed him to the front door.

There was a benefit to not having neighbors. I could wave goodbye to Duke from the front porch completely naked.

"Lock up."

"You know I will." I gave him a mock salute and the motion made my breasts jiggle.

"You're making it hard for me to leave." He wrapped his free arm around me, pulling me into his body for another kiss. There was a new hardness in his jeans, something I hoped might convince him to come back to me early. Or for lunch. But he let me go and sighed. "My house tonight?"

"Sure." I leaned against the doorframe as he jogged down the porch steps to his truck. Then I waved as he got inside. He shook his head and laughed as I stayed right where I was.

When his truck was headed down the gravel road, I went inside and upstairs, my body languid and slow. There was no hurry. I had nothing to do today but wait until Duke was done working. So I took a leisurely shower, dressed in some jeans, then did a load of laundry and washed my sheets.

When my phone rang, I answered before it had a chance to ring twice. "Hello."

"You seem awfully eager this morning," Everly teased.

"No, I'm just happy to talk to you." I plopped down on the living room couch, tucking my feet into the seat.

After weeks of no contact with Everly, lifting the ban on our phone calls had been like the sun shining on a new day.

The day I'd called her, both of us on disposable phones, she'd answered with, "Four-oh-six area code. This better be my best friend."

I'd laughed. She'd laughed. Then we'd both cried and agreed that no one, not even a deranged stalker, was going to keep us apart again.

We'd talked every day since. She hadn't received an email or any word from the stalker. Since I'd refused to check my email account again, maybe there was another picture or maybe there wasn't. If Blake wanted to dig into my accounts, I'd give him access as long as it meant I could stay far, far away.

Everly had contacted Detective Markum as we'd asked. He hadn't been too happy when she'd refused to tell him my whereabouts, but he'd stopped pressing and done his best to help. Until Blake had more time in Nashville, we'd wait to contact Detective Markum from Montana.

My hideout was safe, for the time being. And I hoped it would stay that way for just a little while longer.

"What are you doing today?" Everly asked.

"Nothing. I'm bored. Duke's working. What about you?"

"Nothing." She sighed. "I'm bored too."

Days like this we'd normally spend together. We'd find a show to binge watch. We'd bake cookies and order pizza. We'd laze in our pajamas, making the most of our boredom. And almost always, I'd make her listen to the first draft of a song.

"I wrote a song," I told her. "Would you listen to it for me?"

"Hell yes!" she squealed and clapped. "It's like old times."

"Okay." I got off the couch and picked up the guitar from the corner beside the fireplace. Then I put the phone on speaker and sang the song Duke had heard me singing outside.

She laughed at the comical lyrics, hummed along with the refrain, and when I was done, applauded. "That is priceless. I can hear it on the radio already."

My heart sank.

This one wouldn't be on the radio.

With my identity up in the air, who knew what would happen with my career? Maybe I'd killed it for good by leaving Nashville.

Bottom line—music was important to me. I couldn't stifle that piece of my soul, of Jade or of Lucy, because it was as much a piece of either woman as her beating heart.

Maybe I could beg Travis to let me teach him guitar. So far, he'd been an apt Spanish student, though we'd only had one tutoring session. Duke had bribed him with cash to show up for the first lesson. I was bribing him with cookies to return for a second.

"Um, you got something today," Everly said. "A courier delivered a package to the building from the label."

"What?" I sat up straighter.

"The label sent over legal papers."

"Ugh." I groaned. I'd known it was coming. I was only nine years into my fourteen-year contract and I'd been working on a new album.

"Should I send the papers to you?"

"I can't avoid them forever, can I?"

"Probably not. Unless you really do want to become Jade Morgan."

The more I'd contemplated my options over the past week, the more torn I'd become. It would be easier to stay Jade. Scott could go to hell and I didn't care what my disappearance meant for his career. But my parents hadn't raised me to shirk responsibility. I owed the label the penalty fee for breaking my contract. After all, I'd signed my name after agreeing to the stipulations.

And I had friends working there. The band members who'd traveled with me for years. A few backup singers I'd gotten to know, though since the label chose my backups, most only stuck with me for months or at most, a year. Then there was the studio staff. The sound engineers who'd made creating each album a blast.

At least some of my penalty fee would go toward their salaries—that's what I was telling myself.

"Yeah. Send them to me," I said.

The dust had settled on this adventure and I found myself staring at the horizon, wanting so much to keep walking forward. But first, I'd have to turn back and clean up my mess.

"Okay. Anything I can do to help?" Everly asked. "Want me to slash the tires on Scott's Maserati?"

I giggled. "Don't tempt me."

We talked about her plans for the day—to take a walk in the park and do some shopping—then we ended the call with the promise to talk tomorrow.

I put my guitar away and wandered around the house, wishing our call had lasted longer. *Should I clean? Garden? Nap?*

Nothing appealed.

The restless energy in my fingertips was overpowering and what I wanted was to move. So I swiped my keys from the kitchen counter, climbed in my car and headed for town. The weather was still warm at the end of September so I'd stuck to my flip-flops, a pair of relaxed jeans and a long-sleeved tee. It was white, which meant before I ate anything, I'd have to change or find a bib. With Duke's ball cap on to shade my face, I decided to continue my exploration of First Street since it had been cut short the day I'd gone into the gallery.

As before, the sidewalks were mostly empty. I lingered with every step, not rushing as I passed stores and restaurants. I'd been in Montana for, what, nearly two months? If I didn't find something to occupy my time, I'd go crazy this winter.

Television was fine but I felt guilty watching all day. For as much as I'd hoped to love reading like my mother, none of the books I'd picked up had clicked. Next, I was going to try a thriller or mystery. But even if I became a voracious reader, I craved a challenge.

Maybe a job? The idea sparked when I passed the café and the red and white *Help Wanted* sign caught my eye. I slowed my pace. I was here and might as well inquire about the position. I stretched a hand for the door only to yank it back before my skin could touch the metal.

How was I going to get a job when I couldn't fill out the application? Jade Morgan had no social security number. No bank account for direct deposit. Hell, I didn't even have a valid driver's license.

Duke's phone would be ringing off the hook if anyone in this town suspected I'd been lying to him and that I was trying to con him into . . . whatever. They might have accepted me from a distance, but that man was loved.

Truly loved.

If the Calamity populous suspected I was screwing him over, I'd be chased out of town with pitchforks and torches.

A surge of pride put a smile on my face as I walked away from the café. Duke deserved that loyalty. He deserved to be loved so much.

I reached the end of First Street and crossed the road, walking down the other side to return to the Rover. After today, I finally felt like I had my bearings in town. I could point out the direction to the park where Duke and Travis had played baseball this summer. I'd learned that the school was on one side of town, east of First, and two of the three churches on the west. And I knew the names of most streets and businesses.

For a town the size of Calamity, there was more here than one would expect. It was something that had intrigued me when I'd done my online research, choosing the perfect place to restart my life. The chamber of commerce deserved a pat on their back for an alluring website that showcased the town.

The two-show movie theater was currently featuring an animated film for kids and an action movie. The Mexican restaurant hadn't opened for the day yet, but there was a woman inside, sitting at a booth, rolling silverware in white napkins. The gift shop had put a sandwich board on the sidewalk, advertising forty percent off all summer apparel.

And every person I passed had a smile and a wave.

It was no secret who I was anymore. After the football game last week, word around town must have traveled fast. I was Duke's girlfriend. I was the woman living in Widow Ashleigh's place.

I was Jade.

Blech.

Every time the name crossed my mind these days, a sour taste spread across my tongue.

What the hell had I been thinking? Maybe I could pull this off for others, but for me? No way. I didn't want to live a fake life. I didn't want to saddle Duke with that kind of burden, forever calling me one name in public and another in private. How would he introduce me to his parents? What if we got married?

My dad wasn't here to walk me down the aisle but it would have broken his heart to see me pledge myself to a man with a fake name.

On the flip side, the minute I confessed, the minute Lucy Ross was Calamity's newest resident, it would cause upheaval. News outlets and paparazzi would swarm and probably annoy everyone in the county for information. I'd be flipping on a neon sign to my whereabouts, practically begging for my stalker to head out west.

Music hit my ears, distracting me from the *Jade vs. Lucy* dilemma, and I searched for the source. Ahead, the front door to Jane's was propped open.

A band was playing and as I walked closer, the lead guitar hit a riff that sucked me right in. I matched my footsteps to the beat of the bass drum and I found myself in the doorway, tapping my hand on my thigh to the song.

This was the same band that had been playing the night Duke had brought me here for burgers. I'd been so busy worrying about him and being in public that I hadn't really appreciated the lead singer. He had a smooth voice and a decent range.

"Hey, honey."

I snapped out of my intense focus as Jane came my way through the darkened room. "Hi. Sorry, you're probably not even open. I was just listening."

"Oh, that sign doesn't matter. Come in." She waved me over the threshold and led the way to the bar, which was lined with empty stools. "Want a drink?"

"Water, please."

"You got it." She went behind the bar and filled a pint glass of ice water with a lemon wedge. "You feel the need for something stronger, just holler."

"Thanks." I raised my glass to her, then took a sip, swiveling in my seat to watch the band as she went to the other end of the bar to unload a dishwasher.

My foot tapped on my stool, and when I caught a glimpse of myself in the mirror behind the bar, there was a huge smile on my face.

Once upon a time, I had been the one at the bar rehearsing at ten in the morning for a ten at night show. Those were the early days, when the label wanted me at all the hot spots in Nashville. And those nights, the ones spent just feet away from the crowd, had been the best. When the people listening and singing along to my music made it that much sweeter.

When the band paused for a break, the lead singer set aside his guitar and walked behind the bar for his own glass of water. He shot me a smile and held out a hand. "Hey. I'm Andrew."

"Jade. Nice to meet you."

Jane left the notebook she'd been scribbling in beside the

cash register and joined us. "Jade, you should hop up there and sing."

I blinked, my heart in my throat. Why would she suggest that? "Huh?"

"Heard you singing along. You're good," she said. "Might as well try it behind the microphone."

I'd been singing along? Well, hell. I hadn't even noticed.

I should have stayed home.

"Come on up," Andrew offered. "We're harmless. Think of it like karaoke, but better. And there's no crowd to heckle you."

"Oh, no. That's okay."

"Come on." He set down his water and nodded for me to follow him. "Guys, this is Jade. She's going to sing a song."

The drummer and the bass player both waved me up, so I slunk off my chair, my heart racing as I made my way to the stage.

I hadn't been this nervous to step behind a microphone in years. But damn it, I really wanted to sing. To remember how it felt. To ensure the woman who'd loved to entertain wasn't broken.

Because I had loved it.

I'd loved filling a stadium with my voice. I'd loved singing at the top of my lungs. I'd loved putting smiles on faces as people joined in, feeling the vibration of their claps as they kept time with mine.

My hands were trembling as I stepped onto the stage, dodging wires and amplifiers and mic stands.

I stretched to shake hands with the drummer. Joe looked to be in his forties with a thick white beard to make up for the complete lack of hair on top of his shiny head. Then I introduced myself to Gary, the bassist, who was apparently

Andrew's brother. Both had dark hair and warm smiles and when they told me they were Jane's nephews, the resemblance clicked into place.

"Gary and I started a garage band when we were in high school," Andrew said, slinging his guitar over his chest. "We were awful."

"Either Aunt Jane saw our potential or she knew she'd get us at a screaming deal." Gary chuckled. "She told us we could play at her bar when we learned enough covers for a full set."

"So you've been playing here since high school?" Was that even legal?

"Pretty much." Andrew shrugged. "That was over twenty years ago. We have real jobs and we don't play here every weekend. Gary owns the Town Pump. Joe's a mechanic at the garage. And I'm a freelance writer. We carve out Thursday mornings to rehearse and play a few weekends a month because it's fun."

"Very cool." Had I not been discovered, this was probably what my life would have looked like too. Playing for the sake of playing.

Gary rapped his sticks on a snare. "What do you feel like singing, Jade?"

"What do you know?"

He grinned. "Everything."

"All right." I stood in front of the mic and flipped it on. "You guys know any songs by Dolly or Reba?"

I loved classic country. It wasn't something I'd listened to as a kid but as my career had progressed, I'd found myself more and more drawn to the style and lyrics of artists like Loretta Lynn and Patsy Cline. It hadn't been often that I could play those for an audience—even an audience of one bartender—because when I'd been behind a mic, it was to sing Lucy Ross branded music only.

"Sure." Joe nodded and rattled off a list of song titles. "Take your pick."

I chose a Dolly Parton hit, one that I knew best so I wouldn't stumble on lyrics because unlike karaoke, there was no prompter here and it had been a while.

Gary tapped his sticks and counted off. "One. Two. Three. Four."

Then they played.

And I sang.

Damn, did I sing.

My vocal cords were a little raw and the initial bars were raspy but as I worked them through that first song, they loosened up. By the time we'd played a Reba McEntire song and one from Patty Loveless, my range had expanded and my lungs weren't on fire.

Joe strummed the opening notes of the next song and I froze. "Do you know 'Midnight to Morning' by Lucy Ross?"

I gulped and nodded, then without stopping to overthink or worry, I sang the song I'd written at three in the morning on a tour bus headed from Dallas to Las Vegas. The song lyrics were flirty and dirty. The tune was raucous and loud. It was the one I used to close a show because it was a no-holds-barred screamer with insane vocals. The label had made me tone it down some for the album. *Peppy but not riotous.*

Today, I sang it wild.

The feeling was second to none. Exhilarating. Stimulating. Thrilling. I closed my eyes and gripped the microphone, its handle warm from the heat of my palms. Standing on that stage in a nowhere bar in Nowhere, Montana, it was powerful to just be *me*.

For three minutes and twenty-six seconds, I was Lucy Ross.

Maybe I was bruised. Used. But the pain was fading. And I knew in my heart, I couldn't give this music up. It would crush my soul.

The volume was full blast when I hit the ending. The guys were good and had followed my lead perfectly, letting me stretch where I wanted to and linger a little on my favorite parts. The last note rang through the bar, clinging to air until it finally faded and the only noise was the hum of a fan.

I came crashing back to reality.

Holy fuck.

That. Was. Awesome.

I choked down a laugh. My cheeks were flushed and I couldn't hold my smile. "Thanks, guys. That was fun."

"Damn." Andrew looked at me with wide eyes.

Joe's mouth was hanging open. Gary stared at me like I was a ghost.

"Um . . ." Andrew gulped, finally breaking the silence. "We don't pay much. But, uh, would you like to join the band?"

They didn't have to pay me. The music was enough.

And luckily, Jade Morgan wasn't under contract with Sunsound Music Group and she could most definitely join a band.

"Yes, please."

CHAPTER SEVENTEEN

DUKE

"HEY, JANE," I said, pinning my phone between my shoulder and cheek as I typed the last line on a report for the mayor I'd been working on all afternoon. The music in the background was blaring.

"Better get down to the bar," she said.

My heart stopped. There weren't a lot of times Jane had summoned me, but when she did, I went racing. I shot out of my chair and gathered up my keys, moving for the door. "What's up?"

"Just get down here. You'll see."

"Jane—"

The noise disappeared. She'd hung up.

Shit. Her cryptic call left me imagining the worst.

Was it a fight? A drunk and disorderly? If things were really bad, the band wouldn't have been playing, right? Though it could have been the radio blasting. Jane loved loud music.

Maybe someone had taken their afternoon beer too far and broken a bottle over someone's head. Swear to God, if I walked into that bar and there was a dead body and Jane hadn't given me a better warning, she and I were going to have one hell of a conversation.

The bullpen was empty as I maneuvered past desks. The only deputies in were Grayson and Carla. Gray was pounding away at his keyboard, finishing up his daily report before the evening shift started rolling in within the next thirty minutes. Carla was at her workstation at the front of the bullpen, sitting behind the bulletproof partition that separated her desk from the lobby. She was bent over her phone, thumbs flying over the screen.

"Carla, I gotta go," I told her, not slowing down as I headed for the door. "Jane called me down to the bar."

"Duke, wait!" She jumped out of her chair, following me out the door to the lobby. "I just got this text about Jade."

My feet ground to a stop and she nearly collided with my back. "What text?"

"You know my cousin Harry. He owns the pawn shop. He's my mom's sister's son."

"Yeah." I circled my hand, wanting her to get to the point. I knew Harry. I knew his pawn shop. What I didn't know was why she'd get a text from Harry about Lucy.

"Well, he usually meets some of his buddies down at the bar on Thursday afternoons for a beer. He's down there right now and I guess there's a woman singing with the band. Harry said it's your girlfriend because he was at the football game and saw you two together but I told him that I didn't know she was a singer and maybe he had the wrong lady but he said she's wearing your favorite hat and has quite the voice."

I blinked, absorbing the string of *he said, she said.* Lucy was singing? That had to be why Jane had called me down.

"Thanks. I have my cell." I walked out the door, jogged to my truck and broke every speed limit on my way downtown.

Every parking space in front of the bar was full. So were all those in the three adjacent buildings, on both sides of Jane's. So I circled around to the alley, figuring I'd find somewhere to park in the rear lot. Nope. Full.

What the fuck? It was a Thursday at four o'clock in the afternoon. Was the entire town here?

I finally found a space two blocks away from First and parked. Then I hustled toward the bar, catching the sound of music before it even came into view. It was loud. Damn loud. Jane must have been in her office with the door closed when she'd called because otherwise, I wouldn't have heard a word.

The bar's door was open and when I heard Lucy's voice, my stomach balled into a knot.

What the hell was she doing? Singing, one of her own damn songs no less, was not how to keep a low profile.

I stepped into the bar, giving my eyes a moment to adjust to the dim light.

The dance floor was packed. Couples were dancing the jitterbug and two-step. And beyond them, there she was. The most beautiful, enchanting woman on earth was standing behind a microphone, wearing my hat.

My hand slapped my chest to keep my heart from escaping.

Damn, but she was exquisite. She had the entire room under her spell with that bewitching voice and glorious smile.

The band members on stage with her had never been so into a performance. They looked like they didn't want to be anywhere else in the world than by Lucy's side. She was hitting the high notes on "Ruby River." It was a hell of a song but she was doing it differently than I'd heard on the radio. She'd picked up the tempo so it was a fast song made for dancing.

But it was still *her* song. And she was taking a big risk by singing it.

I tore my eyes away from Lucy and scanned the crowded bar, searching for anyone who might be recording this. Everyone seemed too busy listening to have their phones out. There were a few guys from the bank in slacks, their suit jackets draped over the backs of their chairs. The booths were all full and my guess was that word about the impromptu concert had pulled store owners away from their shops to join the party.

Hell, most of downtown was here. How many stores had closed this afternoon so employees could play hooky?

I weaved my way past the cocktail tables toward the bar where Jane and her weekend bartender were slinging drinks, moving faster than they would on a busy Saturday night. Their tip jar was already packed full of wadded cash.

A single empty barstool remained at the corner of the bar, in a space that didn't give the best view of the stage. No surprise. Everyone wanted a front row seat. All eyes were glued to Lucy.

I sat down and leaned my elbows on the bar, gaze locked on Jane. When she finally spotted me, she jerked her chin for me to follow her into the kitchen.

The two cooks were slammed, flipping burger patties on the grill, plopping them in baskets with fries straight from the fryer. They were too busy to notice me and Jane disappear into her office.

Jane didn't bother sitting at her desk. She just perched on the edge, crumpling the corners of whatever papers were scattered on top. I'd never understand people who kept messy desks, but I suspected Jane knew exactly where everything was in the clutter of her office.

I closed the door, muting the music, and crossed my arms over my chest. There was no use bullshitting with Jane. I knew her expressions well enough by now to recognize she knew exactly what was happening. "How long have you known?"

"Since the night you brought her in."

Fuck. "This is not public knowledge, Jane."

"Haven't told a soul." She held up a hand. "The fact that she's Lucy Ross will stay between us. She doesn't know I know either."

"I'll tell her tonight."

"Good." Jane nodded. "She puts on a good front. I doubt a single soul in that bar recognizes her. But . . ."

That wasn't going to last long. I'd known for weeks we were running out of time. Lucy didn't want to hide away at her house and be a recluse. I didn't blame her. Which meant sooner rather than later, we had to shut off the smoke screen.

But first, I had to make sure she was protected. We needed to give Blake more time to investigate in Nashville and attempt to hunt down this stalker.

"Appreciate your discretion here," I said.

"No problem." The music beyond the door quieted and in its place the bar erupted into cheers.

A proud smile tugged at the corners of my mouth because Lucy deserved that kind of praise. She had a God-given gift and to hide it from the world was a shame. And I hadn't seen her that radiant since she'd come to Calamity.

231

She needed her music, more than she'd been willing to admit.

Jane stood from her desk, ready to get back to her customers, but I stopped her before she could leave.

"Whose idea was it for her to sing?"

"Mine, of course." She gave me a sly grin. "Lucy Ross is sitting in my bar, I'm at least getting a concert out of her, even if people don't know who she is. Tonight's gonna bankroll my whole month of expenses."

I chuckled, shaking my head as she passed, then followed her back through the kitchen and into the bar, where I took up that one empty stool and ordered a beer. There was no point in returning to work, because though I knew she'd be safe here, damn it, I wasn't going to miss this show.

Lucy sang for another hour and a half without a break. When she finally told the room they were taking five, disappointment seeped into the air. The guys on stage were sweating as they huddled around her. Andrew, the regular lead singer, was begging Lucy to do *one more set*.

Lucy didn't hesitate. She nodded wildly, then turned and hopped off the stage. The second her foot hit the floor, she was mobbed.

People stood from their chairs to shake her hand and praise her performance. She returned them all with a wide and gracious smile as she worked her way to the bar.

Jane met her at the cocktail waitress's station and escorted her behind the bar. Then Jane aimed one long finger my direction.

Lucy's eyes followed and when she spotted me, a red flush crept into her cheeks. She walked my way, ignoring the people still vying for her attention. "Hey."

"Hey."

"I, uh . . ." She scrunched up her nose. "I kind of joined the band."

I chuckled and raised up to lean closer, dropping a kiss to her forehead. "I noticed."

"It's stupid—"

"But you need it."

Her eyes softened. "Yeah."

"I get it, baby."

"I know you do." She put her hand on top of mine. "Andrew and Gary asked if I could do another set. I said yes, but that was before I realized what time it was. We don't have to stay."

"Yes, we do. I already ordered a cheeseburger."

Jane slid up to Lucy's side and set a glass of ice water with a lemon wedge beside her. "You two want a quiet space, just head to my office."

"Thanks." Lucy took the water and chugged half the glass. There was a light sheen of sweat on her chest where the V-neck of her tee wasn't covering skin.

The strum of a guitar filled the air. Past Lucy, up on stage, Andrew and Joe were getting into position for the next song. The guys hadn't taken a break, maybe fearful that if they left, the magic would evaporate.

"Short break. Sorry," Lucy said.

"You do what you need to do. I'll be here."

"I'm a lucky woman, Sheriff." She planted her hands on the bar and jumped up, leaning into my space. Then she fused her lips to mine in a kiss that had the people around us whooping and hollering.

The only part of us touching was our lips and our tongues and our noses. And right then, as I kissed this woman, I was the lucky one here. If I spent my life in the wings, watching her sing and spread joy to the world through her music, I'd call it a win.

Finally, she broke away and dropped down on her feet. "One more set."

"Okay." It would be two or three, we both knew that. By the time I took her to my bed, it would likely be well past midnight.

"Any requests?"

"Surprise me."

She grinned and winked, then turned away and sashayed down the bar.

My eyes were glued to her long legs encased in tight denim. Later, I was going to strip off those jeans and that tee and savor every inch of her body. I'd lick her from head to toe until she was breathless and begging me to take her.

The idea of her naked body made my cock jerk. We'd been hot and heavy this past week but no matter how many times I had her, I always wanted more. I took the last of her water, drinking it down, hoping it would cool me off.

Watching her on stage was a turn-on I hadn't expected. She commanded attention. She stood luminous, glowing brighter than any neon sign. Other men in the bar were drooling over her. I tamped down my jealousy because they might want her, but she was mine.

Tonight, she was going home with me.

Lucy Ross was mine.

The band huddled, probably picking the next song, the guys as animated and excited as Lucy. When she took the mic in her grip, a devilish grin spread over her face as she looked my way.

Fuck, she was going to ruin me. If she looked at me like that all night, I'd come in my boxers like a goddamn teenager.

I made an adjustment to my growing erection and signaled for Jane to bring me another beer.

There was no keeping my eyes off Lucy as she started to sing. Her voice, honeyed and erotic, filled the air and the room was hers. The town was hers.

I stared, unable to look anywhere but at my woman. At some point, someone brought me my burger. I don't really remember eating it but the basket was empty when another someone came to clear it away. People approached me to talk but I didn't make much eye contact or attempt any substantial conversation.

My mind was on Lucy, and when they finished their set, I tracked her every step as she waded through the crowd to stand by my side. The man in the stool next to mine stood and offered it to her. As soon as Lucy was seated, Jane brought her a plastic tray heaped with a burger and fries.

"Want something other than water?" Jane asked.

"No, thanks." Lucy popped a fry into her mouth, moaning as she chewed.

"Just flag me down if you do," Jane said, leaving the two of us alone.

Lucy ate another fry and when her tongue darted out to lick her bottom lip, I swallowed hard, doing my best to control myself before I carried her out of here and had my way with her in my truck.

I leaned in and brushed my lips across the shell of her ear. "Watching you sing, baby . . . You'd better be ready for me later."

She shivered and met my gaze beneath the brim of her hat. "Don't worry, Sheriff. I'll be wound up for hours and hours after this."

I grinned and dropped a kiss to a tender spot on her

neck, letting my tongue dart out to taste her sweet and salty skin. I breathed in her cherry scent, cherries and feminine musk, then let my lips linger on her pulse.

Lucy gasped, leaning into my touch.

It took effort to pull away, but if I didn't, there'd be no way I'd last through another round of songs. The bedroom was calling.

I grabbed one of her fries, eating it as she dove into her burger.

A throat cleared behind us and I turned, blinking in surprise at Melanie's face. I hadn't noticed her here tonight—not that I noticed any women with Lucy in the room. "Hey."

"Hey. I just wanted to introduce myself." Her eyes went to Lucy as she held out a hand. "I'm Melanie. Travis's mom."

"Oh, hi." Lucy wiped her hand on her jeans before shaking Melanie's. "I'm Jade. Nice to meet you."

"You're a wonderful singer," Melanie said.

I held my breath, waiting to see how this played out. Melanie had a jealous streak and the last thing I wanted was for anything to wreck Lucy's big night. But Mel simply smiled, her expression genuine.

Maybe she realized now just how special Lucy was to me.

"Thank you. It's been a true joy getting to know Travis," Lucy said.

"Thank you for tutoring him. He, um . . . he probably won't say it, but he's grateful. We both are."

"It's been my pleasure."

"Well, I'll let you get back to your dinner." Melanie looked at me and something crossed her gaze. A flash of pain and regret. Before I could make sense of it, she lifted her hand and waved. "Bye, Duke."

"See ya, Mel."

Lucy faced forward but instead of picking up her burger, she leaned into my arm. "She still loves you."

"No." I put my arm around her shoulders. "Mel might love the idea of us together, but she never loved me." Like I'd never loved her. The two of us would have been better off as friends.

"Why'd you break up again?" she asked.

"Honestly? Because I knew it wasn't going anywhere. But there'd been a lot of pressure at the time, or maybe I'd just imagined the pressure. I felt like the town expected me to settle down. To have a wife and a family. And there was Travis. I realized one day that I was with her because of how we looked from the outside, not because of how I felt. And that wasn't fair. To any of us."

She hummed, settling deeper into my side. "Sometimes, it's easier to satisfy other people's expectations than your own."

Lucy gave me one of those warm smiles that melted me into a puddle. I'd never met a person as empathetic. Maybe that was why people went crazy over her music. Her lyrics were more than just entertaining. They resonated.

"That's not why I'm with you," I said. "I stopped giving a fuck if the town thinks I should be married with two point five kids. You know that, right?"

"Then why are you with me, Sheriff?" She held her breath, the world around us disappearing as those green eyes searched mine.

"Because when you're in the room, I can't seem to focus on another person. Because you consume my thoughts, day and night. Because your smile makes my whole damn day." I bent low, speaking so only she could hear me. "Because I don't care if your name is Jade Morgan or Lucy Ross as long as at the end of the day, you're mine."

A smile tugged at her lips. "We have a lot to talk about."

"We do." There were things I wanted to say and for the life of me, I wasn't sure why I'd been waiting. My feelings for her wouldn't change. "How many more sets are you gonna sing?"

"Two." She leaned in and took my earlobe between her teeth. "Then you can help me burn off some energy."

I took her hand and brought it to my lap, dragging her palm over my rock-hard cock. "Two sets, then you're mine."

Her breath hitched. "Or maybe just one."

CHAPTER EIGHTEEN

LUCY

"FUCK," Duke hissed. His grip bruised my thighs as I rode him up and down. "Get there."

I closed my eyes, my hands on my breasts. My nipples were pinched between my own fingers and I was seconds away from detonating.

Duke let go of a thigh and brought his thumb to my clit. The moment he touched me, my orgasm broke, hurdling me from one body-wracking pulse to another, until I lost all strength and collapsed forward onto his chest.

He rolled us, pinning my wrists to the mattress as he hovered above me, my inner walls clenching around his length. "You feel so good, baby."

My toes curled and I rode out the aftershocks while Duke thrust in and out, slamming our bodies together. My hair was everywhere. A strand was in my mouth and another over my eyes, but I didn't try to pull my hands free to tuck the locks away. Duke had me where he wanted me and I was at his mercy.

He drove in deep, to the hilt, letting the root of his cock

slam against my swollen clit with every move. After such a colossal orgasm, I didn't think I could come again. But the next—the third or fourth, I'd lost count—came over me and I cried out in surprise, arching my back and letting my body tremble as I was lost to anything but pleasure.

My orgasm triggered Duke's and he roared my name through his release, coming inside me with long strokes.

We'd been fucking for what felt like hours. The two of us were dripping with sweat. My bedroom reeked of sex and sin.

"Wow." A smile stretched across my face.

Tonight was one I'd remember for years. Singing at the bar. Finding Duke in the crowd. Riding out the post-show rush in his arms. It was one of the best times I'd had in my entire life.

Duke collapsed beside me, our chests rising and falling in a fast rhythm as we caught our breath. His hand found mine on the sheet between us. "That was hot."

I hummed my agreement. Part of me wanted to drift off into the sexual haze and sleep, but adrenaline from the bar was still coursing through my veins, despite the sated and limp feeling in my bones.

Duke gave my hand a tug, signaling I was not in the correct place. So I used the last of my strength to roll into his side and toss an arm across his abs.

"Do you care that I joined the band? It kind of screws with the routine we've had."

"Care? Fuck no. If you want to sing, sing. Especially if you get all keyed up afterward and let me experiment in the bedroom."

"And the living room. And the landing at the top of the stairs."

"And the truck." The smirk on his face was total male arrogance. *Also hot.*

As were the positions he'd contorted me into tonight. I'd be sore tomorrow, but damn, it had been worth it.

After leaving the bar, we hadn't gone to Duke's place. He'd deemed it too far away, and instead, we'd come to the farmhouse in his truck. My Rover was still parked on First. On the drive, he'd given me orgasm number one with his fingers.

I traced my fingers up and down his ribs. Duke wasn't ticklish, something I'd discovered over the past few weeks. No matter where I touched or how featherlight my fingers skated across areas I expected to be sensitive, he wouldn't so much as twitch.

He mimicked the movement on my ribs, earning a squeal and squirm because I, on the other hand, was quite ticklish.

"Stop." I swatted at his hand with a giggle. "I'm too weak to laugh."

He pulled me close. "You were amazing tonight."

"It was the most fun I've had behind a microphone in a while. Thanks for being there."

"You're there, I'm there. I wouldn't miss a show for anything."

I sighed, sinking deeper into his side. Playing with that band, singing my heart out, had been incredible. And after that last set, I finally had some answers to the questions I'd been asking myself. "I need to be Lucy Ross."

"I know."

I propped my chin on his chest to meet his eyes. "Will people around Calamity hate me for lying?"

"Doubt it. I think most will understand. And if they don't, fuck 'em."

"These are your people, Sheriff."

He touched the tip of my nose. "You are my people."

"I don't want to lose you," I whispered. How could I be me and keep hold of this life in Calamity?

"I'm not going anywhere." He leaned up, taking my lips as he wrapped his arms around me. Then he laid me on my back, tangling a heavy, muscled leg with mine. When he broke the kiss, his hand came to my face, his fingertips tracing the line of hair by my temple.

"I don't know what the future looks like." I wanted to stay in Calamity but I also wanted to create music.

"You don't have to," he said. "We'll figure it out together."

This man was a rock, a mountain of steady strength. Never in my life, not even when my parents had been alive, had I felt this grounded.

"Duke, I swore I wasn't going back to Nashville but now . . ." I wasn't sure I could keep my promise.

"Hey." He leaned on his elbow, locking those blue pools on my face. "Listen. I've had time to think about this. And the bottom line is, I'm not letting you go. If that means I join the force in Nashville, so be it. Or I can work security. Or I can talk to Blake's boss about joining his firm."

I blinked up at him, replaying the words. "You'd come with me?"

"Lucy, from the moment I found you facing off with a buffalo, I knew you were special. Every day, you become more precious to me. I don't care where life takes us as long as it takes me with you."

A sheen of tears filled my eyes. That special moment I'd been waiting for? This was it. "Duke, I—"

"Don't you dare say it first." He put a finger over my lips.

My heart stopped. Even though I knew what was coming, I held my breath. "I love you, Lucy Ross. Jade Morgan. Whoever you need to be, I love you."

"I love you too." I surged into his arms, molding my lips to his.

God, why had I waited to say those words? The moment they were free, I was cloaked in beautiful peace. This sense of belonging I hadn't had since I was eighteen, watching my father twirl my mother around the living room while I played them my latest song on the guitar.

Tears flowed down my cheeks, clinging to his. Did he even know how much I loved him? How much I needed him? How much I'd fight for this, for us, every day of my life?

If he said the word, I'd give up singing immediately. I loved him even more because I knew, bone deep, he'd never ask.

"What's this?" He broke away, drying my tears with his hands. "Why are you crying?"

I sucked in a deep breath, pulling myself together. "Because I've been so lost. Since my parents died, I've been wandering around, searching for a family. I don't even think I realized how much I needed one. Now I have you and it just feels . . . like maybe I'm not so alone."

"You'll never be alone," he promised. "As long as there is a beat in my heart and breath in my lungs, you'll never be alone."

I smiled and another sob broke loose so I buried my head in his shoulder as he held me, crying the tears I'd been holding in for far too long.

The shelter I'd craved for years was right here in his arms.

Duke held me until I had control of my emotions, then

he shifted so his chest was pressed against my back and his big, strong body was wrapped around mine.

"I don't know where to go from here," I confessed. "I don't know how to unravel the truth and meld my old life with the new one."

"We'll start by making sure you're safe," he said. "That's priority one. I'll check in with Blake tomorrow and see if he's found anything yet. Once it's safe, we'll start taking down the wall. We'll let the truth come out and take it one step at a time."

"Okay." I relaxed, happy to let him dictate the next steps.

Blake had been in Nashville for two days. He'd finally wrapped up his other assignment in California and had flown to Tennessee. We hadn't heard from him since he'd arrived but he was working.

Foolish as it was, I had hope for the first time in months. Duke's faith in Blake's skills was contagious. Even though I'd put faith in Detective Markum, after months and months and months with no leads, I'd given up hope.

But maybe, just maybe, we'd end this for good.

Then I'd clean up my mess.

"Do you think it was childish for me to run away?" I asked.

"No." Duke's breath whispered across my cheek. "Not childish at all. You were freaked. You got the hell out of there."

"I *was* scared. Maybe if singing hadn't become so hard, I would have pushed past the fear. But there wasn't enough to make me stay."

The joy from singing had been too far removed. Even now, the anger at Scott and the label for not taking the stalker seriously seethed close to the surface. The frustration that people had wanted me only for my money and talent. The sadness that artists like Everly would never get their due. And the despair that it was out of my control. Hell, I hadn't even been able to choose my own backup singers.

I'd needed to come to Calamity. I'd needed to start down the path of putting the negative emotions aside. Maybe there'd been a better solution than creating Jade Morgan, but as I lay in Duke's arms, I couldn't regret it. Had I stayed in Nashville, I wouldn't have found him.

I wouldn't have fallen in love with Calamity.

"I want to live here."

Duke's arms tightened, like my statement surprised him. "What about singing?"

"I'll find a way to sing. Even if it's just with Andrew and Joe and Gary at the bar. But I don't want to live in Nashville again."

"You sure?"

I spun in his arms so I could see his face as we talked this through. "Absolutely."

"Let's pick a roof. No more back and forth. This place or mine?"

"Yours." I wanted to share his home. I loved the farm-house but it had always been a temporary home. His was permanent.

A grin tugged at his mouth. "Call Kerrigan. Tomorrow."

"Okay. Can I tell her the truth? She feels like a friend. I want her to know my real name."

His eyebrows came together, pondering the decision, but he nodded. "All right."

"And Travis."

"I trust Kerrigan. She's an adult and if you explain the

situation to her, she'll understand and keep it to herself. Like Jane."

"But—wait, Jane? She knows? Shit." I slapped a hand to my forehead. "Maybe I shouldn't have done my own songs tonight."

"She's known since I introduced you the first time we went for burgers. She won't tell."

"Phew." I sighed.

"Now, back to Travis. You know I love that kid. But I don't think he should know. Not yet. He's a teenage boy. Not exactly the breed of human known for keeping shit quiet."

I giggled. "Okay. Not Travis. But soon."

"Soon." He tucked a lock of my hair behind my ear. It was something he'd been doing more of lately, fixing the pieces that wouldn't stay out of my face.

"Will you still love me if I'm blond?"

"No."

I smacked his shoulder.

Duke shifted to his back, laughing up at the ceiling. It gave me the perfect view to appreciate his white smile. And *wow*, it was something. Powerful and pure, it came from deep inside his chest, like he held it close, waiting for the special moments to set it loose.

This moment was mine.

I loved this man with my entire being. If that meant sacrificing my superstar career so he could stay here, where he belonged and was happy, then I'd make that choice. I'd choose him every day, because it didn't really feel like a sacrifice.

One day soon, I'd be Lucy Ross, Duke's girlfriend. Maybe one day, Duke's fiancée, then wife.

And maybe if I wasn't in Nashville, the stalker who'd

tried so hard to tear me away from that life would feel like he'd won.

Fine. I'd admit defeat in that battle.

Because as Duke pulled me into his arms, ending his laughter with a kiss, I knew I'd already won the war.

———

"WHAT DO you want to do today?" Duke asked, sipping his morning coffee.

The two of us had slept in late, having stayed up through most of the night. By the time we'd both finally worn off the adrenaline from the bar, it had been nearly three in the morning.

My voice was hoarse and my throat sore. My vocal cords were not in shape and diving into a performance with no warm-up or rehearsal time had been rough. I sounded like a lifelong smoker at the moment and it wouldn't surprise me if I couldn't speak by the end of the day.

They'd recover, and it had been worth it.

"I'm going to call Kerrigan and tell her I'm moving out but I'll still pay through my lease," I said, sipping my own coffee. "Then I want to start moving into my new house."

He grinned. "Good answer."

I laughed and opened the fridge. "What do you feel like for breakfast?"

"How about we head down to the café for a big breakfast? Then we'll come back and start packing up."

"Sold." I pushed the refrigerator closed. "I'm starving. And I need to pick up my car."

I grabbed my mug, ready to head out, when the doorbell rang.

The two of us shared a look before Duke strode through the house, making sure to block the view as he unlocked and inched open the door.

"Hey there. Remember me?"

I gasped and clapped a hand over my mouth.

I knew that voice.

"Barely recognized you without the bear spray." Duke chuckled, letting me shove him aside to fling the door wide open.

Everly.

Her eyes were shaded by enormous sunglasses. A backpack strap hung from one shoulder and her suitcase rested by her feet.

"Ev?" I wrapped my arms around her for a tight hug. "What are you doing here?"

"I told you I had paperwork from the label. I decided to deliver it myself."

"Come in." I let her go, moving out of the way so she could step inside.

Duke grabbed her suitcase and set it in the foyer.

"Nice place." She looked around, taking in the living room as she walked deeper into the house. "It's even better than the pictures."

When I'd been searching for a place to rent in Calamity, she'd been doing the same. We'd been on the couch in our apartment, both with a laptop balanced on our thighs. She'd actually been the one to find this farmhouse first.

"I can't believe you're here."

"Me neither." She set her backpack down and took off her sunglasses. There were dark circles under her eyes and she'd lost weight that she hadn't needed to lose. Her shoulders were hunched forward, weary, like she'd been awake all night and was seconds away from the crash. "I've been up since three so I could get the earliest flight out. Getting to Calamity before noon isn't easy. And the Uber driver who brought me here from Bozeman seriously needs to lay off the cheap body spray. Two and a half hours of that stench. Blech."

I laughed. "Want some coffee?"

"Is my name Everly Christian?"

I took Everly's hand and led her to the kitchen with Duke following behind.

"How long are you here?" I asked, pouring her a mug.

She shrugged. "Nashville sucks. Especially without you around. Mind if I stay awhile?"

I shared a smile with her, then Duke. "Stay as long as you want."

Maybe I wouldn't have to leave the farmhouse empty after all.

CHAPTER NINETEEN

DUKE

"HEY, DUKE." Carla gave me a puzzled look, then glanced at the calendar tacked to the wall beside her workstation. "What are you doing here?"

"Thought I'd get caught up on paperwork."

"Oh. I thought you'd be spending your day off with Jade."

"Nah. She's got a friend in town. Giving them some space. What's happening here?"

"Nothing." She lifted a shoulder. "Not a single call. Not even a speeding ticket."

"Good." When you were a cop, a boring day was a good day. We all liked it when things were slow. "I'll be in my office if you need me."

She smiled and went back to the game of solitaire laid out on the desk in front of her.

Carla was the type who took initiative without having to be told. When she'd started, she'd spent months alphabetizing and reorganizing our filing system. She'd rearranged and decluttered the storage room to make more space. If she'd resorted to cards, things really were slow.

I'd have to dream up a project for her soon so she wouldn't go crazy.

Before heading into my office, I swung by the break room and filled myself a cup of coffee. I yawned, taking it with me to my desk and sitting down with a sigh.

Last night had been a blast, both at the bar and in Lucy's bedroom, but I wasn't used to staying up like a guy in his twenties. Coffee was going to get me through today and then I was going to bed early.

I pushed up the sleeves of my zip up, one I kept in my small stash of clothes in Lucy's closet. I didn't look at all official today, in jeans, boots and ball cap—since Lucy had stolen my favorite, I was auditioning replacements. But if I could get ahead on some office work, I'd take an extra day off next week and get Lucy moved.

Even with Everly visiting, I didn't see a reason to delay. We wouldn't do it today, but there was no reason we couldn't be living under the same roof by Monday. Everly could stay at the farmhouse or she could take one of the guest rooms at my place.

Our place.

I shook my mouse, waking up my computer, and slugged back my coffee as I worked through the lunch hour and into the early afternoon.

I'd left Lucy and Everly smiling and laughing and practically clinging to one another in the kitchen at the farmhouse. Lucy had missed her friend more than I'd noticed. So while I was here working, they were catching up. I'd promised to bring over pizza and beer for dinner.

"Hey, Duke." Carla poked her head into my office as I

was finishing up the last report on my to-do list. "You got a call on line one. Some cop from Nashville?" She looked at the yellow sticky note in her hand. "A Detective Markum."

My heart stopped. *Oh, shit.*

"Send it through," I said, swallowing the lump in my throat.

"You got it." She nodded and turned to leave.

I stood and quickly shut the door to my office. What the hell did Markum want? How had he even known to call me here? Had Blake reached out to him?

I stared at the phone, waiting for the call to buzz through. On the first ring, I snatched the handset from the cradle. "Sheriff Duke Evans."

"Hi, Sheriff Evans. My name is Detective Brandon Markum. I'm with the Metropolitan Nashville Police Department." He sounded younger than I'd imagined and there was a panicked edge to his voice.

"What can I do for you, Detective?" I did my best to keep my voice calm through my racing heart.

"Well, Sheriff, I'm trying to locate a woman who I believe might be in Calamity at the moment."

"Okay."

Fuck. We'd known this was going to happen, right? Eventually, we were going to have to talk to the Nashville cops. But after last night, I'd wanted just a little more time with Lucy for myself.

"Her name is Everly Christian."

I blinked. Why was he looking for Everly and not Lucy? "All right. The reason?"

"Ms. Christian has been working with me closely over the past month or so. She's been in protective custody for the past five days after an attempt was made on her life.

252

Late last night, she slipped out without telling the officer stationed to protect her and we're trying to track her down. We've pulled credit card records and found an airline ticket she purchased yesterday to Bozeman along with an Uber charge this morning to Calamity. That and the fact that her phone records show a number of calls to your area."

What. The. Fuck.

My jaw clenched and a red haze coated my vision. Everly had promised Lucy that nothing had happened. She'd sworn she hadn't gotten a single email or phone call or text. But that had all been bullshit.

"Detective Markum," I said, "I hope you're sitting down. Because we've got a lot to talk about."

To say he was pissed that I hadn't reached out to him about Lucy would be an understatement, not that I blamed him. By the time I finished explaining how I'd met Lucy and Everly, how Lucy had told me about her stalker and the email she'd received, he was muttering a string of curses into the line.

"I've been working Lucy's case for nearly a fucking year," he snapped. "You didn't think letting the authorities in Nashville know her whereabouts was prudent? What the hell kind of show are you running there, Sheriff Evans?"

"Listen, if I were in your shoes, I'd be angry too. But this was Lucy's decision. Right or wrong, I wasn't going to betray her on this. She's been safe. I've made sure of it personally."

"Wait, are you screwing her? You are, aren't you?"

"Watch yourself, Detective. Or this phone call is over."

He blew a deep breath into the phone. "Sorry. That was uncalled for. I just . . . Lucy disappeared and we've been worried. *I've* been worried. I've been working her case for a long damn time and I'm mad that she didn't come to me first before falling off the face of the earth. Is she okay?"

"She's fine. She's safe. And yes, the two of us are in a relationship."

"And Everly?"

"Arrived this morning. And as soon as I hang up with you, I'll be having a word with her about keeping this from Lucy. But before then, I'd like to know more about what's happened this past month and what you know about the stalker."

"I've worked numerous stalking cases here. This one . . . the guy is a ghost. Never makes a mistake."

"Are you sure whoever came for Everly is the same guy stalking Lucy?"

"Positive. It's the same pattern, though more aggressive. When Lucy disappeared, I suspect the stalker moved on to Everly in the hope of driving Lucy out of hiding."

Which it almost had. Thank fuck I'd shown up at the farmhouse the night she'd been packing her suitcases.

"Any idea who it is?"

"Unfortunately, no. We've got an entire team trying to narrow down a suspect list. But like I said, he's good. And he's off his rocker. I knew it when he killed Lucy's dog. But this attempt on Everly was extreme."

"What happened?"

"He shot twelve rounds through her balcony door from the building across the street."

"Fuck." It must have come from the same place where he'd taken that first photo of her and emailed it to Lucy.

"We suspect he's been breaking into that apartment across the street since Lucy and Everly moved into theirs. He's smart. He knew when the place would be empty.

Didn't leave a trace behind. The tenants never suspected someone had been in their house all day."

"You've got a suspect list, though, correct?"

"We do. It's a mile long. It includes everyone at their record label. Everyone who was on Lucy's staff. Everyone who worked for the tour stage crews. We've looked into them all and have no leads."

If it wasn't someone Lucy knew, then it was probably a crazed fan.

"Shit," I muttered. "What else happened with Everly?"

"Pictures. Texts. Emails. Just in a condensed timeline. Lucy got an email once a week. Everly is getting them daily."

Christ, this was bad. I pinched the bridge of my nose. "He's desperate. I don't like desperate."

And I really didn't like that Everly had come here.

"I assume Everly and Lucy are together?" Detective Markum asked.

"Yep." As soon as I left here, those two wouldn't be out of my sight. They could hang out in an interrogation room while I worked.

If Markum had traced Everly here, there was no telling how quickly the stalker would too.

"I'm going to need a favor, Detective."

"What can I do?"

"Send me everything you've got. For both Lucy and Everly."

"Done."

"Also, I've got a friend in Nashville right now doing some digging too. He's in private security but he's good. If you wouldn't mind, I'd like to share with him too."

"It's not our protocol," he said. "I'll have to run it up the chain of command here."

"That's fine." No matter what they said, I was leaking the information to Blake. I wanted him equipped with as many details as possible as he worked. Besides, I suspected that the files Detective Markum had weren't going to add up to much if they hadn't even shortened the list of suspects.

"Anything else?" he asked after I rattled off my email address and cell phone number.

"No, but let me think on it. I'll be in touch. Appreciate the call, Detective."

"Just keep me in the loop. Please. I don't want to see anything bad happen to Lucy or Everly."

Neither did I. "Talk soon."

I pressed the button in the cradle to end the call, then immediately dialed Lucy's cell.

"Hey," she answered with a smile in her voice. "Are you regretting going to work already? You can always come back and hang with us. We were just talking about opening up a bottle of wine."

"Hold that thought. I'll be there soon and we need to talk."

"Okay," she drawled. "Everything all right?"

"I just got off the phone with Detective Markum."

"What?" I heard her moving, her bare footsteps slapping on the wood stairs. Then the door to her bedroom closed with a familiar squeak to the hinge. "Did you call him? I thought we were going to wait until we heard from Blake."

"He called me."

"Oh, God." She gulped. "How did he find me? What did he say?"

"I'll explain it all when I get there. Just do me a favor, keep the front door locked. You and Everly stay there and stay inside." It was a nice fall day and Lucy loved to go for walks down the gravel road. I didn't want her and Everly out of the house. Or worse, coming into town because they wanted to explore.

"It is already."

"Don't answer it. For anyone."

"You're scaring me, Duke."

"Don't be scared, baby. I'll be there soon."

"Okay." The fact that she let me hang up without demanding answers spoke to how much she trusted me. I'd kiss her for that later, if she'd let me. Because before I kissed her, there was a very real chance I'd strangle her best friend.

The hairs on the nape of my neck stood on end. The nagging feeling in my gut screamed that Everly's trip had basically circled Calamity in red on the stalker's map.

I grabbed my keys and flew from the office, jogging through the bullpen. "Gotta go, Carla."

"Everything okay?"

I didn't answer. I just lifted a hand and shoved through the doors that led me outside. The afternoon sun was so bright that on my way out, I collided with a woman on her way in.

"Duke." Melanie gasped, latching on to my arms since I'd nearly plowed her over.

"Mel? What's up?"

"I can't find Travis."

"What do you mean, you can't find him? It's a Friday. He's at school."

"No, the office just called me and said he didn't show up for his first three periods and I hadn't called to excuse him so they were checking to make sure he wasn't sick." Melanie's hands flailed in the air as the words rushed from her mouth. "After I got home from the bar last night, we got into a fight. He's mad at me because a while back, I was seeing this guy from out of town. Travis didn't like him and made me promise to break it off."

"Did you?"

She shook her head. "It's not serious. We just see each other here and there. Last night after I left the bar, he called and Travis overheard us talking."

"Then you got into a fight."

"Yes. He was still mad at me this morning and wouldn't talk to me before school. But this doesn't seem like something to skip over, does it? Did something bad happen? Have you heard from him?"

"No." I dug my phone from my pocket and pulled up Travis's name. It rang and rang until his voicemail kicked in. "Travis, call me back."

Melanie ran a hand through her hair. "He's not at my parents' house either."

"What about his friends?"

"I asked the school and they're all in class except for Savannah."

I frowned. "Then he's with her. Call her mom. Call her stepdad. Call Hux."

"I did. April hung up on me, Hux didn't answer, and Savannah's stepdad was in a meeting at his firm." She looked at me with pleading eyes. "Will you help me find him? Please?"

Son of a bitch. I needed to make sure Lucy was okay, but I also didn't trust Travis to stay out of trouble, especially if he was with Savannah. That girl could talk him into anything stupid, like ditching school.

"Are you working?" I asked.

"When the school called, I left and took the rest of the day off."

"Go home," I told Melanie. "If he shows up, call me."

"Okay." She nodded. "Thank you. I'm sorry."

There was genuine fear in her face, which meant their fight last night had to have been a bad one. Travis rarely got mad at his mother, at least outwardly.

"I'll find him." I walked to my truck, climbing in and dialing his number once more. When I got voicemail again, I didn't bother with another message but I did send him a text to call me. Then I dialed Hux. He didn't answer.

"Fuck," I spat, turning on the truck and reversing out of the parking lot, driving straight for the gallery downtown.

The peaceful day I'd hoped for, waking up with Lucy in my arms, had slipped through my fingers. With my pulse racing, I had a hard time concentrating on the road.

Where was Travis? I didn't have time to deal with this. Why wasn't he at school? And where was Savannah?

Enough was enough with those kids. My guess was there'd been another incident with Savannah's stepfather, and it was time to step in. That girl needed help and not from another sixteen-year-old.

"Goddamn it." I pounded a fist on the steering wheel as I came up on a tractor on the highway and slowed to a near crawl. "Come on."

The farmer behind the wheel bounced as the large tires rolled.

Rather than wait, I ducked down a side street, flipping on my lights with no siren. I arrived at the gallery and parked in the back lot, hurrying down the narrow stretch in between buildings to get to the sidewalk that ran along First.

The gallery was located across the street from the White

Oak Café. A man I didn't recognize stood out front, staring at me. He didn't wave. He didn't move. He just stood there, wearing a navy polo tucked into khaki pants, and stared.

What the hell? Who was he? I kept an eye on him as I opened the door to the gallery. Still, the man didn't move.

"Hi, Duke," the receptionist greeted me.

"Uh, hey." I walked inside. "Is Hux in?"

"Not yet. He texted that he was up late working last night so I don't expect him until one or two."

"Damn." He was probably sleeping. "Can you have him call me as soon as you hear from him?"

"Sure," she said to my back since I was already walking for the door.

The guy at the café was gone and I scanned the street, looking for him again. My eyes landed on a black car, one block down.

It had Colorado plates. The windows were tinted nearly the same shade as the exterior. There was a man behind the steering wheel, speaking on the phone, but it wasn't the same guy from the café. He was wearing shades and had dark hair, while the other guy had been blond. But like the other man, his unwavering attention was fixed on my face.

I took a step closer, ready to pound on his window and demand some ID, just as he started the car's engine and reversed out of the space.

The knot in my gut loosened for just a moment. He was only a tourist, an innocent man sitting in his car wondering why I was staring at him. No doubt the blond guy was too. Damn it, I was getting paranoid. But with good reason. If Everly had made it to Calamity before noon, her stalker would be here before midnight.

I took out my phone and dialed Lucy's number as I made my way back to my truck.

"Hey," she answered, breathless.

"Hey. You okay?"

"Yes. No." She sniffled.

"Everly told you what's been going on."

"Yeah. I told her that Detective Markum called you and you were freaked out about something. She started crying and . . . Duke, she doesn't cry."

"It's going to be fine."

"Are you on your way here?"

"Not yet. Change of plan. Melanie came to the station because she can't find Travis. He skipped school today because they got in a fight last night. I'm trying to find him."

"Oh, no. Any ideas where he could be?"

"Maybe the park. I'm going to drive there, then search around town for a while. You stay home."

"We will."

"Do you want me to come there?"

"No. You should find him. We're fine. But do you think . . . do you think the stalker is here?"

"Probably not yet," I answered honestly. "But I think at this point, it's only a matter of time."

"Everly promised she was careful. No one knows she came here."

Except she'd paid for a ticket in her own name and with a fucking credit card.

"Just stay put. Keep the door locked. I'll be there soon." Travis was getting an hour. If I hadn't found him before then, I'd pull my deputies into the search.

"Okay. I love you."

"I love you too." And I'd do anything to keep her safe.

261

Even if that meant putting a bullet in the man who'd been making her life a living hell.

The next call I made was to the station. "Carla, can you have one of the guys on patrol drive out to Widow Ashleigh's farmhouse for me?"

"Uh, sure. Why?"

"Just because."

"You got it," she said. "Grayson should be closest. I'll radio him now."

"Thanks." It wasn't the same as being there myself but having someone else's cruiser parked out there was a little peace of mind.

I spent the next thirty minutes driving around town. It was quiet, as it normally was. Kids were in school. Parents were working. The park was empty and the leaves that had fallen from the trees were blowing across the browning grass.

Travis's car wasn't parked at any of his friends' places. It wasn't at Savannah's. Whether he liked it or not, next week I was installing a LoJack system on it, like the ones we had on patrol cruisers.

With no sign of him anywhere, I checked in with Mel. She hadn't heard from him. So then I drove to the high school, wishing I were in uniform and had my gun on my belt because when I interrogated his friends, it would make getting information a hell of a lot easier.

All the while, a nagging dread tortured my gut. I needed to see Lucy and have her with me. I needed to talk to Everly and find out what the fuck was going on and why she hadn't mentioned any of this before.

But first, I was going to find the closest thing I'd ever had to a son.

CHAPTER TWENTY

LUCY

"HOW COULD you keep this from me?" I asked Everly.

She swiped at her teary eyes. "I'm sorry."

I could recall many times like this in our lives. The two of us sitting on a bed, one of us crying. Today, we'd both cried and the bed was in my guest room.

When Duke had called me, we'd just brought her things upstairs and were getting her settled. After I'd told her that Detective Markum had contacted him, she'd spilled everything.

The letters. The gunshots through her balcony. The protective custody.

My fucking stalker could have killed my best friend. And I'd been happily living my life in Calamity, oblivious.

"This is my fault." I put my hand on her knee. "I'm sorry."

"No, it's not. See? This is why I didn't tell you. Because I knew you'd take the blame. But it's not your fault. It's this creep. And I know I shouldn't have come here, but I wasn't sure where else to go."

Her parents still lived in the neighborhood where we'd grown up. If there was any threat of mortal danger, Everly wouldn't drag it to their doorstep.

"You did the right thing, coming here. We're in this together."

She clasped her hand over mine. "I hate this asshole."

"Same." I huffed a laugh. "I can't believe you snuck out of protective custody."

"Ugh." She flopped backward onto the pillows. "It was stupid. I *know* it was stupid. Duke's going to ream me out for that later, isn't he?"

"Oh, yeah."

"Better to face your boyfriend's wrath than stay in that hole where they put me. I was going nutzo. You'd think they'd have something better than a basement with a three-channel television, no books, no nothing, including windows. Fuck that place. I like Detective Markum, but he has no clue who he's after and I wasn't going to live in that cave for the rest of my life. So I waited until the cop on duty went to the bathroom, and then I walked out the front door and made a run for it."

I frowned. "You could have gotten hurt."

"Please. I was in this little suburban neighborhood with white picket fences and kiddie pools in the backyards. And"—she sat up and hopped off the bed, walking to her suitcase beside the closet to unzip it and pull out a can—"I had my bear spray."

"I have mine in the closet." I smiled. "Though since Duke sleeps with a gun on the nightstand, I don't think I'll need it."

She came back to the bed. "How mad is he that I came? On a scale of green pepper to serrano."

THE BRIBE

"Ghost pepper, Ev. He's kind of protective of me."

"Which is adorable," she muttered. "I just wanted to get away and have this disappear. Montana worked for you, so . . ."

"I get it. And so does Duke. But he's going to want to know everything, so don't hold back, okay?"

"Okay." She nodded. "I just wish we had a clue who was doing this."

"Preach. I've thought about it for so, so long. Detective Markum was so sure it was someone I knew, but I think it's got to be a whacko fan."

It could be this nameless, faceless person. I'd performed at so many places, singing for a sea of people. One of them wanted to hurt me. One of them had fired a gun at my best friend.

"But why?" Everly asked. "What did we do to deserve this?"

"You did nothing but be my friend."

And what had I done? I was a nice person. At least, I strived to be a nice person. I was kind to others. If I'd scorned someone, it hadn't been intentional.

"You didn't do anything wrong either." She gave me a sad smile. "No one deserves to live in fear like this."

I scooted closer to wrap my arms around her and rest my cheek on her shoulder. "I'm glad you're here."

"I shouldn't have come." She sighed. "I put you in danger."

"No, I'm glad you did. It's safer here than Nashville." It was safer with Duke. "Let's go downstairs and—"

The doorbell rang.

I gasped and my entire body flinched as Everly yelped and jumped off the bed. I slapped a hand to my racing heart

265

and stood. Then I forced my wobbly knees to move toward the door.

"Where are you going?" Ev hissed.

I put my finger to my lips before tiptoeing out of the room and down the hallway, crouching at the top of the stairs by the banister.

Everly's heat hit my shoulder as she pressed in close.

I held my breath, squinting to make out who was here through the small, narrow window off the front door.

Chances were, it was a delivery. That was the most common reason someone would ring my doorbell. I didn't have visitors or neighbors who dropped by. It could be Kerrigan, checking on the house. But Duke's panicked voice and Everly's brush with death had me freaked.

"I don't see anyone," I whispered and took the first step.

Everly latched on to my elbow, trying to drag me back.

"I'm just going to check."

"No."

I shook her hand loose and took the stairs silently, my eyes glued to that window in case my visitor looked inside.

Which he did. With cupped hands to shield his eyes from the sunlight streaming through, he pressed against the glass to get a glimpse of the entryway.

And the moment I saw his face, my frame relaxed.

Travis.

"It's fine. It's the kid Duke's out looking for." I stood tall and turned, laughing at the canister in her grip. "Put the bear spray away."

"Are you sure?"

"Yes. You're going to freak him out if you carry that around."

"Fine." She spun and ran it back to the bedroom. Then

she hurried down the stairs, a few feet behind me as I flipped the dead bolt and scowled at Travis.

"You are supposed to be at school."

"Sorry." His shoulders sagged. "Is Duke here? I really need to talk to him but my phone died."

"No, he's not. But you can call him on mine." I opened the door wider and waved him inside. "Come on in."

Travis didn't move through the door. Instead he looked across his right shoulder toward the chairs that sat in front of my living room window on the porch. He jerked his chin to the open doorway.

My heart slammed into my throat. Who was out there with him?

I started to close the door when he cursed and muttered, "Savannah, don't be dumb."

Savannah? I peered around the corner. A girl was crouched beside a chair, hiding. She looked exactly like the girl in the gallery painting.

When she saw me, her eyes widened. They were as violet blue as the portrait her father had done but rimmed in red from what looked like hours of crying.

Her face was delicate and soft with youth. She was beautiful, even with the lines of stress etched into her pretty features and her shoulders bunched by her ears.

Savannah would become a stunning woman one day. She had the bone structure. Her long, blond hair was streaked white from summer. In a way, she reminded me of me at that age.

Other than the pain that she seemed to carry in those vibrant eyes.

"This is Jade," Travis said, pointing to me. "That's Savannah."

"Hi." I gave her a little finger wave and the gentlest smile I could summon. "Would you like to come in?"

She shoved off the porch boards, standing and holding up her chin. "Whatever."

Scared to stubborn in two seconds flat. *Teenagers.* I moved out of the way so she could follow Travis inside.

"Duke is out looking for you," I told him. "Your mom went to the station and asked if he'd help find you when the school called her."

"Shit."

"Pretty much." I closed and locked the door, then nodded for them to follow me to the kitchen, where I'd left my phone.

Everly fell into step beside me, leaning in close to whisper, "Think she's pregnant?"

I elbowed her in the side.

"What?" she mouthed.

I shook my head and laughed because no one but Everly could make me smile in this situation.

Travis was right behind us and Savannah stayed on his heels, like she didn't want to be more than a foot away from him.

Okay, maybe Everly was onto something. Was something more than friendship happening with these two? It would explain a lot.

"How much trouble are we in?" Travis asked as we reached the kitchen.

I leaned my elbows on the island. "Depends on what's going on."

Savannah hung her head. "It's my fault."

Please don't be sixteen and pregnant.

"No, it's that asshole's fault," Travis snapped. "He

shouldn't have come after you."

I straightened. "Someone came after you?"

"My stepdad is an epic fucking loser," Savannah said.

It was strange to hear that kind of language from someone with such an angelic face, but there was venom in her tone. Pure poison aimed at her stepdad.

"Did he hurt you?" I asked.

"No."

"He slapped you."

Savannah looked out the kitchen window, her features hardening. "It didn't hurt."

There was a lie. It broke my heart to see a young woman trying so hard to be strong. She was just a kid.

"She was crying in the parking lot when I got to school," Travis said.

"Shut up, Travis."

"No. I'm not gonna shut up. You have to tell someone."

"It's fine," she said through clenched teeth.

"Is that why you ditched school?" I asked Travis.

He nodded. "Her stepdad is a real dick. He was hitting her mom and then smacked Savannah."

"Is that true?" I asked her.

"Yeah." She turned those blue eyes to me. "I didn't want to stick around so I left."

"Where did you go?"

"My dad's."

"Did you tell him about this?" Because Hux should have called Duke, not hidden his daughter away.

"He didn't know I was there," she murmured, dropping her gaze to the island where she traced an invisible circle with her finger. "He stays up late working in his studio. I used my key and snuck in to crash in his spare bedroom. He was still sleeping when I snuck back out this morning."

Why wouldn't she tell her father? I didn't have the time to delve into the complexity of that father-daughter relationship. Not when Duke was out searching for Travis.

"Why did you come here?" I asked Travis.

"We, uh . . . we kind of use your barn as a hangout."

"*My* barn?" I pointed to my chest, then looked out the window to the building in the distance. I hadn't ventured that way since my initial walk around the property. "That one?"

"Yeah. Before you moved in, a few of us used to hang out in the old barn. Since it's pretty much abandoned."

Well, shit. Travis had been here all day.

"How often do you go there?"

He shrugged. "Couple times a week."

How had I not noticed? "How— You know what, it doesn't matter." We'd deal with the barn thing later. "Let's just—"

"Who are you?" Savannah cut me off, her words aimed at Everly. It was so abrupt and demanding, I blinked and closed my mouth.

"I'm Everly. Lucy's best friend."

"Who's Lucy?" Travis asked, looking between the two of us.

Son of a bitch.

"Jade," Everly corrected. "I, uh . . . call her Lucy sometimes? That's her middle name?"

It came out as a question, not a statement.

Everly turned her face away from Travis and gave me an exaggerated frown, mouthing, "Whoops."

I closed my eyes and sighed. We needed to rewind today and start over.

The teenagers weren't buying her lie—no one but a toddler would. Travis's eyes shifted between the two of us, his expression turning suspicious. Savannah's shoulders went ramrod straight as her gaze narrowed on my face.

"I think we'd better call Duke." I swiped my phone off the counter but before I could even unlock the screen, another voice came from behind us.

"Well, well, well. If it isn't my favorite singer. I've been looking for you."

I gasped, my eyes whipping to the intruder.

She stood at the entrance to the kitchen holding a black gun by her side.

Was *this* my stalker? A woman? I blinked, trying to place her face. Her eyes were a muted hazel color. Her brown hair was shoulder length. She looked like an average, pretty woman about my age.

No. No way.

It wasn't a crazy fan. Detective Markum was right. I knew her. But what was her name? Julia? Jessica? Jennifer? She'd been one of my backup singers on my second—or had it been my third?—headliner tour.

We hadn't spoken much at the time and she hadn't stayed with us for long. Maybe two weeks. Then she'd quit and the label had replaced her with someone new.

That's how it had always gone with my backup singers. The label insisted on letting some of their talent sing on my tours. It was Scott's way of auditioning them. If they stood out and had the moxie to move from backup to front runner, the label would fast-track their first album.

This woman had been one of many who'd rotated in and

out. I'd never heard from her again so she must not have gotten her album.

But then again . . . I had heard from her, hadn't I?

Through letters. Texts. Emails.

She'd been the one tormenting me and Everly.

Why?

I'd save that question for later. I stretched my hand across the butcher block for my phone.

"Don't." The woman's eyes narrowed and she clicked her tongue. Then she lifted the gun, pointing the barrel at my nose. "I'll take that."

The gun never wavered from my face as she strode into the kitchen, even as she passed Savannah, Travis and Everly. She swiped up my phone, walked to the sink and dropped it into the drain, turning on the water for a long second. Still the gun didn't so much as shake in her grip, even as her gaze alternated between me and the sink.

"I locked the door," I whispered. I was sure that I'd locked the door.

The woman scoffed. "Please. I've been picking your locks for years."

The clank and grind and scream of metal dragging across glass filled the room as she flipped on the garbage disposal.

Fuck. There went my phone.

My eyes shot to Everly, whose face was stark white. Her phone was upstairs on the bed where we'd been talking. Probably beside her can of bear spray.

The garbage disposal stopped and an eerie silence filled the room.

I held my breath, waiting for a bullet to fly from the gun or words to spew from her mouth.

When she spoke, I expected her voice to sound like nails

on a chalkboard. But it was soft. Soothing, even. "You don't remember me, do you?"

I gulped. "No."

"Cunt." She sneered and the sweet in her tone was replaced with ugly and bitter. "Of course you don't."

What had I done to this woman? How horrible had I been?

How could I not remember?

The tour shows all blended together. We hit city after city as we traveled across the country. There was never any rest. No downtime. The minute the show was over and we were on the bus, I passed out for a few hours just to wake up and work on songs for the next album.

The only people I let travel on my bus were the driver, Meghan and Hank—whenever he felt like acting like my manager and tagging along. All of the other crew members traveled separately.

So if I'd done something horrific to this woman, enough to deserve her brutal punishment, it had to have been at a show.

"I'm sorry," I whispered. "I don't remember your name."

"It's Jennifer. Jennifer Jones." She flicked her gaze to the kids, who were huddled together. "You probably think you're cool, right? Being friends with a famous singer. Be careful. If she thinks you're a threat, she'll ruin your life."

What? What the hell was she talking about? I hadn't ruined her life. I didn't even know her.

I took a step away from the island. Away from Everly and the kids. "Please, put the gun down. We can talk this through. Whatever I did, I'm sorry. I'm so sorry. Let me make it right."

She brought the gun to her temple, using the metal to scratch an itch as she pretended to think the situation over.

This bitch was fucking crazy.

I shuffled away two inches and the gun whipped my way again. I held up my hands. "The kids don't have anything to do with this. Please, let them go."

"I don't think so, sweetheart."

Sweetheart. Bile crept up my throat.

Lookin' pretty today, sweetheart. That would be the caption of me in a pair of sweatpants with my hair all messed up.

You're getting fat, sweetheart. The caption to a picture of me eating.

Sleep tight, sweetheart. A photo of me yawning as I stepped onto a tour bus.

"Why?" I whispered. "I don't understand."

"Don't lie. You know what you did."

"I don't. Please, tell me. What did I do?"

The look on her face turned murderous and the gun began to tremble in her grip. "Admit it. You were so threatened by my talent. Tell them that you were scared I'd steal your fame. I'm the better singer. You know it. I know it. But you were in the spotlight and wouldn't give it up to someone better. Because if I was singing, the world would see you for who you really are. A fake blonde with a mediocre voice who shakes her tits on stage for applause."

I cringed. What the actual fuck? She hated me. No, she *abhorred* me.

"I don't . . . I don't know what you're talking about."

"Liar!" she shrieked, earning a gasp as I flinched.

A sob escaped Savannah's lips. Everly had inched toward the kids and taken the girl's hand, holding it tight in her grip. Travis, that brave boy, was trying to push in front of them both. But Everly was holding her ground, acting as their shield.

"I'm sorry." My chin began to quiver. A deep hopelessness settled in my heart. The only thing to do was make sure Jennifer's anger stayed focused on me. "I don't know what you're talking about."

"You had me fired."

"No, I didn't. I swear. The label didn't let me pick backup singers." Otherwise, I would have had Everly with me on every tour.

But this was still my fault. I'd been so wrapped up in my own career, I hadn't seen what was happening on my own goddamn tour.

Someone had fired this girl. My guess was Scott. And that motherfucker had blamed it on me.

"Such a liar." Jennifer shook her head. "Just like Meghan. I'll shut you up like I did her."

Ice raced down my spine. "What do you mean? Meghan committed suicide."

Jennifer smirked. "Did she?"

No. My stomach plummeted. This crazy bitch had killed my assistant. How, I wasn't sure. But there was no mistaking the evil glint in her eyes. The pride in her actions.

She'd killed Meghan. And she would have killed Everly.

"Why? Why Meghan?" I asked. If I could distract Jennifer, maybe Everly and the kids could make a run for it.

"She belonged in prison," Jennifer said. "She embezzled over fifty thousand dollars from her former employee. Something they never realized. But I found the money. I saw her spending cash and hiding it in her house. Under her mattress of all places. People think they can keep secrets when no one is watching. But I'm *always* watching."

Had Meghan stolen from me too? It didn't matter. None of it mattered. The only thing I was worrying about was getting the others out of here.

I swallowed hard. "What do you want?"

"I want your life. And I would have had it if it weren't for you. So since I can't be a Lucy Ross, I'll rid the world of Lucy Ross instead."

It had always been coming to this. Always. Maybe the reason I'd run from Nashville was because I'd known, deep down, the death threats hadn't been in jest. It had always been about my life.

"Please," I whispered. "Let them go. Then you can do whatever you want to me."

"No," Everly protested. "Lucy, no."

I looked at her, my eyes pleading for her to get the kids out of here.

She shook her head and her eyes filled with tears. Maybe she knew what I was about to do. Maybe she was just terrified.

Please.

A tear fell down her beautiful face as she nodded.

Then I looked at Travis.

He would grow into a good man. Regardless of the trouble he'd been causing lately, he'd become a man like Duke.

My Duke.

I wouldn't get to tell him I loved him again. I wouldn't get to fall asleep in his arms. I wouldn't get to write a song that encompassed the wonder that was Duke Evans.

But there was only one option here.

I wouldn't let this bitch harm Travis or Savannah. They had their entire lives to live. And Everly wasn't going to end up like Meghan.

I faced Jennifer, determination coursing through my veins. Along with defiance and a hatred of my own. This bitch might end me, but she was not hurting the ones I loved.

She noticed the change in my expression and for a brief second, her nasty scowl flashed with disbelief.

I gave her a fake smile. "Fuck you, Jennifer."

Her lip curled and she aimed the gun at my forehead.

The kitchen erupted into chaos.

"Run!" Everly screamed, shoving the kids toward the living room. Savannah had been holding Travis's hand and as she moved, she cried out and pulled him with her.

I lunged at Jennifer, my hands stretching for the gun, just as a flash caught the corner of my eye and a crash filled my ears.

I would have tackled Jennifer, taking us both to the floor.

Except at that moment, a large body threw itself into my path. A body that belonged to the man I loved. Duke had burst through the back door of my tiny farmhouse and thrown himself in front of me.

Just in time to catch a bullet.

CHAPTER TWENTY-ONE

DUKE

"WHY DID YOU DO THAT? Why did you—" A choked sob came from Lucy's throat, cutting off her words as she pressed a dish towel to the blood soaking my shirt. Tears streaked her gorgeous face.

"I'm fine."

"But why did you do that?" she wailed, her hands shaking.

I used my good arm to push up off the floor, ignoring the searing agony in my shoulder and ribs, then took her chin in my hand. "Baby, look at me."

"Stay down." She shook her head as the sobs kept coming. "Everly! Call an ambulance!"

"They're on their way."

Her voice was closer than I'd expected and calmer too. She met my gaze from the edge of the island, her eyes wide and her face drained of color. She swallowed, then her focus shifted past Lucy and me on the floor.

To the other body in the room.

The one swimming in a pool of blood.

I'd caught her bullet in the shoulder. She'd caught mine between the eyes.

"She shot him," Lucy muttered, the towel digging deeper into my wound. "She shot him. She shot him."

"Holy fuck." Travis appeared at Everly's side. He looked at the dead woman, lifted a fist to his mouth and gagged.

"Everly, get them out of here."

No one moved.

"Everly," I barked, causing her to jerk and blink into focus. "Please."

"Come on." She nodded and turned, taking Travis's shoulders in her hands and pushing him away from the horrific scene.

When I heard the front door open, I heaved upright and pressed my back against the island, wincing as I tried to breathe through the pain. The shot had been close range, and the bullet wound hurt like a son of a bitch. It didn't help that I'd broken some ribs when I'd jumped in front of Lucy and smashed into the side of the butcher block.

But I'd take this pain without complaint.

Because it meant that she hadn't taken that bullet in the heart.

"Why did you do that?" Lucy whispered. "You could have . . ."

"Lucy, look at me."

She'd been avoiding eye contact since the gun blasts and even now she was staring at my shoulder.

"Lucy." I put my hand over hers on the towel and lowered my voice. "Lucy."

Her lashes finally lifted, slowly, until those glassy green eyes were glued to mine. "Why did you do that?"

"Because you are my life."

Lucy's chin quivered and whatever hold she'd had on her emotions broke. She collapsed into my chest with body-wracking cries.

I wrapped my uninjured arm around her, holding her tight as I gave my weight to the island at my back.

Then for the first time since I'd arrived at the farmhouse, I breathed.

She's okay. She was okay. She was alive and in my arms.

The last five minutes had felt like a lifetime. Driving up to the farmhouse. Seeing that front door open. Knowing that something was wrong. *Fuck.*

I'd seen some horrific things on the job, but a woman holding a gun to Lucy's face had been the most terrifying sight of my life.

Thank God, I'd made it here in time.

I'd gone to the school to talk to some of Travis's friends. I'd planned on pulling about a dozen kids aside one at a time and drilling them with questions until someone gave me a lead. Turns out, I only had to talk to one kid and drill him with one question.

I asked where Travis and Savannah might be and the kid rattled off three places I'd already checked and one I hadn't.

Widow Ashleigh's old barn.

The little bastards had been sneaking out here to drink beer and vape and smoke right under my damn nose.

I ran out of the school and flew across town to Lucy's. From the gravel road, I saw the front door open, no cruiser in the driveway, and the dread that had plagued me since Detective Markum's phone call spiked.

Lucy wouldn't have left the front door open.

I parked and sprinted toward the back door, gun drawn and ready. My heart stopped beating when I peered through the glass. Without hesitating, I slammed through the door and threw my body in front of Lucy's while pointing my gun at that bitch's face and squeezing the trigger.

In my career, it was the first time I'd taken a person's life.

The woman's death wouldn't haunt me.

The fact that it had almost been Lucy's, would.

A siren wailed in the distance. I closed my eyes, holding Lucy tighter as she clung to me, still crying. I soaked up the precious seconds, letting the relief that she wasn't the woman headed for the morgue soak in deep. Because the moment my deputies burst inside, guns drawn, I had to do my job and get us off this floor.

Grayson was the first inside. He took one look at the scene and his expression hardened. There would be no tears and no vomit from him anymore. He'd learned how gruesome it could get and he'd made the choice to stick it out.

Years from now, that kid was probably going to take my job as sheriff. I'd happily hand over the star when I retired.

"I didn't know, Duke." He swallowed hard. "Carla told me to drive out but I was in the middle of a traffic stop and—"

"It's okay." The fault was mine. I should have told Carla it was an emergency. "Help her up, Gray."

He held out a hand for Lucy but she didn't budge.

"Come on, baby. We need to get out of the house."

She nodded into my chest but didn't let go.

"Lucy"—I kissed her temple—"I can't get up with you on top of me."

"Okay." She tore herself away, and when she saw Grayson's outstretched hand, she shook her head and shoved to her feet alone. "Just help Duke."

Grayson bent and gripped me under my arms as I leaned

forward, then he carefully helped me to my feet, holding me until my head stopped spinning.

"Good?" he asked.

I sucked in some air and focused on taking one step. Then another.

"Don't touch anything," I said as we made it to the living room, Grayson supporting me on one side and Lucy on the other. "Tape the house off and don't let anyone inside. Then get on the phone and call Jess Cleary in Jamison County. Tell him I need him to run an investigation for me."

Jess was a long-time colleague and sheriff in the county that bordered mine. Being neighbors, we'd always tried to work together and stay in touch. He was a damn good cop and a man I could count on to do this investigation. To make sure that all of the details were noted and the report honest.

The last thing I wanted was for Lucy to suffer any more from this. I wasn't sure who my assailant was, but I'd seen families take action against police officers when they felt like a death hadn't been necessary.

Jess would make sure that this didn't blow back on me. Because I knew, deep in my heart, that the only reason Lucy and I were walking away from this today was because I'd taken the kill shot.

The woman would have kept firing. She wouldn't have stopped until Lucy, me or both of us were in the ground.

"Sure, Duke," Grayson said when we reached the porch. "Anything else?"

More sirens came blaring with lights flashing down the gravel road. I spotted the county ambulance with two other deputy cruisers. "Call the coroner."

Grayson nodded, then left me with Lucy.

I scanned the driveway, searching for Everly, Travis and

Savannah. They stood beside the garage, huddled together. Everly had her arms around Savannah, who was crying. Travis stood close to both, his hand in Savannah's.

Those kids had seen things today I wanted to erase from their minds but that would take a once-in-a-lifetime miracle and I'd already cashed mine in to save Lucy. Now all I could do was be there to help see everyone through it.

Lucy eased me toward the stairs as the ambulance pulled into the driveway. The EMTs hopped out and rushed my way.

"Hey, guys," I said as they took Lucy's place for the last two steps.

"What are we dealing with, Duke?"

I jerked my chin to my shoulder. "Gunshot wound at close range. Bullet went through and through."

I'd shoved the arm not holding my gun at Lucy, knocking her over. Otherwise, that bullet might have grazed her too. Instead, it had passed through my shoulder and was now embedded in a kitchen cabinet.

The blood had seeped down my shoulder to my hip, causing my shirt to stick to my skin. The bullet hole hurt, but fuck, my ribs were almost worse.

"I'd say I've got some broken ribs too." I winced as one of the EMTs took my elbow to help me into the back of the ambulance.

Lucy stayed by my side, sitting on the gurney and watching in silence as the EMTs stripped off my shirt and started cleaning the wound.

"You're going to have to go to the hospital," one of them said.

"Later. For now, just clean me up and shove some gauze

in there to slow the bleeding." I'd drive myself to the hospital when I knew this crime scene was under control.

"Is there anyone else inside who needs medical treatment?" the female EMT asked.

I shook my head. "No."

She nodded and pulled a white bandage wrap from a drawer, then began the painful process of wrapping my ribs so tight I could barely breathe. Maybe my body was going into shock, but once they were done with both wounds and my arm was in a sling, the pain began to subside. Or maybe that was the numbing shot I'd talked them into giving me. Whatever the combination, it was enough that I could get out of the ambulance on my own.

"Do me a favor, baby," I said to Lucy. "Go check on Travis."

"He's fine."

"Please?"

"I'm not leaving you."

I eased in close and dropped a kiss to her forehead. "I need to be the sheriff for a few minutes. Please? I'll be right here. And I'm worried about Travis."

She sighed. "Fine. Five minutes."

"I'll hurry." I kept my back straight and hid the pain from my expression until she reached Everly and the kids. Then I sagged, wincing as I gulped another string of deep breaths. When I stood straight again, Travis gave me a sure nod, then took Lucy's hand in the one not already attached to Savannah's.

Once this was over, I was going to hug that kid so damn tight. Then I'd strangle him and insist that Melanie ground him until college. Later, I'd get the details about what had happened before I arrived, but I suspected Travis had come here to find Savannah. Then he'd gone to Lucy.

My heart thumped a beat too hard and I brought a hand to my chest, rubbing at my sternum as I tried to catch my breath.

I could have lost them. I could have lost all of them today.

There was work to be done but I couldn't bring myself to look away from those faces.

"Sheriff?"

I pushed the fear aside at the sound of a familiar voice, then let training and experience take over.

My deputies were lined up in the driveway, silently waiting for me to tell them what to do. Grayson jogged over from his cruiser with a hoodie in his grip. He helped me shrug it on, then I zipped it up and blocked out everything else but protocol.

Thirty minutes later, Carla was inside, photographing the crime scene. The beams that bracketed the porch had a line of caution tape strung between them. And a truck that looked a lot like mine but with a different county's emblem on the door came rolling down the gravel road.

Jess Cleary stepped out of his truck and pushed his sunglasses into his hair. He strode over, his tan uniform shirt rolled up his forearms. "Duke."

"Hey, Jess. Thanks for coming so quickly." The trip between Calamity and Prescott was an hour. He must have stood on his accelerator the whole way.

"'Course. I was out on a call in the country when dispatch sent your deputy through. Good timing. So what can I do?"

"Lead this investigation." I gave him the quick rundown of what had happened today.

I told him that I suspected the woman inside the house was Lucy's stalker and that I didn't want any of my deputies to question Lucy. Not that they'd do something wrong, I just wasn't risking a future lawsuit because I hadn't handed over this investigation.

"That your girl?" He jerked his chin at Lucy.

I nodded. "Yeah."

"Got it." He put a hand on my good shoulder, his touch gentle for a man who was as big as I was. Then he strode over to the garage, shook Lucy's hand and escorted her to a quiet corner.

Some of my tension eased now that Jess was here. He'd take care with Lucy. He'd ask her a few preliminary questions at the scene, then follow up with her again later. Jess would talk to me separately too. He'd question my deputies and step in to give orders.

I shuffled over to the porch steps, collapsing on the bottom one as my head throbbed. Sooner rather than later, I needed to get to the hospital. But Lucy wouldn't let me go without her, and I wasn't keen on leaving her side either. Once she was done with Jess, we'd take off.

The adrenaline was leaving my system and the pain was back with a vengeance, so I closed my eyes, dropping my head between my knees.

"Duke?" Travis's sneakers appeared in my line of sight.

"I'm okay," I promised. "Just need a minute."

He sat by my side. "I'm sorry."

"For what?"

"You were out looking for me. If you had been here, then—"

"This is not your fault." I sat up and put a hand on his knee. "Get that out of your head."

He glanced over his shoulder to the front door. "She was going to kill Jade."

"Yeah."

"You jumped in front of her."

"I did."

He looked at me, his eyebrows pulled together and his forehead furrowed.

"I would have jumped in front of you too. I love you both."

Travis's eyes filled with tears and he dropped his chin to hide them, leaning his shoulder against mine.

"Hey." Savannah hesitated to approach. "Um, that other cop is talking to Everly."

"Have a seat," I said. "Jess will want to talk to you too."

"Okay." She plopped down beside Travis and wrapped her arms around her waist.

When the dust settled, we'd have to talk about why she hadn't been at school and why she and Travis had been in Lucy's barn. But now wasn't the time. First, I wanted to give Jess the chance to get everyone's statements. Then we'd have to call parents.

The moment word of this spread past the highway, this place would be swarming with people. Hell, we were lucky that someone hadn't already noticed the commotion and stopped by to check things out.

I could hear the buzz already. *The farmhouse shooting.* This would be the talk of Calamity for months to come.

"Savannah, you okay?" I asked as her chin began to quiver.

She shrugged and wrapped her arms tighter.

That was a no.

Before I called her mother, I was calling Hux. Savannah needed a supportive parent and maybe this incident would freak Hux out enough to take the right next step.

A shadow crossed my face and I looked up to see the most beautiful woman on earth.

Lucy crouched in front of me and put her hand to my cheek. "You don't look so good."

"You're okay, so I'm okay."

She gave me a sad smile as Travis and Savannah shifted down on the step to make room for her to sit. Lucy looped her arms around mine and dropped her cheek to my shoulder.

Then we sat there as my deputies bustled around us with the afternoon sun warming our faces and the slightest fall breeze blowing the smell of grass and pine through the air.

"I love you, Duke Evans," Lucy said, hugging my arm tighter.

I kissed her temple. "Love you too, Lucy Ross."

"Not Jade, huh?" Travis asked. "Who are you, anyway?"

"I'm Lucy Ross."

"Why'd you tell everyone your name was Jade Morgan?" Savannah asked. "I don't get it."

"She's famous," I answered.

"Like an actress or something?" Travis studied Lucy's face, clearly not having a damn clue who she was.

"She's a Grammy Award–winning singer. Don't you ever listen to the radio in my truck?"

Travis's face soured. "That's country."

"Ew." Savannah scrunched up her nose.

And Lucy tipped her head back and laughed, a sound so musical it chased away the pain.

In that moment, I knew that no matter what happened, we were going to be okay. No more dread. No more lies. No more secrets.

Just Lucy Ross on my arm.

And in my heart.

———

"HEY, JESS," I answered as I drove toward home.

A whimper came from the crate in the passenger seat so I stretched an arm across the console to pat the cage, cringing at the burn in my ribs.

It had been two weeks since Jennifer Jones had tried to take Lucy's life and my injuries were far from healed. The black and blue marks across my torso were only now just beginning to fade to an ugly greenish yellow.

"Got a sec?" Jess asked over the truck's speaker.

"Yeah."

"Just wanted to let you know I sent in my final report. Emailed you a copy."

"Appreciate it." I didn't need to ask what was in the report. Jess had been keeping me apprised of the details as he'd put it together this past week. "Give Gigi my best."

"Same to Lucy."

I ended the call and blew out a deep breath.

It was over.

Technically, it had been over since the day I'd killed Jennifer Jones, but today, with the case closed, it was truly behind us. Detective Markum was still tying up loose ends in Nashville but that was his problem. The past two weeks had been an epic shitshow.

As soon as we'd given Detective Markum the stalker's name, he'd surfaced a ton of information in Tennessee.

Jennifer Jones had been stalking Lucy for nearly two years and was the definition of batshit crazy. Markum raided her home and discovered hundreds upon hundreds of photographs of Lucy. There were nearly as many of Meghan Attree and a growing collection of Everly.

Jennifer had cataloged their every move, along with her own. Electronic journal entries depicted her plans to kill Meghan and stage the woman's death as a suicide. Then after the fact, the macabre details were noted along with photographs and a video of Meghan begging for her life.

Markum sent me copies.

Part of me wanted to know so I could relay the important details to Lucy. I didn't want her seeing that shit. And the other part needed to know, beyond a shadow of a doubt, that the woman I'd killed had been beyond salvation.

Jennifer Jones had belonged in a mental institution.

She'd enjoyed killing Meghan. She'd enjoyed killing Lucy's dog. She'd enjoyed tormenting Lucy and had thrived on causing fear. When Lucy had disappeared from Nash-ville, the journal entries had become desperate and incensed. Jennifer had gone into a rage over losing her favorite toy.

Detective Markum had been hours from closing his own case file on Lucy's and Everly's stalking—until Blake had shown up at Markum's precinct with a file of his own.

Like Blake had said from the beginning, this case inter-ested him. He didn't stop when we identified the killer. He went deeper into Jennifer's connections, and low and behold, Meghan hadn't been the only one feeding the bitch information.

Jennifer's ex worked for the Nashville PD as a rookie

cop, something she'd kept out of her journal entries for reasons unknown. My fear that there had been a leak in the police department had been justified after all.

Jennifer had known that Everly had booked a flight to Montana on her credit card because the ex had been monitoring Everly's accounts. Like he'd been monitoring Lucy's. Jennifer had been on the same damn flight as Everly to Bozeman and in an Uber of her own to Calamity, trailing not too far behind. Had Lucy not lived on cash, Jennifer would have gotten to her before I'd even had a chance to fall in love with her.

Of course, the ex had a string of excuses when his superiors hauled him in for questioning. Turns out, Jennifer had been blackmailing him for years. She'd agreed to stay silent about an unsolved sexual assault he'd committed in college in exchange for information.

And Blake didn't only find the ex.

He met with Lucy's producer and after five minutes decided the guy was as greasy as a shop rag after an oil change. So he investigated Scott Berquest.

Lucy had known that Scott had kept Meghan as his mistress. What she hadn't known was the many other women he'd lured into his bed. Blake discovered a trail of scorned women, nearly all of whom were former employees of Lucy's record label. Scott's favorite hunting ground had been Lucy's shows.

He'd fucked—and fucked over—almost all of her backup singers.

Including Jennifer Jones.

Scott would promise them stardom. He'd promise an album and gush over their talent, anything to get them in bed. And when he'd had his fill—something that seemed to last anywhere from two weeks to three months according to the women Blake spoke to—Scott would fire them.

And the bastard would blame it on Lucy.

He'd tell the woman it was Lucy's request and as the headliner, she was in charge.

He'd probably told Jennifer that she would have made it big if not for Lucy Ross.

When I'd told Lucy the news, it had been in the kitchen while she'd been making dinner. She'd picked up a plate and smashed it on the floor.

I'd offered to call the label and report the news, but she'd insisted on doing it herself.

Blake had returned to California and was still refusing to let us pay him for his time. His boss, Austin, wasn't much help either.

With Jess's report complete and stating that Jennifer's death had been a justified police shooting, the case was closed. Permanently. It was another step to putting this behind us.

And today, I was taking one more.

I turned off the street and eased down my driveway, the crate rattling beside me as I parked in the garage beside Lucy's Rover.

"You ready for this?" I asked my new puppy as I shut the truck off.

She whined and looked at me with brown eyes too big for her little face. When I didn't move, she gave me a little bark.

"Remember your job here, okay? Don't pee on her."

That earned me another bark.

I got out of the truck, my pulse racing as I rounded the tailgate for the passenger side. Then I hefted out the crate, not caring about the ache in my side. My nerves were too jacked to feel much other than excitement. With the puppy loaded, I walked inside through the mud room off the garage. I didn't bother with my boots.

"Lucy!" I called. "Can you help me a sec?"

"Coming," she called back.

Deep breath. God, I hoped this wasn't a mistake. I knew the question I was about to ask was the right one. I knew she'd say yes. Mostly, I was worried she wouldn't like the dog.

She rounded the corner from the living room and walked through the kitchen. She was barefoot and wearing jeans. Her gray V-neck sweater was too big and draped over her shoulder, revealing the strap of her neon-orange bra.

She was stunning. And the smile on her face nearly dropped me to a knee then and there.

Lucy had lost some weight these past two weeks, thanks to stress and sleepless nights. Her cheeks were hollower than normal. But for the past two days, she'd seemed to regain her appetite, and she snored quietly into my side as she slept. The dark circles under her eyes were fading.

"Are you okay?" The smile on her face fell, probably because I was about to have a damn heart attack.

"Yeah. But wait right there." I raised a hand before she came closer.

Her steps stopped beside the island as she drawled, "Okay."

I turned to the crate and unlocked the latch, then stretched inside to retrieve our two-month-old German shepherd puppy.

The puppy's collar dinged as she wiggled, her tongue darting out to lick my hands. When I put her on the floor, she instantly scrambled, her paws struggling to find traction on the smooth marble tile, but once she had a grip, she took off.

And ran straight away from me and into the kitchen.

Lucy gasped and dropped to a crouch, catching the puppy as she jumped onto her hind legs.

Tail wagging, tongue licking—a puddle of pee forming beside Lucy's feet—the dog was everywhere.

And I stood and waited for my girl's reaction.

Lucy's eyes flooded. "Is she for real?"

"If you want her."

"Yes." She beamed, laughing as she scratched the puppy's ears. "She's perfect."

"Good." I crossed the distance between us and crouched down with Lucy, the dog bouncing between the two of us. "Let's take her for a walk. Grab some shoes."

Lucy nodded and rushed to step into some boots in the mud room while I tossed a wad of paper towels on the piddle puddle and picked up the puppy before she could disappear deeper into the house and find a shoe to chew on or poop in.

With Lucy busy with her boots, I dug out the leash from the crate and clipped it onto the puppy's collar.

Along with something else.

"Here." I handed over the leash and let Lucy lead us to the front yard.

"She's so sweet," Lucy said as we meandered. The puppy's nose was pressed into the grass, sniffing as she took in her new home. "Thank you."

"Welcome." I laced my fingers with hers. "How was your day?"

"Better now." She smiled up at me and stood on her toes for a kiss. "Yours?"

"Busy."

We walked, hand in hand, enjoying the evening glow and the cool October air. The tinkling metal of the puppy's collar rang across the yard, and I waited for Lucy to notice. I followed as she walked behind our dog, in our yard, at our house.

I'd refused to let her step foot inside the farmhouse again. After it had been cleared as a crime scene and cleaned of blood and gore, I'd gone over alone and packed her things.

She hadn't protested.

Around us, the leaves were orange and yellow. They'd started falling this week and my boots ruffled those on the grass as we walked.

As I waited.

"You're quiet." She nudged my elbow with hers. "What's up?"

I simply shrugged. If she knew how loud my heart was beating, she'd know the reason I couldn't speak.

The tinkling continued as the puppy pulled on the leash, going left, then right, leaving no blade of grass unsniffed. Then finally, she plopped down on the lawn and sprawled, her little teeth chewing at a leaf.

Lucy smiled down at her. "What should we name—"

Her sentence cut off as the solitaire diamond ring on the puppy's collar caught the fading sunlight.

I bent and fished it off the puppy's collar, and since I was close to the ground, I stayed on one knee.

"Oh my God." Lucy's hand flew to her mouth. "Duke."

"What would you say to a bribe?"

She laughed. "The terms?"

"Marry me and I'll give you this ring."

"That's it?"

I fought a smile. "And I'll love you for the rest of my life."

She tapped her chin, pretending to think about it for a moment. Then she dropped to her knees and framed my face with her hands. "I love you, Sheriff."

"That a yes?" I didn't wait for an answer before taking her left hand from my cheek and sliding the ring onto her finger.

"That's a yes."

The last word was barely out of her mouth before I sealed my lips on hers. I kissed her like I'd kiss her every day. Like I'd love her every day.

With everything I had.

The kiss was cut short, thanks to the dog. She yipped and bounced at our thighs, demanding to be included. I petted her ears as Lucy pulled away, laughing and swiping tears from the corner of her eyes.

"I was going for a cheesy proposal. Something your dad would have done for your mom. Not sure I got there but . . ."

"It was perfect." Lucy's hands skimmed over the puppy's soft fur. "He'd be proud."

"What should we name her?" I asked. "Jade?"

Lucy laughed. "How about Cheddar?"

EPILOGUE
LUCY

FOUR MONTHS LATER...

I was standing in the middle of the Calamity High School gymnasium in utter shock.

The rafters, the walls, and even the basketball hoops seemed to be cheering as I let the last note of the national anthem ring through the air. The sound of applause was deafening. The bleachers shook beneath the weight of hundreds of spectators on their feet. Clapping and whistles echoed off the shiny yellow floor.

Just like they did for the football team, the Calamity community showed up and showed up big to support the basketball team.

This was the third time I'd sung the country's anthem for a home game, and with each, the crowd got into it even more. Or maybe that was just me.

I spun in a circle, giving everyone a wave, then walked toward the end of the gym as the Cowboys jogged by in their warm-ups.

"Good luck." I raised my hand for a high five as the coach passed me on his way to the bench.

"Great job, Lucy!" someone hollered from the stands.

"Thank you." My cheeks were flushed and my spirits soaring as I climbed the stairs, slid into my row and sat in the empty seat beside Duke.

"You got 'em pumped tonight." He kissed my cheek. "Sounded great."

"Show off," Everly teased on my other side.

I laughed and elbowed her as I took the bottle of water Duke had waiting and gulped it down.

The sounds of dribbling basketballs, squeaking tennis shoes and spectator chatter surrounded us, chasing away the last of my nerves.

I wasn't sure why I got nervous, but three times in a row, my stomach had been in knots when I'd stood behind the microphone. The anxiety was probably because I didn't perform as much as I once had. Or because the faces smiling back at me were familiar. Or because I didn't want to let down a single person in this community, the kids especially, with a subpar introduction to the game.

The reason aside, by the time I'd finished my bottle of water and the buzzer had sounded, signaling the start of the game, my feet were no longer bouncing and my hands had steadied.

It was the end of February and the Cowboys were poised to head to the playoffs for the State Class C Championship. There were only two home games left until the tournament started and they were penciled into the calendar at home. Duke and I had been to every home game this season. If the Cowboys made it to the championship, we'd caravan with the rest of Calamity to Bozeman to watch the final game.

"Do you want something from concessions?" Duke asked.

"Nachos and cheese pizza, please."

Everly leaned forward. "I'll take the hot dog she really wants but can't eat."

"Brat." I elbowed her again.

"Be back." Duke dropped a kiss to my lips and stood, returning waves and handshakes as he made his way down the stairs and disappeared to get our meal.

I rubbed my belly, not sure if the churning was still from nerves or if my hormones were making me sick. Morning sickness seemed to hit me hardest in the evenings, go figure. But at almost ten weeks pregnant, my doctor had assured me the nausea would soon begin to fade.

In the meantime, I craved the foods and beverages I couldn't have. Hot dogs. Coffee. A cold ham and turkey sub sandwich. And sushi, not that we had a sushi place in Calamity, much to Everly's dismay.

"Ooh, there's Kerrigan." She pointed five rows below ours where Kerrigan was waving at us from her seat beside her parents.

She held up her fingers, thumb to her ear, pinky to her lips, and mouthed, "Call me."

Everly and I both nodded.

The three of us had become good friends over the past four months. Kerrigan had been incredibly understanding after the incident at the farmhouse—and the fact that I'd lied to her about my identity—and had let me out of my lease.

I'd still paid her through the end of our agreement, despite moving in with Duke before the wedding. And though the farmhouse sat empty at the moment—maybe it was cursed—Kerrigan did have a new tenant in another one of her properties. Everly.

Kerrigan had cleaned up the studio apartment above the space she'd been converting into the women's gym and Everly had been in need of a new address.

My best friend and I had lived together all our lives. That wasn't changing.

Our lives in Nashville were over. Everly hadn't even returned to pack her things. We'd had our belongings shipped to Calamity—on the label's dime. They'd been kissing our asses these past few months, ever since Blake had discovered Scott's behavior.

Just thinking that asshole's name made my nostrils flare.

Maybe if he'd come clean, we would have learned about Jennifer before it had escalated so far. Maybe we could have prevented Meghan's death. But he'd used Jennifer and tipped her fragile mind over the edge.

Considering all that she'd put me through, pitying her was an odd emotion to accept. So I did my best not to think about how differently things could have been and focused on making the best of a terrible situation.

When I'd found out about Scott's behavior with my backup singers, I'd made a phone call to Sunsound's CEO. I'd told him that if I wasn't let out of my contract, penalty free, I'd take my information on Scott to the press—to every morning, evening and nightly news show that would let me—and drag his and the label's name through bison shit.

He'd agreed immediately, fired Scott—whose wife, I'd learned, was in the process of divorcing him and taking every penny of his worth—then offered both me and Everly an album deal.

Everly had declined. Whatever desire she'd had to be a professional singer had vanished. Whenever I asked her about it, she changed the subject. Whenever I invited her to sing with me and the band at Jane's, she invented conflicting plans.

But I could understand her feelings. I'd shut myself off from the music for a while too, and maybe it would come to her in time.

Maybe she just needed someone to inspire her to sing again, like Duke had for me.

I'd walked away from Sunsound too and into the arms of their biggest competitor. Last week, I'd inked a two-album deal with one of the top country music record labels in the country and this time, the contract was on my terms. My songs with my arrangements would be recorded in my new studio, the one Duke and I were adding on to the house.

I had no deadline or pressure to write. When I was ready, I'd record. There'd be no tour. No press exhibitions. Just me and the music. Any funds they would have reserved for a concert tour would be spent on marketing.

If I had a few hits land on the radio, I'd call it a success. The fame and flash of entertaining had lost its appeal for me, much like it had Everly, but I wasn't ready to give up the music.

The only concerts I'd be performing would be here in Calamity. At least until after the baby was born.

Duke strode across the floor, his arms loaded with food. His faded jeans molded to his bulging thighs with every stride. His biceps strained at his sleeves. My stomach growled and I licked my lips—for the man and the food.

My appetite for him never seemed to be satisfied, which

was probably why we'd gotten pregnant less than a month after we'd married at the courthouse in town.

Everly had been my maid of honor. Travis had been Duke's best man. I'd worn a white, sleeveless satin gown, the dress sleek and sexy and elegant and simple. The neckline had come to my collarbones in the front, but the back had opened in a plunging scoop that revealed the length of my spine. Duke had stunned in a charcoal suit that I'd ordered custom made from a tailor in Bozeman. I'd ripped that suit off Duke's body without remorse hours after the judge had pronounced us husband and wife.

He was delicious, my husband, whether he was wearing Italian silk or American flannel.

"Here you go, Ev." He tossed her two hot dogs wrapped in foil when he reached our seats.

"Thanks, babe," I said, shoving a chip overloaded with gooey cheese into my mouth.

"So good," Everly moaned.

I waved off her bragging. "What did you do today?"

"Not much." She shrugged. "Cleaned. Did a load of laundry. Got married."

"That's ni—" My brain screeched to a halt.

Duke leaned forward, a bite of pizza showing in his gaping mouth. "What did you say?"

"I got married." She wadded up the foil wrapper from the hot dog and stood. "I'll tell you all about it later. Thanks for the hot dog."

"But—"

"Bye." She patted me on the shoulder as she shuffled past our knees, then did the same to Duke.

He swallowed his bite. "Did she say married?"

"I think so?" I could only stare as Everly's dark hair swished down her back as she descended the stairs. "Maybe it was a joke."

She reached the base of our section, her gaze searching until it landed on her target. She lifted her hand and waved to three familiar faces. Travis. Savannah.

And Hux.

"I'm thinking that wasn't a joke," Duke muttered.

Hux kissed his daughter on the cheek, then left her behind as he strode to meet Everly, taking her hand and leading her to the exit.

My paper boat of chips nearly slipped from my grip. I caught it at the last second, but not before a blob of nacho cheese landed on the calf of my jeans.

"That spill was on Everly," I mumbled, taking one of the many napkins Duke had brought with the food. "You don't think . . . Everly and Reese?"

"I don't know, baby." He put his hand on my thigh. "But give her some time. She'll explain."

Duke had seen the changes in my best friend over the past months too. The same patience he had for me, he extended to her as honorary family.

This man truly was a dream. He'd given me a home. A family. Soon, a baby. And a puppy we'd named Cheddar.

I had no idea what was happening with Everly, but if Reese Huxley hurt her in any way, I'd burn his gallery to the damn ground.

"I'm worried about her," I said.

"I know." Duke looped his arm around me. The movement was fluid, finally free of the stiffness the shooting had caused. He'd healed quickly, save for a scar he'd have for the rest of his life. Even if evidence of Jennifer's bullet wasn't there to remind me daily, I doubted I'd ever get the image of his bleeding body out of my mind.

I went back to my food, drowning the stress of Everly's announcement in processed calories.

Travis stood, spotted us and came up to join us, taking Everly's empty seat at my side. "Hey, guys."

Duke handed him a spare hot dog. "How's it going, bud?"

"Good. Got a job today."

"You did?" I bumped my shoulder into his. "Congrats. Where?"

"The movie theater."

"Guess we'll have to go to more movies," Duke said, finishing his last bite of pizza.

I handed him my nachos, not wanting any more. My stomach still wasn't in a good place, and with the knot in it— courtesy of Everly—I'd probably just eat cold cereal when we got home.

Travis didn't inhale his food like normal. Instead, his hot dog rested in his lap while his gaze drifted to the rows below, where Savannah slid into a seat beside a couple of other boys. The moment she was seated, his posture drooped.

"What?" I asked.

"Nothing," he muttered, finally eating. He demolished the hot dog Duke had given him, then devoured my pizza slice. With him around, I didn't have to worry about wasting food. Travis came over once a week for dinner and there were never leftovers, no matter how much Duke and I cooked.

Melanie had put him in counseling after the shooting.

He'd gone, begrudgingly at first like he had with our Spanish lessons, but after a month, the complaining had stopped.

Except for tonight.

Travis grumbled something under his breath. I ignored it, until two minutes later he did it again.

"Okay, spill," I ordered. "What's wrong?"

He sighed. "I want to ask Savannah out."

"Aren't you dating already?" Duke asked.

"No. We're just friends. I guess. We were. I don't know. Girls are complicated."

That girl especially. "Does she like you?"

"I thought so. She kissed me in the parking lot when we came in, but then she wanted to sit with Jordan Brown."

"Maybe she's not sure that you like her," I said. "If you asked her out, what would you do?"

"I don't know. Go out to eat, I guess. Get cheeseburgers or grilled cheeses or cheesesteaks."

Duke leaned his forearms on his knees, looking at Travis like he'd sprouted wings. "That's awfully specific."

"Well, I don't know." Travis tossed up his hands. "You guys are always talking about cheese. I mean, you named your dog Cheddar."

I pulled in my lips to keep from laughing but my darling husband didn't even try to spare the boy's feelings.

Duke burst out laughing, leaning close to bury his face in my hair.

My blond hair. After four months of careful lightening treatments, I was almost back to my natural color.

"So, um . . ." *Don't laugh, Lucy. Don't laugh.* "That's not why we talk about cheese. It's just an inside joke. I'll tell you about it later."

Duke's laughter turned into a roar, growing so loud that he drew attention from the others around us.

I elbowed Duke in the side. Hard. This was not how to be supportive of Travis's love life.

"Just ask her out to dinner," I told Travis. "Take her somewhere nice."

"And get your ass down there." Duke sat up straight, shaking his head as he continued to laugh. "If she's sitting with another guy, you'd better be right beside her so she knows how you feel and that Jordan kid does too."

Travis contemplated the advice for a few seconds, then shot out of his seat and practically leapt across us to jog down the stairs.

"I had no idea tonight's game was going to be so dramatic," I told Duke.

"Small-town life, baby. You're in the thick of it now."

Small Town Life. I'd been struggling with a title for my next album, but that was it.

"I love it." I leaned into his side.

I'd soak up every moment of this simple drama if that meant we'd live this life together, waiting to welcome the child in my belly into our arms.

"You're humming." Duke leaned in to whisper.

"Huh?"

"You're humming." He smiled that handsome, sexy smile that made my heart melt and my body ignite. "That usually means you're happy."

"I am." Happier than I could have imagined in my wildest dreams. I laid my head on his shoulder. "I love you, Sheriff."

"Love you too, baby."

We sat there, Duke cheering on the team and me humming the song that would end up becoming Duke's.

Because a man like Duke Evans deserved one hell of a song.

———

The Calamity Montana series continues with Everly and Hux in *The Bluff*. Subscribe to Willa's newsletter to receive new release alerts and the latest news.
www.willanash.com/newsletter

BONUS EPILOGUE
LUCY

I threw my arms in the air and screamed, "Thank you, LA!"

A wave of sound rocked me on my heels and stretched the smile on my face even wider.

It was a rush, being on the receiving end of such pure, unfiltered fun. It was a thrill to stand on stage in an amphitheater like this one, with thousands of people screaming my name. Especially when my family was backstage watching along for the first time.

Past the edge of the stage, Duke waited on my right.

His smile was as wide as my own. He looked so happy and maybe even a little bit awestruck.

I was a little stunned myself.

When we'd flown to California three days ago to start rehearsals, I'd been a ball of anxiety. I'd had no idea how this show was going to go and I'd mentally prepared for a flop. The label had asked—begged—for me to participate in this charity concert. My manager, Alison, had promised it would be easy. Just one show featuring a stellar lineup of popular country artists who'd perform and raise money for a good cause.

I'd agreed but my nerves had been a mess over the past two months as I'd prepared.

We'd kept the set simple. There were no aerobatics, pyrotechnics or crazy choreography moves. It was just me with a band from the label, playing and singing our hearts out for the live audience and the ones at home watching the broadcast networks or online streams.

I'd feared that people had forgotten me since I hadn't toured in years. I'd done two albums with my new label since moving to Calamity. Both had landed me massive hits. Duke had told me it was absurd to think people wouldn't want to hear me live, but I was so out of practice and you needed a certain charisma to keep thousands of people engaged. I'd worried I'd lost my edge.

But he'd been right, per usual. The crowd's excitement was like jet fuel. Maybe the people at home had switched the channel, but everyone here was absorbed with the show.

It was a win.

If tonight was my last big show, I'd be happy, knowing I'd ended on a good note.

I closed my eyes, raising my arms as the cheering continued. I let it seep into my skin and swirl in my blood for a long moment before the band started the opening riffs of the song I'd insisted I perform last.

Duke's song.

I rocked my head and tapped my hand on my thigh to the beat of the drums. I shot Duke another smile, earning a laugh and a shake of his head, then raised the mic to my lips and sang to my husband.

"Slow Down Sheriff" was fast and loud. It made you

want to clap your hands, stomp your feet and dance with wild abandon. Some might have expected a ballad for the love of my life, like the ones I'd written for my children. But Duke had come into my life like a tornado, sweeping me off my feet. Nothing but a rocking beat and clever lyrics would have suited my husband.

I twirled across the stage, singing and keeping up with the energy from the fans. And when that last note rang through the air, I was overpowered by the applause. I threw my head back and laughed. My hair dangled down my back and past my waist. I screamed with them, cheering for the man who had saved my life and made it whole.

When the cheering finally began to subside, I spoke into the microphone but looked stage right. "Y'all want to meet my real-life sheriff?"

The noise was earsplitting.

Duke shook his head.

I waved him onstage.

He mouthed, "No."

And I waited. Because he might protest but that man would come out on stage and stand beside me because he knew it would make the moment even sweeter.

Duke hung his head, then one boot stepped in front of the other, unhurried, as he emerged from the shadows and into the limelight. His gaze never strayed from mine.

I flipped off the mic and set it on the stage floor, then I opened my arms wide to catch the little boy who didn't walk if running was an option.

"Mommy!" Theo launched himself into my arms.

I caught him under the arms, spun him in a dizzying circle, then settled him on my hip.

At four, he was getting too heavy for me to swing around.

He was tall for his age and he'd inherited his father's strength. In most ways, he was Duke's miniature, though he had my green eyes.

Bella, our one-year-old daughter, had Duke's blues. She clung to him, her cheek resting on his shoulder as she looked out at the crowd with wide eyes.

Where she was timid, her brother had no fear. Theo raised a hand and waved, earning his own booming cheer. Thank God, both kids were wearing the huge earmuffs Alison had brought for them.

Duke stepped close and gave me his sexy grin. The crinkles around his eyes deepened.

I ran my fingers through the hair by his temple, fluffing the gray strands that threaded through the tawny brown. He teased that I was the reason for those grays. He wasn't wrong.

But he was as handsome now as the day I'd met him under the big, blue Montana sky. And those eyes would always be my safe haven.

He put his free arm around my shoulders and leaned in to speak into my ear. "Hell of a show, baby."

"Thanks, Sheriff."

"Miss it?"

I scanned the sea of people before us, their arms raised. Phones were held high, taking pictures. Some weren't paying us any attention. It was beautiful chaos.

Did I miss this life?

No. I didn't need stadium lights when I could play with the guys at the bar once a month. I didn't need other people cheering my name when the word Mommy filled my heart.

It was fun to revisit. Maybe I'd do this again. But this

would never again be my life. Not when I had the life of my dreams waiting in Calamity.

Duke bent to kiss me and when I didn't think the applause could get any louder, the amphitheater proved me wrong.

I smiled against his lips. "This was fun. But let's go home."

―――――

The Calamity Montana series continues with Everly and Hux in *The Bluff*.

―――――

Get new release alerts and the latest Willa Nash news by subscribing to her newsletter!
www.willanash.com/newsletter

ACKNOWLEDGMENTS

Thank you for reading *The Bribe*! This book started as a short story for an anthology. I'd only intended to write about five or six thousand words, and it was going to be its own little entity with a neat and tidy happily ever after within fifteen pages. But the moment I introduced Lucy and Duke in Yellowstone, I knew there had to be more. So here we are, at the beginning of a new series. A new adventure with me, Devney Perry, writing as Willa Nash. Thanks again for reading and I hope you'll come along with me to more stories in Calamity.

I'd like to give special thanks to the incredible team who contributed their talents to this book. My editor, Elizabeth Nover. My proofreaders, Julie Deaton, Karen Lawson and Judy Zweifel. My cover designer, Sarah Hansen. Thanks to Kimberly Brower, my agent.

Thanks to Kristen Proby for being Willa Nash's first fan. To Jennifer Santa Ana and Natasha Tomic for always picking up the phone to talk things through. To Danielle Sanchez. And thanks to the Goldbrickers for holding me accountable to show up every day for my two thousand words.

To the bloggers who have taken the time to read and post about my stories, thank you! I am so grateful for all you do. And a huge thanks to the members of Perry Street, whose love and excitement about my books makes me smile every day. I am so blessed to have such wonderful readers.

And lastly, thank you to my family. To my husband for not looking at me like I was crazy when I dreamed up this idea. And to my kids, who don't mind a little extra screen time so Mommy can finish writing for the day.

Will and Nash. This pen name is special for so many reasons, but its inspiration comes from you. You two are the lights of my life.

ABOUT THE AUTHOR

Willa Nash is *USA Today* Bestselling Author Devney Perry's alter ego, writing contemporary romance stories for Kindle Unlimited. Lover of Swedish Fish, hater of laundry, she lives in Washington State with her husband and two sons. She was born and raised in Montana and has a passion for writing books in the state she calls home.

Don't miss out on Willa's latest book news.
Subscribe to her newsletter!
www.willanash.com

Made in the USA
Monee, IL
03 July 2023

38605998R00187